To John

Bes...

Jessica Porter.

STEEL DROPS

Jessica Porter

Pen Press

First published in Great Britain by Pen Press

All paper used in the printing of this book has been made from
wood grown in managed, sustainable forests.

ISBN13: 978-1-906710-49-1

Printed and bound in the UK by Cpod, Trowbridge, Wiltshire
Pen Press is an imprint of Indepenpress Publishing Limited
25 Eastern Place
Brighton
BN2 1GJ

A catalogue record of this book is available from
the British Library

Cover design and photograph: David Carroll

STEEL DROPS
IS DEDICATED TO THE MEMORY
OF
VIN CONBOY
1920-2001

This is a work of fiction but I hope Vin's friends
will read between the lines and remember him

ACKNOWLEDGEMENTS

I would like to thank my cousin Kay Smith for typing my first book, Unbridled Love, which started me on the long journey down this road.

My thanks also go to Adam Jervis Smith and Jonathan Jervis Smith for their advice when writing my second book, Saving Time and for reading it.

Ken Smith was the inspiration for various characters and still is!

Anne Jervis and Harold Jervis supplied the most important ingredient in the production of all my books. Loving support.

Without these special members of my family, I would have probably given up.

CHAPTER ONE

Lacy fingers of moisture caressed his face as the rain blended with his tears. The mammy was holding his hand. Her hand was cold and it felt like a piece of wet tripe. But it was his only lifeline and he clung to it like a barnacle clings to the bottom of a boat. Nearby, buffeted by the wind, a seagull perched on the rail. Dermot McCoy waved to them from the dockside.

'See! Wave to the daddy.' Kathleen waved like mad. Alarmed by her antics, the seagull hurtled up into the sky.

Danny had no intention of waving. His body was stiff with fear. He was trying to remember what he'd heard the mammy and daddy saying just before the packing started. The memory was fading fast. Part of the problem was that none of it had made any sense. And it still didn't make sense now but Danny knew summat was up. The black greasy waves were churning, just like his stomach. Slapping against the side of the boat. Slip! Slop! He was mesmerised by the sound and by the dark chasm that was appearing below.

'Jesus, Mary and Joseph!' Kathleen crossed herself. 'Sure an' you're not going to be sick? Lean further over the rail.'

Danny leaned and gasped and heaved but nowt came up.

His mother unbuttoned her wool coat and used it as a canopy to protect him from the cold wind.

The coat helped a bit in spite of its threadbare state. He sighed with relief as his frozen flesh absorbed some of her body-heat.

'Sure an' didn't I tell you to eat your breakfast?'

Oh aye! So it could all come back, thought Danny.

'Come an' sit down.'

They sat on the hard slatted benches where they were more sheltered but Danny just felt worse as he watched the unfamiliar city of Liverpool fade into the distance. Soon he couldn't see any land at all. Why were they on this boat? Where were they going? He tried once more to remember that conversation.

'He can't stay here. A public house ain't the place for a little'un, Kathleen. He'll be better off in Ireland. Remember those velvet green hills and cornflower blue skies? Remember fishing in the lovely lakes of Leitrim? Remember Galway Bay, Kathleen? Sure an' don't you remember paddling in the sea?'

Danny recalled the wheedling tones of his daddy's voice and he remembered hearing his mammy giggling. They'd have killed him if they'd found him sitting on the floor in the hall, listening to them when he was supposed to have been in bed. Now here he was on a smelly ol' boat with the rain lashing down, trying to work out why he was here at all. Why was his ma taking him away? An' what did his da mean by paddling? And then he suddenly remembered what paddling meant. Oh dear!

'I'll paddle your backside if you cheek me again.'

That's what he'd heard Tony's ma say and she had. Tony couldn't sit down straight after. Tears like October cabbages welled up in his eyes. He stared anxiously at his ma. 'Please don't hit me.'

'God love us. What for goodness sake are you talking about? I'm not going to smack you just because you're not feeling well. Come on. We'll go and get you a nice cup of tea and a bite to eat. Dry toast. That's what you want, sonny boy.'

Danny wrinkled his nose. He couldn't think of anything more revolting than dry toast except the rice puddin' his ma made him eat every Sunday.

He stared at the crumbs on his plate. The dry toast hadn't gone down at all well. He gulped the hot strong tea. More thoughts scampered through his head like startled mice. They were leaving home. They must be going to America. Time stretched endlessly. Eventually his eyes started to close.

'Come here.' Kathleen pulled him closer.

Danny leaned against her and dozed off.

He woke up. 'Where are we?'

'Dublin.'

Danny was none the wiser. Where was Dublin? The train journey wasn't much better. 'Where we goin'?'

'I've told you once already. Leitrim.'

Danny was terrified when he found all the hoards waiting for them were foreigners. He couldn't understand a word that was being said. His mother was enveloped in clouds of emotion. All these people! Danny hated them. She let go of his hand. He flapped about in a vain attempt to keep hold of that lifeline. He grabbed her coat.

Her hand made contact again as she pulled him forward. 'See Danny! Your Auntie Eileen and here's your Uncle Joseph and Uncle Michael.' She was speaking in English but the names were rolling off her tongue as fast as falling rain. Hundreds of them! 'Uncle Patrick. Cousin Neil. Cousin James. Sean and Seamus.'

Danny's head was spinning. He fixed his eyes on the ground. Raindrops were falling all around him. They looked like tears. They were tears. They were his tears.

'Poor little lad. He's overcome with tiredness from the awful journey, so he is.' His Uncle Patrick scooped him up and carried him out of the station, to the pony and trap. Some of the McCoy family rode in the trap. Some ran behind.

The farm was only a mile from the village but Danny could hardly keep his eyes open. They put him between cream linen sheets and as he laid his head on a pillow filled with the softest goose feathers, he fell into a dreamless sleep.

Breakfast was a confused affair and Danny felt he needed to keep a careful eye on his mother. He knew he must be ready. The moment she showed signs of moving from the table, he was ready to jump up and follow her.

'Did you like Dublin, Danny? How did you like the steamer? Cold was it? Never mind. See! The sun's out today.'

The questions were endless. Danny didn't answer any of them. He just kept watching his mother.

'Eat your breakfast, Danny,' said Kathleen.

'Don't bother the lad. There's no hurry. Sure! When God made time, he made plenty of it,' one of his uncles quipped.

There were even more of them sitting round the table this morning. His mother had made him kiss them all.

4

'See! This is yer daddy's daddy and yer daddy's mammy, Granddad and Grandma McCoy. One day I'll take you to see my own mammy and daddy over in Cavan.'

Danny didn't pay much attention. All that had been before breakfast. Now the talk ebbed and flowed over him.

'He hasn't got much to say.'

'He's shy. Poor little lad.'

'He'll get over it.'

'More of our Eileen's potato cake, Kathleen?'

'You'll need some sustenance for that long journey home.'

Danny pricked up his ears. Good! They must be going home soon.

'An' don't I just know it. I'm dreading it but Dermot needs me back as soon as I can get. You'll look after the boy, won't you?'

Her face looked weird, thought Danny, sort of crazed like the path round his school. Maybe she's got a bellyache like I sometimes get, he thought to himself. His first realisation that all was not right was when one of his uncles picked him up, just as the mammy was getting in the trap.

'No! No! No! No!' Danny screamed and struggled. 'Ma! Ma! Ma! Ma!' He wailed and yelled but the trap was gone.

They carried him indoors and held him down. 'The mammy told you she was goin' and she told you we was goin' to look after you.'

Danny was inconsolable. He'd been locked in his own secret world while his ma had been rattling on in the bedroom and as usual he'd not heard a word she'd said. He'd not even noticed that she was only packing her own clothes. All he knew was, he'd been abandoned. He didn't believe the McCoys when they told him, over and over again, the mammy was coming

5

back for him. Fearfully he watched the road for the trap to reappear.

For two whole weeks, every morning, as soon as he got up, he would run to the window and plant his nose against the glass. The beauty of Leitrim's hills went unnoticed. They had to drag him away at mealtimes. His lonely vigil went on and on and on until…

'Come on outside, Danny.' Six-year-old John was trying hard to persuade his cousin to go out into the farmyard. So far, everyone had failed to penetrate Danny's stiff Yorkshire indifference. He tried to ignore his cousin but John got hold of his hand and tugged it with a surprising show of strength.

Reluctantly, Danny dragged his nose from the tiny patch of condensation and let his cousin lead him outside, into the farmyard. A little coloured pony stood between the shafts of a small tub. His grandfather held out his hand and several willing children pushed Danny up.

'See Danny. Hold the reins like this.' Down the farm track and onto the lane leading to the village they went. 'We'll just pop into Clancy's and see what they've got for a little 'en. Then we'll come straight back.'

The sweets eased the pain in his heart and, as he held both reins on the way back, he felt quite grownup.

'Pull the left hand rein to turn left.'

Danny was amazed when the pony did what he asked. He had no idea his grandfather had spent hours schooling it.

The tub turned neatly into the farmyard. 'Can we go out again?'

'Well we'll have to give this little chap a rest but he'll be ready to go out again tomorrow, sure he will.'

'Come inside Danny. I've just this minute taken some bread out of the oven and I've got some nice farm butter and home-made jam you can spread on it.' Granny McCoy helped him get down.

Later that afternoon his cousins dragged him down to the river. Danny watched them while they built a small dam with some fallen tree branches. It quickly formed a little pool, deep enough to swim in. That's deep enough to drown in, thought Danny. He backed away. He'd only ever been in the bathtub at home.

'Come on, Danny.' Sean and Seamus coaxed him in. 'We'll teach you to swim.'

The days and weeks passed in a blur. They were so full of enjoyable things to do. The whole family took off to the Fair of Muff in County Donegal. It was a real eye-opener for Danny. He watched children no bigger than himself riding the horses, bareback. They were showing their paces: walking, trotting, cantering and galloping. And they were at it from morning till night. There were hundreds of them.

'I wish I could ride like that, Uncle Peter.'

'You will, Danny. I'll teach you mesel', sure I will. See these hosses, Danny? They're Ireland's greatest export,' he paused and added, 'next to Guinness, that is?'

'Who's Gynnys, Uncle Patrick?'

'I'll teach you about that an' all, when youse a bit older.'

When it happened, it was such a surprise. Danny couldn't believe his eyes. He'd quite forgotten it was supposed to happen. There she was: stepping down from the trap. 'Ma! Ma! Ma! Ma!' He flung himself into her outstretched arms. He couldn't get the words out fast enough. 'Ma! I can drive a tub! Ma! I can swim. Ma! I've got me own pony! Come and see me pony! Come and see the cows, Ma! We get our milk from 'em.'

The family watched the reunion with tears in their eyes. There was a sudden stillness in the farmyard. Everyone was caught in a spangled web of happiness. Kathleen had her arms wrapped tightly round Danny and was showering him with kisses.

Danny pulled away. He didn't want to look like a right softy in front of all his cousins. 'Ma! You've not come to take me away, have you?'

'Not this time, though it breaks my heart that you don't want to come home.'

'Aw! Ma! I didn't mean…'

She was laughing at him. 'I'm only teasing you. I'm staying for a couple of weeks and then we'll go home.'

The years passed. Each summer Danny came back from Ireland with his head full of dreams. Sheffield was ok for the time being but Ireland was in his blood. He'd almost forgotten where he'd been born because, to Danny McCoy, it felt like he was just marking time in England. As soon as he was old enough to leave home he was going to live in Ireland. 'I'm going to be a farmer like Uncle Patrick when I grow up. I'm going to have my own horses like Uncle Peter. When I grow up I'm going to go and live in Ireland.'

'Is that so?' Dermot smiled at his nine-year-old son. 'Well before you go off to Ireland; Frank's here to see you. How's yer mammy today, Frank?'

'Hi Mr McCoy. She's still not so good. Me dad says I've got to stay out of the road because the doctor's comin' to see her.' He turned to Danny. 'You comin' out to play?'

'Go on. Off you go lad. Drayman's comin' today so you can keep out of the way and keep out of mischief an' all.'

Danny followed Frank outside. 'Where we going?'

'Hunter's Wood. Saw Bert and his lot headin' that way.'

'Good idea! Let's go then.'

Hunter's Wood was strictly out of bounds but, for the kids who lived round and about the Green Archer, it had an irresistible magnetism. It was a bit of land that the trams passed on their way to Fulwood Church. No one really knew why it was called a wood because there weren't that many trees. But it was full of rather exciting hillocks and crevices. When it rained, the depressions filled up with water. The kids loved it and pretended it was the Grand Canyon. It was a source of irritation to their parents because their children always came back covered in muck if they'd been playing there.

'Is it like this in Ireland?'

'Nope! It's tons better. It's bigger than this in Ireland. And you can go fishing and swimming and you can play on the sands. Last summer we went to...' Danny had got onto his favourite subject yet once again but he suddenly found he was talking to thin air.

Frank, now bored with hearing all about Danny's precious Ireland, was already running down the first mound, banging his hip with his right hand, pretending to be one of the cowboys in the films they watched at the Tivoli every Saturday morning.

'Wait for me,' screamed Danny as he grabbed a small piece of wood from the ground. He held it up in the air. 'Bang! Bang! Bang!' He galloped down the slope on his imaginary horse, firing his imitation gun at all the Red Indians surrounding them. They caught up with Bert's gang and played all afternoon until their bellies told them it was teatime.

Kathleen was waiting for them at the bottom of Eccleshall Road.

'Ooooh! Heck! We're in for it now,' said Danny, covered in mud.

'I'm off,' said Frank, racing past Kathleen and leaving Danny to face the music on his own. The strange thing was, Danny's ma didn't look mad. In fact, she looked like she'd been crying.

She took his hand. 'Come on Danny. We'll walk along to St Mary's. I see you and Frank have been playing in Hunter's Wood.'

'Yes Ma. I'm sorry Ma. I'm sorry I'm dirty. I didn't mean...'

'Never mind about that Danny.' They'd reached the little stone wall that surrounded the church. 'Sit down here a minute. I've got some bad news.'

Danny's heart froze. A vision of his pony swam before his eyes.

'Frank's mammy has just died.'

Danny turned the words over in his mind. Frank's ma! Dead!

'You mean she's gone to heaven to be with Jesus?'

Kathleen crossed herself. 'Yes son. She'll soon be in her eternal rest. Now Frank's going to need a friend like you. There'll be the Requiem Mass to go to and the funeral.'

Oh no! Not a funeral. Danny knew what that meant. All that crying an' talking an' sitting around an' having to be quiet. An' she'd probably make him go and look in the coffin. Frank's ma'd be cold and white like Mister Thomas who'd died last year. Mister Thomas had been the oldest regular at the Green Archer. Everyone went to his funeral. There had been a procession of people at least half a mile long, walking behind the hearse. Everyone had gone to have a look at him in his coffin. So here we go again, thought Danny. We'll surely be going to see Missis Turner. There'd be no getting out of it. All the curtains would be closed an' the gloomy parlour would smell of mouldy old flowers and stale green soil and death. 'I don't need to go to the funeral, do I, Ma?'

'Yes you must, Danny. You can't ignore the fact that Frank's mother has gone to Heaven. We'll all go and rally round. It's a mark of respect.'

Danny knew it was pointless to argue. There was something about a funeral that seemed to turn his mother into stone. They'd always got to do "the right thing" so they'd be going round to Frank's to look in that coffin. And the grownups would be sitting round in the parlour, drinking! And then they'd all be having to sit on those hard benches and they'd have to kneel on the floor for ages and ages while the priest prayed for her eternal soul. And when they got back to the house, him and Frank would be expected to keep quiet and sit still and there'd be no playing out for quite a while. Oh heck!

That summer, Danny's ma asked Frank's daddy if Frank could go to Ireland. Danny had no idea how she managed to get Mister Turner to say yes but she did and now here they were, on the steamer to Dublin. 'See. Lean over the rail,' said Danny, feeling quite superior as he watched Frank sick up his breakfast. 'See! I told you not to have any breakfast.'

'Come on Frank.' Kathleen put her arm round him. 'Come and sit down in the sunshine. You'll soon feel better. Danny! Go an' get a cup of tea from the cafeteria and ask the lady behind the counter to put some extra sugar in it.'

Frank hung back as Danny and Kathleen were gathered into the arms of Dermot's family but it was only a few minutes before Kathleen pulled him forward and introduced him. They were soon on top of the trap and driving down the road.

Granny McCoy was waiting for them and as usual the table was laden with good farm produce.

Frank's eyes were wide with appreciation but Danny had something other than food on his mind. 'When can I see me pony?'

'Sure an' you can nip and see him now while we're all sitting down. Be sure an' wash your hands when you come back.'

Everyone was sat down when Danny got back. There was an empty seat next to Frank and he popped himself into it. 'Where will Frank be sleeping?'

'In with you and John. You'll be all right in that bed. It's plenty big enough for three little nine-year-olds, so it is.'

'Can we go out and play?' John asked when they'd all finished eating.

'If you've all finished,' said Granny McCoy.

'Don't be out too long. I want you in bed at a respectable hour.'

'Leave the little lads alone, Kathleen. They're on their holidays. What will you be doin' boys?'

'Showin' Danny and Frank how to fight.'

Danny waited, with baited breath, for his ma to hit the roof. He wasn't allowed to fight. There was no reaction whatsoever. His mammy had started telling his granny about his daddy. He pushed his chair back ever so quietly, got up and followed his cousins out of the room. Frank trailed after him.

'Put 'em up,' said John, dancing round them with his fists in front of his face.

'We're not supposed to fight,' said Danny.

'This ain't fighting. It's boxing,' replied John.

'Come on,' said Neil, 'behind the barn. That's where we fight. We'll show you some good moves. Have you ever boxed before?'

'Nope,' said Frank.

'Not likely,' said Danny. 'I'm telling you, Ma'll kill us.'

'No she won't,' said Uncle Patrick, who had just emerged from the long, low, whitewashed farmhouse. 'Boxing's a fine sport, so it is and it's a good time for you both to start learning. I'll give you some lessons.' He followed the children round the barn, took off his jacket, hung it over the bottom half of the barn door and rolled up his sleeves. Before long all the boys were throwing punches and dancing around.

'Bedtime everyone!' Granddad McCoy appeared round the corner of the barn. 'Come on Danny! Yer mammy's fussing a bit. They'll be plenty of time for a few late nights when she's gone back to Sheffield. How's the boxing?'

'He's doing pretty good, Granddaddy.' The young James McCoy poked Danny in the ribs. 'Just think, if you get good enough you can get into the ring and then you can make plenty of money and you'll be famous.'

'What do you mean? Get in the ring?'

'The boxing ring. You can make a lot of money in a boxing ring. More than you can in a boxing booth.'

'What's a boxing booth?'

'It's a booth at a fairground where men bet on the outcome of a fight,' said his Uncle Patrick.

'You wait till Uncle Frankie comes over from America. He's a famous boxing manager, isn't he Daddy?'

'Aye! So he is. He's got a gym in New York. He'll give you a few good pointers all right.'

Danny couldn't wait to meet his Uncle Frankie. What with the boxing and the swimming and his pony, life was pretty good.

Even when he was back in Sheffield, Danny was forever thinking about his pony. He always pricked up his ears when the talk turned to Ireland. He listened with concern as his ma and pa talked about all the troubles. And they were always going on about how the granddaddy and grandma were short of money. Anything spare from the pub takings, went back to Leitrim to help the family. Danny hoped they were spending some of the money on food for his pony.

Each summer, on the way back to Ireland, he worried in case things had changed and the summer of 1930 *did* change things. When he got back to Leitrim that year, he found he'd finally grown too big to ride his little pony and the family had decided to give it to his younger cousin.

'...an' don't be bothering about it, not at all,' his granddaddy said, 'for we've got you a hoss to ride instead.'

14

There was a young horse standing nearby. Its coat was the colour of mahogany.

'Now Danny,' said Uncle Peter, 'jump on his back and see how he feels. He's an Irish Draught hoss. He'll do anything for you. He'll jump, work, race, drive. He's fearless and powerful but he's so well behaved you can drive him wi' a piece o' cotton. You wait till you take him out on the roads, lad. He'll frighten you to death. He lifts his feet so high and proud-stepping, sparks fly off his shoes.'

'What's he called?'

'Tommy.'

That summer was the best summer of his whole life. At least that what he thought in 1930. But then each year seemed better and better. He learned to ride like a jockey. 'I'm going to ride in the Derby, when I grow up, Ma.'

'What about being a farmer?'

'I can do that as well, can't I?'

His father laughed. 'I thought you were going to be a boxing champion?'

'Oh aye!' Danny frowned: concentrating on the poser his da had just set him. 'Well I've plenty of time to do that, as well.'

Life in Ireland was idyllic. There was so much time and so many wonderful things to do and making his mother's life hell was one of them. Like the time he rode Tommy past her bedroom window, scaring her half to death.

Every morning about seven o'clock he went down to Tommy's field to catch him. The field where he grazed ran down to a lake. It was one of the lakes in the song "Leitrim, Lovely

Leitrim" that the daddy liked to sing. There were fifty-two verses and the daddy always did it on Christmas Day while the mammy sat crying over the dirty pots and her glass of Guinness.

This particular morning the sun hadn't quite risen and the lake was a dark steel blue. Danny jumped up onto a nearby boulder, about three-foot high, left by the last ice age. Then he shouted, 'Tommy! Tommy!'

As soon as he heard his master's voice, the lovely big bay horse came cantering over. Danny slipped the halter over his head; jumped on his back and away they went; galloping across the glistening white shingle to the water's edge.

By the time Danny was ready to head back, the colour of the water had changed from indigo to sapphire and the rising sun was criss-crossing the surface of the lake with diamonds. The olive-green hills were bathed in its golden light. It was Danny's own private Paradise. He would take one last look before turning Tommy towards the lane leading to the long low farmhouse. Up the dirt track they would gallop: Tommy stretching his legs just like a racehorse. Then they hit the cobblestones that led into the farmyard. Going at a fast gallop, as he was, Tommy's shoes pounded over the cobbles. What a racket! He seemed to know just what to do. He missed the old stone gatepost by a whisker and he was going at breakneck speed.

Kathleen was just getting up when she saw her son shoot past her bedroom window. She started screaming at the top of her voice. 'Oh! Oh! He'll be killed!

Having dismounted, it took a few minutes to put Tommy in one of the stables. But when he went into the kitchen the mammy still hadn't recovered. The grandmammy and his Auntie Eileen were bending over her with the smelling salts.

'Promise! Promise me! Promise you won't ever do that again.'

But Danny did do it again. It was such fun. Tommy was expert at missing that stone post by an inch. Any closer and Danny's leg would have been ripped to shreds. Eventually though, he had to cut it out. His ma said she couldn't get to sleep at night.

'I can't stand it any more. I'm awake all night, dreading the morning coming, knowing you're going to appear on the scene!'

When Danny was sixteen his holiday in Ireland came to a brutal end due to the fact that his father broke his leg. Danny rushed back to the Green Archer to help out but he promised himself he'd get back to his granddaddy's farm as soon as possible. Then something happened that was to delay his return for quite some time.

CHAPTER TWO

Danny and Frank were sitting on a rocky outcrop up Wincobank Hill, gazing over the distant chimneys of Sheffield.

Danny lit up. 'Want a fag, Frank?'

'Aye! I don't mind if I do.'

'So how's the job going?'

'Well, it's a job. Can't say as I'm right keen. You don't know how lucky you are, bein' able to work for your old man.' Frank had been down the mine since he was fourteen whereas Danny had been working at the Green Archer ever since his dad had broken his leg.

'It's not what I want to do. I should have been in Ireland by now but the accident put paid to all that.'

'Yeah but he's better now, isn't he?'

'Aye.'

'So why not go to Ireland now?'

'Because I'm thinking of joining up. They'll call me up anyway so I might as well get it over with.'

'What? You? Join up? You're never going in the army?'

'Nope! I'm goin' in the RAF. I've always fancied a bit of flying.'

'Don't you have to a bit clever for that? I heard you have to take an entrance exam.'

'Yeah! But I'm not thick. Anyway, I've bin told that they like a bloke who's a bit sporty. I reckon my boxing record will get me in.'

'Do you think I could get in?'

'What do you wanna get in for? Miners'll be exempt.'

'Same as you. I fancy a bit of flying now you mention it. Be better than being stuck underground. D'ya reckon we're getting into a war with Germany then?'

'Nowt's more certain! When we get back down there, I'm going straight to that recruitment office.'

'I'll come with you. How d'ya rate my chances then? I've not done as much boxing as you.'

'No but you're much brainier than me and I can say that you've always been my sparring partner. Anyway, what can we lose? If we fail the entrance exam, well, so what? It won't matter much. They'll grab me for the army and you'll still have a job down the mine. But if we do get in, it'll be a bonus. Listen. Better not mention this to anyone. Don't want to look right idiots if we fail, do we?'

They passed the exam. Easily! They were in!

Kathleen went mad. 'We'll never see your likes again!'

'Leave the lad alone. He'll be drafted into the army afore too long. At least he'll be safer, up in the sky, than on the ground.'

'Your ma isn't keen on you joining up, is she.' Frank and Danny were propping up the bar. 'She could be right, you know. It might not be that glamorous. And I'm not keen on getting shot down by a Jerry.'

'Well, if you stick wi' me you won't get shot down. I've got a very important date, straight after we finish Jerry off.'

19

'Oh aye! Who with?'

'My Uncle Frankie. He's promised he's taking me over to New York. A boxer can make millions over there. Then when I've made my fortune I can set up in Ireland.'

'You and your dreams. All you ever think about is Ireland. What about girls? You could have your pick, what with your looks and your successes in the boxing ring and your Irish blarney.'

'I've told you over and over again, I'm not letting any female get her hooks into me. I've got plans for my life and they don't include settling down wi' a woman. You know what happens when you get involved wi' a woman?'

'No but no doubt you'll tell me.'

'Within five minutes you've got a pile of little nippers hanging onto your coat tails and dipping into yer back pocket. I need to be fancy-free for what I'm going to be doing.'

'What's that then?'

'I keep telling you. I'm going to be a boxer.'

'Well, forget all that and take a look at that girl over there?'

'Why?'

'Because she's been watching you all night. I reckon she fancies you.'

'Yeah? Well she can watch all she likes. I'm not interested.'

Frank could see the girl was smitten and who could blame her. Danny was a very good-looking bloke. His dark brown hair was cut short and slicked back. His deep blue eyes were mesmerising. There was a strong determined look about him and his ever-present cheeky smile told everyone he hadn't got a care in the world. Danny McCoy had everything going for him.

Frank had followed Danny's example and there they were: in the RAF. All through the war they stuck together. They were just like brothers. And their friendship carried them through the most ghastly horrors a man could experience. They were really bad times. Course there were some good times, like when Danny became the squadron's boxing champion.

Danny was on his way back to his quarters when he ran into his Commanding Officer. 'Been doing a bit of training?'

'Yes sir.'

'Ready for Saturday night?'

'Yes sir.' Danny was fighting a boxer from Chicago.

'Hope you're well prepared. He's got a bit of a reputation over in Chicago and we don't want to give them Americans another reason to feel superior, do we?'

'No sir. Don't worry sir. I've seen him box. He's not anything special. He's had a lot of easy fights. I can handle him, sir.' The Americans had flown over in readiness for the daylight raids that were being planned. A boxing match had been laid on between one of their boxers and Danny. The pride of the RAF was resting on this fight and Danny knew it. But he wasn't a bit bothered. 'I reckon I'll have him laid on the canvas in the third round.'

'Good! I'm glad to hear it. Best of luck.'

'Thanks sir.'

'Now. Your lot are going out tonight and the Wing Commander is just briefing them. You'd better cut along now. Don't bother to get changed. You can change later.'

'Yes sir.' Danny hurried along to the briefing hall.

'Good. You've just made it in time. I know you've been training. Don't worry about your state of dress. I'll excuse you today.'

Danny sat down at the back. He listened intently whilst the Wing Commander went over the usual information about that night's raid. It was pretty much routine. Then he pricked up his ears as he heard that there were a few changes to the crews.

Danny and Frank always flew with "Johnny" Johnson so Danny wasn't at all pleased to find that he was in another squadron and flying with Squadron Leader Charles Barrington instead. Him and Frank hung back till everyone else had gone. 'Sir? Can we speak to you?'

'If it's about the changes to the crews, there's nothing I can do. You know I don't like splitting a good team but if a Squadron Leader doesn't have a navigator, he can't go out. It wouldn't look too good if we had to ground a flier of Barrington's calibre, would it?'

'No sir,' muttered Danny, wishing he wasn't a navigator.

'So run along, get showered and changed and get some tea.'

Frank stared across the table at Danny. 'I don't know what you're bothered about. He's a brilliant pilot, you know. Far better than Johnson. He's got three DFCs and…'

'They're two a penny. We all got a DFC in that last raid. Every time we go out they feel obliged to give us one. And I ain't interested in medals.'

'Well you might not think much about a DFC but Barrington's got a VC.'

'I don't dispute that he's a brilliant flier. I just don't like change, that's all. It's unlucky. You an' me: we've always flown together.'

'Don't worry about it. You'll probably only have to do it this one time. You'll be all right. Trust me.'

It was the worst raid that Danny could remember. The ack-ack was so fierce; it sent one of the men crazy. He was screaming and careering all over the place.

'Sort that boy out, Yorkie. Get that fire extinguisher and knock him out.'

Danny did as Barrington had told him and hit the bloke several times on his helmet, making no impression whatsoever.

Then Barrington looked over his shoulder. In spite of all the commotion he was as cool as a cucumber. 'Yorkie! Listen to what I'm telling you. Will you take off his helmet? A sharp glancing blow to the temple will be far more effective than what you're doing.'

As soon as the plane landed, Danny was out faster than he had ever moved in the boxing ring. Within minutes of landing he was pummelling his way into the control tower.

'Hang on McCoy. You can't go in there. There isn't room for a flea, never mind a big heavyweight like you.'

'I'm a middleweight,' muttered Danny automatically. 'Let me in. I've got to find out what's happened to "Johnny" Johnson. We heard on the radio that they've only got one engine.'

One of the officers came out. 'Johnson's crew all bailed out over Lincoln.'

'Are they all right?'

'They should be. They all got out. Someone counted the parachutes coming down.'

'Thank God,' said Danny, crossing himself.

It was the night of the big fight. It was in the third round that it happened. Danny felt his anger explode. He was suddenly fed-up of flying. He was fed-up of dropping bomb after bomb, to no effect. He was fed-up of going out on endless missions and flying for sixteen hours at a time. He was fed-up of sitting at a metal table in a freezing tin can. He was utterly fed-up to the back teeth of the bloody war and he wished he'd never joined up.

He had the American up against the ropes and he was punching him as hard as he could. The referee was trying to pull him off so the American could get back into the game. Danny ignored him. The bell went for the end of the round but Danny never even heard it. Against all the rules he carried on belting his opponent. He wanted to kill him. There was a red haze in front of his eyes. The crowd was screaming and booing. Danny didn't hear them. It took the referee and several officials to drag Danny away. The fight was stopped and the decision awarded to the American.

Next morning Danny was told that the Wing Commander wanted to see him. He had to report to him as soon as he'd had his breakfast.

'I don't want to do anything that might spoil your unblemished record in the RAF and that's why I'm ordering you home on sick leave.'

'Yes sir!' Danny saluted.

'Dismissed!'

Danny caught the train at midday. It was the first train he'd been on for six years that wasn't late on arrival. He walked into the Green Archer just as the daddy was pulling a pint. He felt an enormous sense of relief at being drawn back into the bosom of his family. But that was all he felt. He felt no pride in fighting for his country. As far as Danny was concerned it was just a bloody waste of time and lives. The mammy and daddy could boast all they liked about the medals on his jacket. They were heavy but not as heavy as his heart.

A few days later, he walked to church. The medals were burning a hole in his pocket. He stopped off at Hunter's Wood. There was plenty of time. He lit a fag. Shrouded as they were by a thin cloud of his smoke, he could still see the two little lads as they galloped down the slopes. It all came flooding back.

'Bang! Bang! You're dead!'

'That's not fair. I weren't ready.'

'Aw Danny! You're never ready. You're always standing around dreaming of Ireland.'

The scene changed. Danny watched Frank as he pulled his first fish out of the river. 'Look at me Danny! I've caught a fish! I've caught a fish!'

'Will you stop waving the rod like that,' shouted Sean.

'See! Get that fish off the hook before he loses it,' said Uncle Patrick.

Sean just managed to grab the fish before Frank danced away.

'See, look over yonder, boys.' Kathleen pointed. 'There's the dockside and there's your daddy, Danny.'

'When can we go back again?' Frank's eyes were shining.

'Maybe next summer.' Kathleen smiled down at him.

But Frank never did go back to Ireland. He went down in the mine instead. And that's what decided him to go and fly up in that bright blue expanse above the clouds, with his best friend, Danny. 'Ay! It's not bad up here.'

'Better than going down that mine?'

'A million times better, I'd say. I can't believe we're doing this.'

Danny dropped the fag and ground it under his heel as he stared at the children. They were playing the same old games. Some of them saw him standing there: tall, slim and immaculate in his smart, beautifully pressed slate-blue uniform.

They ran over to him. 'Here mister! You killed any Germans?' They gathered round him like he was a film star.

The admiration in their eyes was almost too much to bear and Danny felt like telling them to get lost but he hadn't the heart. They were as scruffy as the children he'd seen running barefoot in Ireland. Yet their eyes were filled with a bright shining ray of hope. So he stayed a while and with the expertise of an Irishman, he wove them tales about his life in the RAF.

And now he was late. He walked faster. They were all there at the church. All the lads from Squadron No 83 of Bomber Command No 5 Group. There must have been forty-five medals on view that day. They shone in the pale February sunshine, against those slate-blue uniforms, pressed till they looked like new.

'Come on Yorkie. We've been waiting for you.'

'Right boys.' "Johnny" Johnson arranged them all. 'On the count of three. One! Two! Three!' The chosen six hoisted Frank's coffin onto their shoulders and marched slowly into the church.

As Danny walked into the church, questions filled his mind. What was he doing here? A young man just turned twenty-three, carrying his best friend's coffin. What was it all about? No one answered him.

Danny had decided to keep Frank's medals for himself. They were in his pocket. But when he looked at the broken and bent figure of Frank's dad, he knew that he couldn't do it. Slowly he pulled them out. 'I was hanging on to these until I could catch you on your own.' He handed them to Mr Turner.

Frank's dad took them and went to the sideboard. Reverently he laid them in front of the photo of Frank in his uniform. 'He nearly made it, didn't he?'

'Aye Mr Turner. He nearly made it.'

'If only he hadn't landed on that railway truck. They said he wouldn't have known anything about it.'

'No! That's what they said.'

'What I don't understand is; why did he have to go all through the war without a scratch and then break his neck just bailing out?'

Danny knew it was his fault that Frank was dead. He'd made a choice and then he'd persuaded Frank to make the same choice. It had been the wrong choice. And it had killed his best friend. It was that knowledge that had sent him mad in that last fight. And he knew that whenever he stepped into the ring he would always see Frank's face in front of him. He knew his boxing days were over. He wasn't fit to go in a boxing ring ever again.

CHAPTER THREE

The black waves did nothing to improve his mood. The trip hadn't come up to his expectations. It was the mammy who persuaded him to go. She thought it would be good for him. He'd been pretty depressed after his de-mob. He missed Frank more than he could possibly have imagined. He missed his other RAF pals as well. The war had changed his attitude to life. Before the war, he'd been a free spirit. But now he felt the whole world was against him. Life in Sheffield was boring all because his dreams of becoming a boxer had been crushed.

The situation at home had worsened while he'd been in the RAF. The Green Archer was really run down. The daddy was plagued with arthritis and the food situation was still diabolical thanks to government restrictions. Even now, in 1952, rationing was still going on. It was the rationing that had prompted Danny to go into pig farming. The rules were that you had to rear two at a time: one for your own use and one for the Ministry. So they now had a plentiful supply of bacon. He was rearing them on the spare land at the back of the pub. A voice cut through his thoughts.

'Excuse me?'

The girl had an English accent with a slight twang that Danny recognised but couldn't quite place.

'Didn't we see you on the station at Leitrim?'

Danny remembered seeing her waiting for the train. You couldn't help but notice her. He'd wondered fleetingly if she was a film star with her blonde curls and those baby-blue eyes. Her clothes looked like they'd been designed in Paris so either she was very rich or her mother was a gifted dressmaker. But he didn't want to get into a conversation with her so his reply was very off-hand, 'Aye! I was there, so I was.' During the war he'd managed to steer clear of women. He'd seen most of his RAF pals marched up the aisle by girls that had plenty of tricks to trap a fella but they'd never caught him, thank God.

'Are you Irish?'

Damn! She wasn't going to be brushed off so easily. Well, with a bit of luck, as soon as she found out he wasn't one of those romantic Irishmen, she'd be off like a shot. 'No! I'm from Sheffield.' He turned his head away and blew his cigarette smoke over the rail. That should terminate the conversation, he thought to himself. But it didn't.

The word "Sheffield" opened the door for Connie. 'Oh blimey! I can't believe it! Guess where we're from?' She ignored his silence and carried on. 'We're from Chesterfield. Whereabouts in Sheffield do you live?'

That explained the accent. She was what you might say, a next-door neighbour and he wasn't going to get rid of her so easily, thought Danny, irritably. Since it was a small boat, it didn't look like he'd be able to escape so he decided to answer her question. 'I'm from the Green Archer. It's near the A625 going out towards Castleton.'

'Good heavens, you're a barman! That's marvellous!'

He wondered why she thought being a barman was so marvellous. He didn't get a chance to tell her he wasn't a barman, not that he wanted to.

'My parents own the Wellington.'

'You mean the one near Brimington? The one with the bowling green?'

'Yes! That makes us neighbours. Let's get out of this rain. You must come and meet my parents. They're in the cafeteria.'

To his surprise, Danny found himself following her as she tottered along on her high heels.

She suddenly stopped and turned round. 'I say! I haven't even told you my name. It's Connie Green. What's yours?'

'Danny McCoy.'

'I thought you said you weren't Irish?'

'Well I'm not: not really. My parents are. They were born in Ireland but I was born in Sheffield.'

'Oh bad luck! Ireland's such a beautiful place, isn't it?'

'Most beautiful place on earth, so it is. I spent most of my childhood there. Mind you, things have changed since the war.'

Connie pulled a face. 'You can say that again. The war changed everything for my family. My three brothers were killed in that war. Mam and Dad still haven't got over it. That's why we went on holiday to Ireland. It was supposed to make them forget but it hasn't.'

Danny found himself warming to her, especially since she'd lost her brothers like he'd lost Frank. Perhaps his first impressions were wrong, this time. Maybe she wasn't just another dumb blonde. 'By the way, there's summat I ought to tell you. I'm not actually a barman. I live at the Green Archer because my dad's the landlord there.'

'Good heavens! There's another coincidence. Both our parents own a pub. We must have been destined to meet.'

'Well actually, my parents are only tenants. It's a Barkers pub.'

'Oh well! It's virtually the same. Anyway, come and meet my parents.' She set off again, almost stumbling into the cafeteria. 'Mam! Dad! Guess what? This is Danny McCoy from the Green Archer in Sheffield.'

And that was the start. Docking in Liverpool; they all caught the train together and suddenly…

'We'll just walk down to the restaurant and leave you two young things to talk.' Sylvia Green dragged her husband from the compartment.

Danny was alone with Connie.

'So where did you go in Ireland?'

'Well first off, I went to Dublin, to my uncle's place and then we went to see the farm where I was brought up. It was nowt but a ruin.' Danny's voice shrunk to a whisper as he remembered the farm buildings.

'Oh no! That's awful! Doesn't anyone live there anymore?'

'Not since the granddaddy and the grandmammy died.' Danny found himself telling Connie all about his life in Ireland. 'My Uncle Peter gave me an Irish Draught horse. I called him Tommy. He'd do anything I asked.'

'So did you see Tommy when you were there?'

'Nope! He died while I was away in the RAF.' Danny's voice was hoarse with pain. 'I saw his grave. Uncle Patrick had buried him in the field by the lake, where I used to ride him. I'd go out on him everyday; more than once an' all. I was only a little kid but I was bent on being a jockey. Mind you, me weight would have been a problem. I suppose I could have been a farmer and I might if summat else hadn't come along'

'What?'

'Boxing. That's what. My uncles taught me to box and suddenly all thoughts of being a jockey or a farmer or anything

32

else for that matter went right out of the window. Me and me best friend used to spar all the time, back in Sheffield. That's what got him into the RAF. I got in because I was a sporty sort of bloke and Frank got in because he was my sparring partner. Then Frank got killed.' He suddenly stopped speaking.

Connie didn't press him to go on. She could see Frank's death had affected Danny badly but Danny continued.

'I promised mesel' I wouldn't fight again after Frank died.'

'Frank died in a fight?'

'Good God no! He'd been out on a bombing raid. Got safely back all right but they had engine trouble. Plane was going down and they all bailed out. Everyone got down OK all except for Frank. He fell bang on top of a railway carriage. Broke his back. I was fighting in a match, a few days later. I went a bit berserk. I tried to kill the other bloke and they had to stop the fight. It's the only fight I ever lost. I was the squadron champion before that. Anyway, I made a vow not to box again so my career was over before it got started. The trouble is, I was born to box. It's the one thing I'm really good at.'

'Then why don't you go back to it?'

'Can't trust mesel' in the ring. Frank and me, we'd been together ever since we were nippers. I know I'd just keep seeing his face and I might lose control again.'

'Well, you don't have to fight. Why don't you go into training or managing?'

It was like she'd hit him in the face with a wet dishcloth. This girl didn't know the first thing about him or his dreams of being in the boxing game yet she had just presented him with the answer to all his prayers. Train boxers! Yes! That's exactly what he would do. He had this strange feeling that he mustn't lose touch with Connie. They were on the same wavelength. He heard himself making arrangements to meet her…

33

'Where?'

'Outside the Palace. You know the one?'

'The Palace in Sheffield?'

'Aye that's the one.'

'I'll have to bring my girlfriend.'

Danny knew she was just being cautious. She didn't want to go on her own in case he stood her up. But he'd no intention of standing her up. 'Yeah, right! See you next Saturday night. Seven o'clock.'

It was just a casual date. That had been six months ago and now Connie Green was meeting Danny McCoy on a regular basis. Her mother loved him. Her father hated him!

CHAPTER FOUR

George Green passed him the change from his fiver.

'Thanks George.'

George's grunted reply was unrecognisable.

Danny was used to him. He took a mouthful of Guinness before picking up the gin and tonic. There was no point in taking umbrage. George was all right, really. He just didn't think anyone was good enough for his daughter. He doesn't need to worry, thought Danny, to himself. I've got no intention of marrying her. 'There you are, love.' He put the gin and tonic down on the table.

'Did Dad say anything?'

'Like what in particular?'

'Anything about us?'

'What about us?'

'He doesn't think I should be going out with you.'

'Why? What's up wi' me?'

'He thinks you should get a job.'

'I've got a job. I help out at the Green Archer. The mammy and daddy think I'm doing great.'

'You're surely not going to spend the rest of your life there? What happens when they retire? Barkers'll want another married couple in.'

'I'm not that bothered. I don't want to run a pub. Anyway, I've got me pigs and I'm making a bit on the side breeding greyhounds.'

'My dad doesn't think I should be going out with a pig man. You ought to get a proper job. I thought you were going to train boxers?'

'Yes, well. So I am.' Danny was halfway down his glass of Guinness. 'It just takes some setting up. Anyway! I'm not just going to train them. I'm going to do everything for them. You know? Lay on their fights. Manage them. See to them when they're injured. I'm going to be in full charge of everything.'

'What d'you mean? What does "see to them" mean?'

'Hurry up wi' that drink. I'm about ready for another.'

Connie downed her gin and tonic and put the empty glass down. 'What d'you mean about "seeing" to your boxers?'

'You know. Give 'em physio and all that stuff. My Uncle Willie's an orthopaedic surgeon in Dublin. He taught me all about injuries when I was a lad. I'm going to apply for a trainer's licence and I'll get it.' His voice held a ring of determination. 'You'll see! The only problem is: where to set up the gym.'

'I know somewhere that would be perfect.'

'Never!' Danny couldn't believe his ears. Connie knew nowt about the boxing game. So how could she know of anywhere suitable for a gym?

'Yes I do.' She pointed upwards. 'There's a whole empty floor up there.'

'Oh yeah! Empty bedrooms. You do know a bedroom won't be big enough for a gym, don't you?'

'I'm not talking about the bedrooms although it's true, there are some bedrooms but most of the first floor is taken up by a massive ballroom with a heavy duty sprung floor. We

36

used to have a dance every month before the war but after the boys were killed Dad closed it down. It's completely empty.'

'And d'you really think he'd let me use it?'

'Well he might…' Connie paused and then she grabbed the opportunity she'd been waiting for, all her life, '…if we were courting.'

Danny's brain assessed the situation faster than the speed of light and a speculative look crossed his face which, luckily for him, Connie didn't notice. He leaned across the table and gave her a passionate kiss. He got several wolf whistles from the locals and a glare from George. 'What d'ya think this is then? As a matter of fact, I've been thinking of asking if you wanted to get engaged. How about it, girl?'

'Oooh! Danny! Do you mean it? I know Mam and Dad will be pleased, especially if we tell them about your idea. It's a proper job, not like keeping pigs.'

'Oy! Watch it! Them pigs have done us all proud. I've kept the mammy and daddy in bacon since the war and your old man's done nicely out of it an' all. There's not many folk round here have been able to put their hands on a nice bit of bacon as easily as us lot and I never charge your dad the full price. Can't think why he's against me being a pig man when he's doing so well out of it.'

'I didn't mean it like that. I just meant there are better prospects in training boxers than in breeding pigs and dad will be better pleased if he knows I'm marrying a boxing manager.'

'Here! Hang on a minute!' Danny was panic-stricken. 'I never said owt about marriage. I've got to make a go of things, get on my feet, like, before we get hitched. Got to be able to give you a decent home and all the paraphernalia that goes wi' it.'

'But we can live here.'

This was going down like a lead balloon. Danny could see his freedom vanishing over the horizon like a runaway racehorse. 'Go easy girl. I need to concentrate on the boxing first. I need to make a name for mesel' and get mesel' noticed. I'm not getting married till I can afford to give you everything you deserve.' This seemed like a good tack. 'Tell you what, let's get engaged and see how things go. You can help me set up the gym and everything else, proper, like.'

Connie sighed. 'Oh! All right!' Her tone brightened as she said, 'When can we tell everyone we're getting engaged?'

There was no getting out of that one. 'Soon as you want. Better tell your folks first but wait till they've closed up, tonight.' He suddenly realised that he'd better try a bit harder to convince her he was sincere in his intentions and he ran his fingers up and down her arm. She giggled and out of the corner of his eye, Danny saw George watching. He ignored him.

George picked up some dirty glasses and stormed off into the kitchen.

In a tiny meeting room, above a public house, in Derby, a small group of men were gathering their notes and preparing to go home. The chairman of the council for Area No 8 of the British Boxing Board of Control looked up, 'Will you represent me at the next Board meeting in London, Father Murphy? I won't be able to attend. I've got that hospital appointment on the same day.'

'You'll be getting that wisdom tooth seen to at last then?'

'Aye! Can't put it off any longer. So will you stand in for me?'

'Certainly I will. Who else is going?'

'Billy Battle. Sorry about that.'

Father Murphy's forehead creased as he beetled his eyebrows. No one liked the local inspector, Billy Battle. He was a real troublemaker but it didn't make any difference to his decision. Someone had to go. 'Don't worry Arthur. You just get that tooth seen to.' He thrust his arms into the sleeves of his coat and throwing his scarf round his neck, he went to the door. It had been cold before the meeting and as it was now after eight it was likely to be even colder.

He walked briskly to his car and drove back across the moors, through the little pit villages, to Chesterfield. He parked near the presbytery, underneath the streetlights. He flung his coat and jacket on to the front seat and rolled up his sleeves. There were a number of young boys on a piece of scrap land. To a casual passer-by, glancing through the gloom of the winter's evening, they might have looked like they were brawling but Father Murphy knew better. He recognised some of them. Four of them were Sammy Clark's boys. They were trying to box but they didn't know the first thing about it. He went to join them. Having been born in Ireland, he knew a bit about the old game and there were a few good moves he could teach them. He wished with all his heart that he could find somewhere proper for them to train. He only needed some rooms because he'd already found a man who could make a much better job of teaching them.

Sylvia emerged from the kitchen with a tray of hot pies. She placed it on the bar. She got some plates from the plate-warmer. 'Here George, grab these and take three pies in there.' She nodded towards the snug where three miners were drinking ale 'Careful! They're hot.' She took another plate out, put a pie on it, grabbed some cutlery, salt, pepper and sauce and made her way to Danny's table. 'Danny, my love. Get this down you while it's still hot.' She perched on a stool. 'I'll just rest my weary legs for a moment.'

'Great! You spoil me, Sylvia. You know the only reason I come in here is for your pies.' He winked at her.

'Danny! You are cheeky.' Connie thumped his arm.

'Hey up girl. Leave us alone. You know I need to be in one piece for later on.' He smiled meaningfully at her and Connie edged her stool nearer to his.

'What's going on?' Sylvia eyed them keenly.

'D'you think we could talk to you and George, after closing time?'

'Is it about what I think it is?' Sylvia could hardly contain her excitement.

'Might be. Oh go on, tell her.'

'Me and Danny want to get engaged.'

Sylvia's face was wreathed in smiles. 'I'm so pleased. I won't breathe a word till you've asked George,' she cocked her head in his direction, 'and don't worry about him. I know how to handle him.'

'We're going to the pictures. We'll be back at eleven'

'You have a good time,' said Sylvia, getting up, 'and, like I said, don't worry about a thing. See you later. I'll get on and collect some glasses.'

'Blimey Danny! You've gone and done it now!'

'I meant to. I'm not one for hanging about once I've made me mind up. You an' I we're going to make a great team. Now go and get your coat while I finish this pie. The sooner we get out, the less chance there is of your father giving me the third degree.'

George was just locking up as Danny and Connie returned from the pictures a few hours later. 'Humph! You're back early.' He glared suspiciously at Danny.

His daughter kissed him on the cheek. 'Don't be grumpy Dad. I've brought Danny back for a bit of supper. Come on through Danny.'

George watched them go behind the bar and then he slammed the door shut, slid the bolt with a bang and followed them. He found Connie, Danny and Sylvia standing there. Waiting. 'What's up with you lot. You look like you're part of the Gunpowder Plot.'

Danny took the plunge. 'We've got summat to ask you.'

'Oh aye? What's up now?'

'We've really come to ask you…' Danny paused.

'Come on lad. Spit it out.'

'Will you let the lad speak,' said Sylvia.

Connie blurted it out before Danny had time to change his mind. 'Danny and me want to get engaged.'

Sylvia pushed forward before George could speak. 'That's wonderful, isn't it George. We're so pleased. Now George. Bring a bottle of bubbly up from the cellar while I get some glasses.'

'Oy! Hang on a minute! I've not said owt yet. What d'you mean? We're pleased? I've not said I'm pleased in fact I'm bloody well not pleased.'

'Dad! You can't stop me. I'm twenty-two. I don't need your permission.'

'Oh! Right then!' George was shouting now. 'So I don't count, ay? So you won't be wanting a contribution from me towards the big day, ay?'

Sylvia could see that things were turning nasty and the tone of her voice sharpened. 'Calm down George! I'm not having

41

our Connie upset. Danny's a nice boy. You're just being awkward.'

'The boy as you like to call him is thirty-three an' he hasn't even got a proper job. She's not getting married to someone who can't support her.' He turned to Danny. 'You can't marry her till you've got a proper job.'

Connie was in tears. 'He's getting a proper job.'

'That damn pig job's no good. I'm not letting you marry a pig man.'

'Danny's going to be a physiotherapist.'

'A boxing manager.'

'Right! That's it!' George was really yelling this time. 'I'm not having my daughter travelling round a load of fairgrounds, in and out of boxing booths.'

'What's that?' Sylvia didn't look quite so pleased now. 'You've never said anything about fairground work, Danny. I don't want Connie working the fairs.'

Now it was Danny that was shouting. 'Will you all be quiet. I'm not going on any fairground. I want to set up my own gym, here in Chesterfield.'

This sounded a bit better to Sylvia. 'Now look here. Everyone calm down. Everyone sit! That means you an' all, George!'

George sat down.

Danny and Connie perched on the two-seater.

'Now look here, George. I'll look after Connie. I know you're worried about me not having a proper job but it's not been easy since the war. When I got out of the RAF I had to help the mammy and daddy. Their pub isn't half as busy as yours and wi' me dad's leg being bad, pub were a bit run down. But I've got everything running nicely now.'

'I hope you're not thinking of applying for the tenancy. I don't want our Connie beholden to Barkers. She'll get this pub when we're dead and gone and this is a Free House.'

'George, will you stop interrupting.' Sylvia got a glare for her trouble.

'I don't want to run the Green Archer. I've no intention of running a pub for anyone. I want to go into sport. I want to train boxers and fix fights for them. It's not like you think. Boxing is turning into a respectable game now that the British Boxing Board of Control is in charge. For a start off, all boxers have to pass a medical. Look, George, there's a lot of money to be made but it's not just the money I'm after. Boxing's in me blood.'

'Listen to me, George,' said Sylvia, keen to split the men up for a few minutes, 'go and get some bubbly like I asked you to.'

George pulled a face but went out of the room.

'Just give him a bit of time. He'll get used to the idea.' Sylvia smiled reassuringly at her daughter.

George returned with the champagne and the discussion started up again.

'My idea is to train and manage boxers but I'll also be able to help them when they get injured. My Uncle Willie's a surgeon. He's taught me a lot about injuries and how physiotherapy can help. My boxers will be the best in Britain. I was a junior champion in Ireland and an amateur champion in the RAF. I know all about boxing and they're crying out for proper training facilities round here. I can get plenty of them young miners signing up. I'll have the pick of the talent for miles around.'

George was beginning to look convinced and Sylvia scenting victory seized her chance. Pushing a glass of champagne into his hand she said, 'Let's raise our glasses to Danny and Connie. Health and happiness to you both.'

George spoke grudgingly, 'Aye! All right. I give in. Here's to you both. But I still want to know more about these plans of yours, Danny.' The atmosphere was a bit calmer. 'So come on, Danny, tell us what you're going to do.'

'Well first of all, I'm going to get a trainer's licence which is a bit of paper that will entitle me to train my own boxers. I've already submitted my application to the local area council of the Board of Control. As it happens, Father Murphy's on the committee. He got me the form and he's going to give me a recommendation when I go in front of the committee.'

'Well, that's good,' said Sylvia. 'Let's hope you do get a licence from them.'

'So d'you think you will get one?' George asked.

Now is the time for a bit of bullshitting, thought Danny. 'Oh aye! No sweat! Then I'll need to buy some punchbags and speedballs. I'll get those from Goldberg's Emporium. I'll need to borrow a van to pick 'em up. They'll not fit in the car. I'll also need a good solid physio couch and some heat lamps. They'll cost me a bob or two. Might have to hire them or buy some second-hand ones. And I'll have to hire a portable boxing ring.' He turned to Connie. 'That's why I don't want to rush into marriage straight away. It's going to be a real struggle at first.'

'This is all very well,' George cut in. 'You've got all these plans but where are you going to set up? You haven't got a gym.'

There was a few minutes silence as Danny looked at Connie.

'Well Dad. I've come up with a really good idea. You know the old ballroom upstairs…'

'No!'

'Oh please Dad!'

'No!'

'Listen George,' Sylvia started on him, 'You're not going to stand in the way of two young…'

'No! It's out of the question!'

'But Dad, it can soon be turned back into a ballroom. Anyway, you don't use…'

'No! No! No! I'm not having my lovely ballroom turned into a sports hall.'

'Oh come on George. These youngsters need our support and…'

'No! He's not having my ballroom and that's my final word. Subject's closed!'

CHAPTER FIVE

A week later, Danny and Connie were sitting on a wooden bench, outside the committee rooms of the Midlands Area Council of the British Boxing Board of Control.

'They're a long time in there, aren't they? What did they ask you?'

'I've already told you. They just asked me why I wanted to train boxers and what experience I'd had.'

'No need to be so touchy. I'm only trying to find out what's taking them so long. It must be something you said. Did you tell them about your Uncle Willie?

'Yes! And I told them I was a junior champion in Ireland and squadron champion in the RAF.'

'Anything else?'

Danny knew Connie was referring to his Uncle Frankie. 'You know very well! I told them about Uncle Frankie.' He stubbed out his cigarette and lit another.

'You want to stop that chain-smoking.'

'Will you be quiet. My nerves are shot at. I reckon I shouldn't have told them about Uncle Frankie. They'd already heard of him. I saw it in the expressions on their faces.'

Behind the closed doors, the committee was still deep in debate and now the inspector was speaking. 'I'm telling you!

You give Frankie McCoy's nephew a licence and you're asking for trouble.' Billy Battle was red in the face with frustration.

'Look Billy.' Father Murphy tried to talk him round. 'He's not in the same league as Frankie McCoy. Anyway, this isn't New York. We operate far differently to that lot over in America. As an inspector you should know we're going to be keeping a tight rein on everything now.'

'I don't see as how you can say he not in the same league. It's the same family, ain't it? You give Danny McCoy a licence and it's an open invitation to Frankie McCoy to jump on a plane. He'll be here and running the show before you can say...'

'No! You're absolutely wrong, Billy. I'll vouch for young Danny. For goodness sake, he's a war hero. He flew in the RAF. That alone should tell you the sort of man he is. Give him a licence and I promise you all: I'll see to it that Frankie McCoy stays in America.' He mentally crossed himself because he knew that Frankie McCoy was a law unto himself.

Outside in the corridor, Connie was still interrogating Danny. 'What d'you mean, you shouldn't have told them about your Uncle Frankie? He's famous.'

'More like infamous.'

Connie's voice rose several octaves. 'What d'you mean? Infamous?'

Danny clapped a hand over her mouth. 'Shut up, girl. I'll tell you what I mean when we're back in the car.' He stubbed out his umpteenth cigarette and lit another.

'You said you were giving those up. You said they affect a sportsman's lungs.'

'Leave me alone.' Danny got up and started pacing the floor.

Suddenly the door of the committee room opened and Father Murphy came out. 'The council is recommending to London that you be given a licence and it's ninety-nine per cent certain that you'll get one. Mind you: I had to promise that we wouldn't see your uncle over here so mind you tell him to lie low if he feels like visiting you. Anyway, the licence should be in the post to you in the next few days. As soon as you get it, you'll be able to start training them boxers. Well done my boy!' He slapped Danny on the shoulder. 'You can start by finding some rooms for a gym and maybe I can help you with that.'

Connie had jumped to her feet and was kissing Danny. 'Well done!'

Danny shook hands with Father Murphy. 'There'll be a Guinness waiting on the bar for you, tonight, Father.'

'God bless you Danny. I look forward to that.'

'Maybe you could work on my father,' said Connie. 'We've all been trying to persuade him to let Danny use the ballroom.'

'Well I didn't know about that. And here's me thinking of asking about some rooms at the church. They wouldn't be as good as the ballroom at the Wellington. You'd be right on the spot. Sure an' you leave the old man to me.'

'Thank you Father.' Connie was almost dancing down the corridor.

As soon as they got outside, Danny grabbed Connie, lifted her up and whirled her round and round. 'That's it! I'm on my way! I'm on my way to the top and I'm taking you wi' me.'

'Ooooh! Danny! It's wonderful. You've got your licence. You're a boxing manager now.'

Danny planted several passionate kisses on her lips before opening the car door. 'Come on. Get in. Let's get back and tell your parents.'

She scrambled in and he closed her door. As soon as he got in the driver's seat and closed his door, she started on him. 'What did you mean about your Uncle Frankie?'

Danny started laughing. 'He's the best boxing manager in the world and the whole world knows it but his methods are a bit suspect. Course they turn a blind eye over there because he treats his boys like they were his sons. The thing is, they use stuff over there that's banned over here.'

'What stuff?'

'Mmmm! Just stuff!' Danny tried not to answer the question fully. 'You know. Substances like.'

'What substances?'

'Just substances.' He shrugged nonchalantly. 'Listen girl! You don't want to know. What you don't know about, you can't talk about. Trust me!' He turned on the ignition.

A couple of days later and George was surveying his precious ballroom. 'Well! Here it is Danny. Will this do you?'

'It's just the ticket. I'll not forget what you're doing for me. I'm really grateful.'

'It's not thanks I want. What I really want is for you to make my lass happy. Losing three sons in the war like that, well, I feel like I've got to look out for our Connie all the more. She's all we've got. Now don't keep her hanging on too long. The sooner she's married, the sooner you can be giving her a few babies to keep her occupied.'

Danny tried not to let his real feelings show. This wasn't part of his plans at all. He'd fully intended to coast along as Connie's fiancé not her husband. He reckoned that after a few years she'd get tired of waiting for him and she'd be casting her net again. Then he'd be free to pursue a career in sport without any interference from anyone. So what George had just said was a real shock to his system. 'I appreciate what you're saying but I thought you'd want me to be making a decent wage before you let me marry Connie.'

'Yeah well! I know that's what I've always said. On the other hand it strikes me that if you're going to be working here, you might as well be living here. There's ten bloody rooms up here and they're all empty. It makes sense for you and Connie to be using them. You can spread yourselves out and there will still be plenty of room for an office and a treatment room. I don't mind altering things a bit. I'll put in some doors to separate the living quarters from the gym. Your boxers can use the back stairs.'

Danny turned it all over in his mind. This was a fantastic opportunity. He couldn't really afford to turn it down. But marriage! Was it worth that? The whole ball and chain bit. On the other hand, Connie was a bloody good looker. Any man'd be proud to have her on his arm. His ma would be pleased. His da would be pleased. Sylvia would be pleased. Connie would be ecstatic. He had the feeling that he'd been trapped but he'd just have to play along. 'It's real decent of you to do this for us. I never expected this. Mind you,' and here he was clutching at straws, 'Connie might not be keen.' His hopes were dashed.

'You'll have no trouble with her. You're the first man she's ever shown more than a passing fancy towards. Sylvia was getting to think she'd never get any grandchildren. And, if you haven't already guessed, it was them women folk that forced my hand. And then Father Murphy got on the bandwagon and had a go at me. He doesn't half take advantage of that dog collar. Anyway, since you've been making all these plans I've come to the conclusion I'd like to be more involved. You know that bowling green out there? What's to stop us covering it with a tarpaulin, erecting a boxing ring and some tiered seats and staging our own boxing matches? I reckon we could get about four thousand punters round. Think about it Danny. We'd be the only ones in this neck of the woods putting on open-air boxing bouts. We could make a killing.'

'Now you're talking!' Danny was amazed that George had come up with such a fabulous idea. 'I could get some of my Uncle Frankie's friends to come and give exhibitions. There's Randolph Turpin and Johnny Williams. They'll come and get us started. And I've already spoken to Bruce Woodcock about my plans. He's an old family friend. He said he's going to send me some of his boxers. He's just taken on a couple of promising lads but he can't find the time to sort them out properly.'

'Just gone into retirement, hasn't he?'

'Correct! Undefeated European Heavyweight Champion. Since he retired, everyone's asking for his help. He says he hasn't got enough hours in the day. He'll be glad if I take over a couple of his lads. He's already told them that he's got every confidence in me. He knows my Uncle Frankie.'

'He's the one in New York, isn't he?'

'Yeah! He's sending me a couple of youngsters as well.'

'You're really going to make a go of this, aren't you?'

'Aye!' Danny had a sudden brainwave. 'It's thanks to you that I can so why don't you come in with me as my partner. Proper legal contract an' all that. You can have a share in everything. I'm more grateful than I can say. So will you share all this with me?'

'Aye Danny. I will and I appreciate the gesture. But as far as the boxing itself and any negotiations: that's your department. I'll not be interfering on that score. Oh aye! One more thing. Get that date set for taking my daughter up the aisle then we can all relax and concentrate on this boxing lark.'

Danny was standing on the steps of the Wellington waiting for Connie.

As she emerged from the pub she frowned at him. 'Why haven't you changed?'

'Listen girl. I've been at it all day. We've never stopped. I haven't got time to change. If you want to come with me you'd better get in the car now. I want to get there before the shops close. Anyway, I don't know why you're dressed up like the dog's dinner.' He dragged her, tottering on her high heels, to the car.

Danny was lucky. There was a parking space right in front of Goldberg's Emporium in Knifesmithgate. Connie had her door open before he'd even turned off the engine.

'Where d'ya think you're going?' Danny yelled after as she set off down the street.

She turned round. 'To the jewellers. You said we were getting a ring.'

'So that's what you're all dolled up for. Well! You can just get back in the car. I'm here to hire a portable boxing ring not to buy an engagement ring and if Irwin Goldberg sees me with a bird dressed like a bloody film star, he'll double the hire fee.' He ignored Connie's tears and stalked off.

The doorbell pinged. Irwin Goldberg looked up. 'Danny McCoy! A nice surprise! How are you today? I hear you've been granted a licence. Good luck to you.'

'News travels fast, Goldie. Thanks anyway. So you'll know why I'm here. I need some speedballs and some punchbags and I've been looking at some portable boxing rings in this.' He pulled a catalogue from out of the pocket of his overcoat. 'But if I'm going to get the lot from you, I want a decent discount.'

'Danny! Danny! Would I treat you badly? All I ask is that you send your boxers to me for their gear. I'll treat them well. We can do each other a lot of good. Come with me into the back. We'll have some privacy.'

Half an hour later and Danny was just finishing his business.

'Danny! Danny! You want that I should drop twenty pounds? Should I make a loss? Go out of business?'

Danny was killing himself laughing. 'Come off it Goldie! Even with twenty pounds off, there's still plenty in it for you.'

'Danny! Danny! You're breaking my heart. I've a Bar Mitzvah to pay for in November.'

'Oh aye!' Danny's tone was sceptical. 'So how many's this then?'

'Danny! Danny!' Irwin Goldberg put on a good act of sounding hurt. 'You know. Everyone knows. I have four boys. This is my youngest. You want that he should have to go without his Bar Mitzvah? I'll tell you what: I'll take off ten pounds and I'm giving it all away.'

'Right! Done! Thanks a lot, Goldie. Me and George will be down with a van to pick it up. Give us a bell at the Wellington when that portable ring comes in. Leave a message if I'm not around.'

'You got a good deal there. How am I going to eat next week?'

'My heart bleeds for you,' said Danny, laughing. 'Don't worry. You'll get it all back. I'll give you the nod when there's good money to be made on any of my boys.'

'Might be waiting a long time for that,' replied Goldie, gloomily.

'It'll be well before that Bar Mitzvah, don't you worry.'

Danny threw himself in the car and banged the door. 'I've got everything I need and I managed to pay cash for it all. Goldie gave me some good prices. Mind you, he knows there'll be more business coming his way.'

Connie wasn't speaking to him and she had her face turned to the window.

Danny started up the car and drove a few blocks down the street. He parked, got out, went round to her door, opened it and dragged her out. 'Come on.'

'I'm not going anywhere with you, Danny McCoy. You're a pig and I hate you!'

Danny ignored the insult and dragged her into the doorway of the jewellers.

As soon as she realised his intentions Connie flung her arms around his neck.

Danny took full advantage of her ardent kisses. Might as well enjoy the situation, he thought to himself, seeing as a ring was going to cost him a pretty penny.

CHAPTER SIX

Danny and Connie had been engaged three months when Frankie McCoy turned up, all the way from New York.

'So? You'll be marrying this girl then?' Frankie was sitting in the snug with his nephew. They were drinking the usual Guinness.

'Looks like I've got no option. Who'd have thought it? Me! Danny McCoy! Getting caught like this!'

'Well lad! You've had a good run, so you have. You're thirty-three and you've managed to keep fancy-free all this time. You should count your blessings.'

'Aye! Maybe! But I've not much longer to count 'em if she's got owt to do wi' it.'

'I don't know what you're looking so glum about. What d'you think you're going to be missing? It's not like you've been playing the field.'

'No. I know that. It's just that I'm not the marrying kind. I want to concentrate on boxing. I've got no time for romance and all that rubbish.'

'Well you couldn't get hitched to a nicer lass. She'll not give you any trouble. She's a bonny looking bird with a landlord for a father. I wish I was twenty years younger. She's the answer to a bloke's prayers.'

'I quite agree. She's a bobby-dazzler and now George has come up trumps with that ballroom, it looks like I'm going to get a gym. I just wish there were no strings attached.' Danny drained his glass. 'Want another?'

'I t'ink I will and I'll pay. Will you take some over to those two young fellas in there?' He nodded towards the main bar where his boxers were playing darts with two of the locals. 'Get them other lads a drink, an' all. 'T'is good of them to take my two boys under their wings like that.'

Unaware that she was the subject of the conversation in the snug, Connie was feeling quite relaxed. She was sitting with Sylvia, listening to the Third Programme on the radio. 'You like this musical stuff don't you, Mam?'

'Yes I do. By the way, why has Frankie McCoy come all the way from New York? Bit of a surprise, him turning up like that this afternoon, wasn't it? And who are those fellas with him?'

'Those are two of his boxers. He's brought them over for Danny. It's to get him started, like.' She popped a chocolate in her mouth.

'That's nice of him. Danny seems to have a very nice family.'

'Yes he does. They're ever so tightly knit. Uncle Frankie is the one who taught Danny to box, when he was in Ireland. And he arranged all his fights for him.'

'Is he staying for the wedding then?'

'No, I don't think so. As far as I know, he's off to Ireland next week to see Danny's family.' She held out her left hand and fluttered it so the light could catch her engagement ring. 'I love this ring.'

'Maybe Frankie will come over with the rest of Danny's family.'

'Mmm! Maybe he will.' Connie was still gazing fondly at her diamond ring.

The two men in the snug were still deep in conversation.

'Just see that I get an invitation to that wedding.'

'You know as well as me, you don't need one. All you have to do is turn up. Don't go disappearing off to New York. I want you here to see me married. I'll never forget what you've done for me; both in the past and now. Bringing these boys over will give me a great start.'

'It's helping me as much as you.'

Danny looked puzzled. 'How's that then?'

'I'm having problems getting anyone to fight Johnny, over in the States.'

'Why?'

'Because he's so well respected over there. He came to me with a fantastic reputation. Originally I paid for him to come over from New Zealand. I'd been reading some magazine or other, about all these boxers from Tonga, that were fighting in New Zealand. It said in this article, as far as I can remember, Johnny had only lost one fight.'

'Never!'

Frankie got up and went to the door of the main bar. 'How many fights did you lose back home, Johnny?' Frankie shouted.

Johnny Halanara shouted back, 'One out of ninety Boss and that was only on points.'

Frankie came back and sat down. 'See what I'm telling you? All true! And since coming over to me, he's won every fight that I've ever arranged for him. So no one wants to fight him now.'

'D'ya think anyone will have heard of his reputation over here?'

'Shouldn't think so but they'll catch on pretty quick so you'll need to get plenty on the first time he fights. Anyways you got two good boys there. Now I've fixed a couple of fights for them, up in Newcastle, in five weeks time. It's the week of The Hoppings. We need to have a talk about a training plan for these two lads so go and get another round of drinks in, will you, Danny?'

Fate has a strange way of bringing people together from completely different walks of life and over in Skegness, the wheel of fortune was beginning to turn. Bert Shaw, owner of the coconut shy, was knocking some stakes in the ground. 'Ger a bloody move on, yer brainless object,' he shouted to a midget who was unrolling the tenting material. 'At the rate you're going, by the time you get it sorted, it'll be time to take everything down again.'

'Yes Boss!' The midget speeded up as best he could.

'Gimme that bloody rope and be quick about it.' Bert Shaw had walked over and he smacked the midget on the back of his head. Shaw was a big brute of a man and he had managed to inflict as much pain as possible. The midget was reeling about in agony.

Frankie was telling Danny about Carlo Santini, the little Italian he'd brought over. 'He's not very experienced but he's good and fast. He's not been over-exposed in America and I think he's just coming into form. He'll do even better with you. Now, Danny. Remember! I'm giving these boys into your care.

You've got to look after them and always treat them proper. These are your boys, Danny. You be good to them and they'll be good to you.'

'Don't worry, Uncle Frankie. I won't let you down. I'll look after them. I'll treat them as if they were my own sons: just like you do.'

'Good lad. Now listen to what I'm telling you. Be sure and get plenty of money on these two boys, the first time they fight. You'll get a good price because they're unknown over here. This'll be your one and only chance to make a packet on them so see you do. And don't forget, get someone else to put the money on for you.'

Next morning, Danny and his Uncle Frankie were watching Johnny Halanara working with a punchbag in the new gym. Carlo Santini was beating a tattoo on a speedball.

'Just give them an easy time these next few weeks. Let them acclimatise. Build them up gradually. Then they'll be ready. Now! Watch out for that Abe Rosen. He's a devious bastard. Don't get into any deals with him. You listening to me?'

'What? Oh yes. Sorry! I was watching Johnny. He's bloody good.'

'Wait till he really finds his feet. Then you'll see how good he is.' Frankie raised his voice and shouted over to the two boxers. 'Carry on with the good work, lads. Remember! Danny's the boss now. He'll look after you.' He turned and spoke quietly to Danny, 'Have you got somewhere we can talk in private – somewhere we won't be overheard?'

'Aye. We can go in the office.'

Frankie gazed round Danny's new office. 'You're well set up here. Get behind that desk. I want to take a photo. I'll be seeing your Uncle Willie this time next week. He'll want to know how you're doing.' He took a camera out of his bag, took the photo and stowed the camera back in his travel bag. Then he sat down opposite Danny. 'There's something I've got to tell you about Johnny.'

'What's that then?'

'You know how I've always told you, everyone's got a dodge?'

'Yeah! That's what Uncle Willie used to say.'

'He got it from me, so he did. Anyways, you know what we mean by a dodge, don't you? We don't mean a trick or an angle.'

'Yeah! A dodge is a problem.'

'That's right. It means everybody's got something that bothers them. Might be they're scared of spiders or might be that they get nightmares. Might be they've got a weak knee or a tendency to break out in spots before a fight. Never had a boxer with spots thank God!' He crossed himself. 'Anyway, when you're training sportsmen, the trick is, to find their dodge. As soon as you find that dodge everything becomes so much easier because then you know what you're up against. Are you following me?'

'Yeah!'

'Well, Johnny Halanara, he's got a dodge and it's this. He bleeds easily and quite badly.'

'That's not a problem, Uncle Frankie. I know how to use that adrenaline.'

'Well, it's not adrenaline you'll need. It's tarmacadam.'

Danny burst out laughing.

'I'm not joking. If Halanara gets the slightest blow to one of his eyes, he's off. It doesn't affect his performance but as soon as the referee sees it, he'll be after stopping the fight. And when Johnny starts bleeding it's just like a tap. Your job of course is to turn that tap off, immediately. Whatever happens, he's got to take his chance up in Newcastle. The boy I've fixed him up with is good. He's a potential world champion. Johnny Sullivan.'

'Phew! He's bloody good. We'll do well to draw, especially seeing he's on his home ground.'

'Draw!' Frankie exclaimed. 'I'm telling you: our boy can win, as long as the fight isn't stopped. They'll never have seen anything like Johnny Halanara here in England. I've fixed up this fight with Sullivan so that in the eventuality of us winning, our boy's next fight could be against the world champion himself.'

'Bejasus!' Danny crossed himself.

Frankie followed suit.

'That's aiming high, Uncle Frankie.'

'Danny, trust me! I'm telling you. Our boy can win easily against this Johnny Sullivan. But if the worst should happen and Sullivan gets in a lucky blow, it's possible our boy might start bleeding. So if he does, I want you to use these.' He took a wooden box out of his bag and placed it on the desk. It looked just like a box from some fancy New York perfume house and it had a wax seal shaped like a flower. 'You got a penknife, Danny?'

Danny searched in the top drawer, found one and handed it to his uncle. He didn't dare say a word. He knew instinctively what was in the box and he didn't like it.

Frankie chipped at the wax. 'Luckily I wasn't searched coming through your Customs. Mind you, they wouldn't have

61

realised what this was, See! Look at the name. Here!' He showed Danny the name on the box. 'My contacts know just how to make things look kosher. This box looks just like the ones that firm uses. Only there ain't perfume in this little bottle.' He'd opened the box and now he was holding up a small glass phial. 'You'll need an empty adrenaline bottle. Put a few drops in and keep it handy. Keep it in your pocket not your first-aid box. What? What you looking so po-faced about?'

'Are those them Steel Drops they're using in America?'

'Yes! So what! I know they're banned over here but there's nothing wrong with them. Sure an' I don't know what all the fuss is about. They don't enhance a boxer's performance. They're just more efficient than adrenaline. Quite honestly, I don't know why they're banned over here.'

'Well they are.'

'So don't tell me you're too scared to try a bit of subterfuge?'

'No I'm not scared but they'll be watching me and if I get caught, I'll lose my licence.'

'Why are they going to be watching you? You've only been in the game a minute or two, so you have.'

'They'll be watching me because of you being my uncle. Father Murphy said there's an inspector called Billy Battle on the local committee of the Board of Control. He tried to stop me getting a licence because of you.'

'Never heard of him.'

'Well he's heard of you.'

'Well then, you'll just have to be extra careful, Danny boy. Anyway, good luck to you. By the way, I'll certainly be back for this wedding, so I will.'

Frankie had caught the train for Liverpool just after lunch. Danny looked at his watch. It was six o'clock. Frankie would be in the middle of the Irish Sea by now, lucky bastard, Danny thought, wistfully. He wished he'd gone with him. Maybe he could swing a trip to Ireland for the honeymoon. Better work on Connie. He was just checking his equipment when she came in with some clean towels.

'Where do you want these?'

'Shove 'em in the office. I'll put 'em away when I've finished here.'

Connie disappeared. A few minutes later she was back. 'Oooh! Danny? Is this perfume for me?' She had the wooden box in her hand but she hadn't opened it.

Danny moved like greased lightening. 'No it isn't.' There was a slight struggle but he did manage to grab the box.

'Then who else are you buying perfume for?' Connie's eyes were flashing blue fire.

'It's not perfume. It's something Uncle Frankie brought over for me.'

'Then why is it in a perfume box? I recognise that name. It's a famous perfume.' Connie was screaming at him by now.

'It's in that box in case the Customs searched Uncle Frankie.'

Connie's voice fell to a frightened whisper. 'What are you up to? Dad'll kill you if you get into trouble and spoil things.'

'Then keep quiet about it.'

'So what is it?'

'You don't want to know. What you don't…'

She interrupted him. 'Yeah! Yeah! Yeah! I know what you're going to say. What I don't know about, I can't talk about.'

'Got it in one.'

63

'What are you getting into, Danny McCoy?'

'Don't you worry your pretty little head about my business. You just worry about all that lovely money I'm going to be spending on you.' He pulled her into his arms and silenced her protests with a long passionate kiss.

CHAPTER SEVEN

It was eleven o'clock in the morning and Sylvia was sitting in front of the dressing table, re-touching her make-up. Connie was lounging on one of the twin beds.

'I'll tell you what, Mam. This room is nice and the bed was really comfy. I had a good night's sleep and so did you, judging by the amount of snoring you were doing.'

'Don't be cheeky. I don't snore.'

'You certainly do, Mam. You were at it all night.'

'How d'you know, if you were asleep, like you say you were?'

'Because I got up a couple of times to use the toilet and you were at it then all right. Dad's always complaining that you snore. Anyway, forget all that and tell me what you think of this hotel.'

'It's very nice and so it should be. It's a five star, according to the RAC sign outside. But we're only in here because I put my foot down. If I'd left it to those two fellas we'd have been staying at some flea-pit or other.'

'Well, thank goodness you did put your foot down. It might be the only venue we get to go to. Danny'll not want to fork out like this again. I think he was a bit put out that we all wanted to tag along but I told him; his first public appearance was too special to miss.'

'Where did they all beetle off to so quickly, after breakfast? I thought the weigh-in wasn't till four o'clock?'

'Danny wanted to walk round the fairground. I was going to go with him but he didn't wait for me. He's such a pig.'

George, Danny and Mac were just passing the coconut shy. Lewis McBrayn or Mac as everyone called him, was a big tough ex-middleweight from Glasgow.

Danny stopped and backtracked. 'OY! What thee hell d'ya think you're doin'?'

George and Mac stopped and turned round.

'Mind yer own business,' shouted Bert Shaw. 'Clear off, yer busybody or yer'll get some of the same.' He carried on kicking a midget, who was prostrate on the ground.

Danny looked at George and Mac, who'd come back to see what was going on. 'I'm not standing for that. I'm not leaving that poor little bugger to that bully. Are you with me?'

'I'm right behind you,' snapped George.

'Me an' all,' said Mac.

The three men ran down the path between the two stalls. Danny walloped Bert Shaw and he collapsed in a heap. While this was going on, Mac and George grabbed the midget and carried him away.

'Find us a taxi, Danny,' shouted George. 'This little bloke's going to need some hospital treatment. He's unconscious and he's bleeding badly an' all.'

Connie and Sylvia were sitting at a table in the hotel bar. Father Murphy had just come in.

'Over here, Father,' called Sylvia, waving her hand in the air.

He walked over and sat down.

66

'Thank goodness you're here, Father.'

'Sure an' why would I not be here? I said I was coming.'

'What I mean is, thank goodness you're here because George isn't. He's missing.'

'Missing? Is he?'

'So are Danny and Mac,' Connie chimed in.

'They're all missing. George, Danny and Mac. Something must have happened.' Sylvia was starting to panic. 'They all went out at nine o'clock and we haven't seen them since. That was four hours ago.'

'Don't be upsetting yourself, Sylvia and don't you be crying, Connie. T'is sure I am that they'll be back before the boys are having to weigh in. Did they say where they were going?'

'Yes Father. To the fairground.'

'Then they'll most likely have spotted a bit of talent and they'll be trying to sign him up. Don't take on. I'll get you both a drink. A nice sherry should calm those nerves.'

George and Mac were at the bedside. Danny was talking to the doctor at the end of the bed. 'I'm very grateful for what you and your staff have done, Doctor.'

'It's our job to do our best but it's nice to be thanked. Not sure what we've done is going to be of any benefit to him. He was pretty badly beaten up. Those broken ribs will take a bit of time to heal and he'll not be walking on that leg for a while.'

George joined Danny. 'Yeah well I wish we could have done a proper job on that fairground bloke,' he growled. 'Bloody bully. Danny only got one punch in. I would have liked to break both his legs but we wanted to get the little fella away.' He nodded towards the midget, who was just coming round.

'Can you keep him here till The Hoppings are over?' Danny asked.

'He'll be in here a lot longer than that.'

'Well, here's my name and address, Doctor.' Danny was scribbling on a page of a small notebook: something he always carried with him in case he needed to get a new boxer to sign up. 'This is for you to give to the police should they get wind of anything.'

'Thank you,' said the doctor, taking the page, 'but I don't think you need to bother. I can't see that fairground bloke reporting it to the police. They're a law unto themselves, unfortunately.' He looked down at the address. 'You're a long way from home.'

'Aye! We're up for the big fight. Two of my lads are on the bill.'

'So I might be seeing you again?'

'Not likely. The only boxers you might see in here are the ones who are fighting my lads. If I were you, I'd get a sizeable bit of money on 'em.' He took back the piece of paper and wrote the names of his boxers on the back. 'Keep it to yourself Doctor. We don't want the prices plummeting.' Danny noticed the midget had his eyes open. He went to the side of the bed. 'Look after yourself mate.' He touched his shoulder. 'Get yersel' a better job, well away from that bully. Next time you might not be so lucky.'

The injured fella's eyes were the only things visible beneath the swathes of bandages. He watched Danny and his friends leave the ward.

'Where the hell have you been?' Sylvia was livid.

'Thank God you're back,' cried Connie, throwing her arms round Danny.

'We ran into a bit of trouble.' mumbled George. 'We'll tell you about it over lunch. Let's get into that dining room before there's nowt left to eat. Aye! Aye! Father! You find your way here all right then?'

'That I did. Father Delaney pointed me in the right direction. It was handy being able to spend last night at the presbytery. Gave me a chance to catch up on all the gossip. As you know: this was my first parish.'

'You'll be coming back with us on the train, I hope.'

'I surely will. Be nice to be travelling back with the winners.' He lowered his voice so only George could hear. 'You got that money?'

George used the same hush-hush tones. 'Sure have. Speak to you about it later, when we've got rid of them women.' He raised his voice, as they followed Sylvia and Connie into the dining room. 'You two girls going shopping later?'

It was eight o'clock and the hall was packed to the roof with fight-crazy Geordies. They were hanging on the rafters, screaming and shouting. Danny and his two seconds, Mac and George were in the ring, waiting for the bell to go for Round One. Carlo Santini was on his stool in his corner. He was fighting another lightweight called Jack Jarvis. Connie, Sylvia and Father Murphy were in the front row.

'Seconds away!' The referee shouted.

Danny, George and Mac climbed out as Carlo got up, crossed himself and walked into the centre of the ring.

'Now lads! I want a good clean fight.'

DING! DING!

No sooner had Danny sat down than Connie dropped her programme. She bent down and scrabbled about and…

69

BANG! Santini got in a lucky punch. Jarvis sprawled on the canvas and the referee counted him out. The crowd went crazy.

Connie sat up. 'What? What? What's happened?'

The spectators who'd got money on Santini were cheering. The ones who hadn't were booing. The ones who hadn't bet at all but thought they were paying good money to see a good fight go the full time were standing up and shaking their fists at the referee. It was absolute pandemonium.

Father Murphy had jumped up and was screaming, 'We won! We won! We won!'

Danny, George and Mac were looking dumb-founded.

In the dressing room of a nearby theatre, Eddie Calvert stared into the mirror and wiped the sweat off his face. Two men hovered anxiously behind him.

'You haven't got time to be going to a boxing match.' The House Manager was clearly worried by this sudden turn of events.

'Listen,' said Calvert's manager, 'there's only about half an hour before the Second House.'

'That's plenty,' said Eddie. 'I'm only going to say hello to Johnny Sullivan. He's from my hometown.'

'No he's not,' said the House Manager. 'He's a local boy.'

'He might have been born here but he's based in Preston, where I come from. Now I can't be appearing just down the road from him and not go and say hello, can I? I'll be back before you've even noticed I've gone.' He grabbed his golden trumpet. 'Look! I'll take this with me and then if it's a bit tight, I can go straight on stage.' He shot out of the door.

'What's he mean by "a bit tight"?' The House Manager was starting to panic. 'There's half an hour. How long does he need to say hello?'

Eddie Calvert's manager spoke soothingly. 'Don't worry. It'll be all right. I'm sure he'll be back in plenty of time.'

George was watching Danny bandaging Johnny Halanara's hand.

Danny looked up. 'It's a good job we got all that money on both our lads, before Carlo fought. The price on Johnny's come right down. They're making him favourite, which surprises me, seeing as Sullivan's a local boy.'

'What d'ya mean, a local boy. He's from Preston, ain't he?'

Mac, who was leaning against the wall, grinned. 'Most people think that Johnny Sullivan comes from Preston because he's living there now. What they don't know is, Johnny's the son of a fairground boxer who used to work the fairs with his boxing booth. Battling Sullivan he was called. The story goes: Johnny junior was born here, on Newcastle Town Moor, while the family was here for The Hoppings. So all that lot out there will be rooting for him and that's where the money should be going.'

'So why isn't it?'

'Dunno. There must be someone in the know: someone with big money who's putting a pile on our boy. That's all I can think of.'

'What's the matter Johnny?'

Johnny Halanara was rolling his eyes.

'Not getting cold feet, are you?'

'Don't like all dat money restin' on mah shoulders, Boss.'

'Yes well you can forget about the money. Just get out and fight.' Danny looked at Mac. 'Actually, that's not the real problem.'

'Why? What is? What d'you mean?' George spoke sharply. 'No one saw you putting that money on, did they, Father Murphy?'

'Absolutely not.'

'It's not the gambling I'm on about. What I'm really bothered about is that bastard Billy Battle sitting out there on the front row.'

'Who's Billy Battle?' George asked.

Mac and Danny spoke in unison.

'Inspector for the BBBC.'

'Local inspector for the Midlands Area of the Boxing Board of Control.'

'If he's from the Midlands Area, what's he doing up here? Doesn't Newcastle have its own area inspector?'

'He'll have come up here specially to keep an eye on me.'

'You? Why you?'

'Because he knows about my Uncle Frankie.'

'What about your Uncle Frankie?'

'He's got a bit of a name for himself in New York.'

'What d'ya mean? A name? A name for what?' George wasn't leaving it alone.

'Just a name for a few dodgy techniques, that's all. It's nothing to do with me, George. Honestly. I'm clean. I swear to you.'

'Well in that case, why are you bothered about that fella being here then?'

'I just don't like him. He's a troublemaker.'

'Well forget about him and concentrate on getting your man in the right frame of mind for his fight.' George had no time for shilly-shallying.

It was almost the end of Round Five. Danny had been on pins right from the start. He was convinced something was going to happen. It was sod's law. Both boxers were dancing around, in the centre of the ring. They were equally matched and each had landed one or two good punches but Danny thought that if they both saw out the contest then his boy would win on points. He was, by far, the better boxer. Suddenly there was an accidental clash of heads just as the bell went for the end of the round. The two boxers retired to their corners as Danny, Mac and George climbed into the ring.

Oh my God, thought Danny. He'd never seen so much blood. A large cut had opened above Halanara's left eye and the blood was literally gushing out. 'Settle down now, Johnny. It'll be all right. George, gimme that medical box. I need my adrenaline.'

'Adrenaline's no' gonnae do the trick on that, Boss. It's no' use. This bleedin's no' gonnae stop.' Mac was obviously worried.

George passed him the medical box.

Danny opened it. He hesitated, but only for a second. Then. 'Mind out! Let me get to him! Mind out!' Surreptitiously, he reached inside his jacket pocket for the tiny bottle. When he'd put it there he'd prayed that he wouldn't have to use it and that was even before he'd known that Billy Battle would be sitting in the hall. Even now, he still didn't want to use it. Then he looked into Johnny's eyes and he knew he couldn't let him down. His hand closed around the tiny bottle of Steel Drops and then he pretended to reach inside his box for his adrenaline. Bending over Halanara, he quickly applied a tiny drop of the magic agent to the cut. Immediately, even before Danny had time to replace the stopper on the bottle, the bleeding had stopped.

'Hey! Look at that!' A fan shouted from the front row. 'Bleedin's stopped!'

The words rippled, like a giant wave, all through the hall. 'Bleedin's stopped! Bleedin's stopped!'

DING! DING! The bell went for Round Six and the seconds climbed out. The fight continued. A few minutes later Halanara hit Sullivan with the devastating "right-left-right" combination that was his trademark in the South Pacific. Sullivan fell onto the canvas and was counted out. The crowds went berserk. Eddie Calvert had completely forgotten about the Second House. He'd been given a complimentary seat at the front. He climbed into the ring and put his golden trumpet to his lips. When he started playing "O Mein Papa" the place erupted.

Eventually Johnny Halanara and his team were allowed to leave the ring. They were fighting their way through the mob of wildly cheering spectators. Suddenly, a hand fell on Danny's shoulder. He looked round. It was Billy Battle and the local stewards.

'Right McCoy! We want the bottle containing the substance you've just used on that eye.' Billy Battle was triumphant. He was about to prove his journey hadn't been a waste of time and money. And he knew all about the legendary Steel Drops and their effect.

'Certainly!' Danny matched him with a confidence he didn't feel. 'With pleasure! It's in my box. If we can get out of this crush and down to the dressing rooms, you can help yourself. Take anything you like. I've nothing to hide.'

They fought their way through the screaming fans and into the corridor leading down to the dressing rooms. They were passing some toilets when Danny had a flash of inspiration. 'Just a tick! Is that a toilet? I've been dying to go. Must be all the excitement! I won't be two seconds. Here! Hold the box till I come out.' He thrust his medical box into Billy Battle's hands and ducked into the toilets.

Into a cubicle! Slammed the door! Whacked home the bolt! Good! He was safe for at least a few moments. He rolled up his sleeve and then he took the bottle of Steel Drops out of his pocket, where he'd managed to transfer it when the fight resumed. He shoved it into the toilet and pushed it right under the U-bend. He pulled the chain. 'Right! That's that! Be somewhere down the Tyne by now,' he muttered. But just to be on the safe side, he shoved his hand under the U-bend again just to make sure it had gone. As he emerged into the corridor, he smiled at the stewards. 'Phew! I do feel better for that!' He took his medical box back from Billy Battle and they continued down to the dressing rooms.

Meanwhile, outside a certain theatre in the centre of Newcastle, a crowd of very angry people was trying to lynch the House Manager and calling for his blood.

'I'm telling you! You'll all get your money back if you wait patiently.'

Inside the dressing room, Danny put his medical box on a chair.

Billy Battle pounced on it. 'Ah! Yes! Here it is!' He grabbed the bottle of adrenaline.

'Oh aye! My adrenaline.'

'Adrenaline!' Battle laughed, fanatically. 'Never seen adrenaline work as fast as that!'

'Well, I only use the best. My Uncle Willie told me never to use any sort of second-rate gear.'

'Then you won't mind if we take this bottle to analyse the contents?'

'I don't mind at all but I want a drop in another bottle, sealed and signed by you, so there's no funny business.'

Battle looked disconcerted. Then he said, 'We haven't got a bottle.'

'Well you'd better go and get one.'

Billy Battle wasn't daft. He suspected Danny had just pulled the wool over his eyes but he didn't know how. And Danny wasn't daft either. He knew as long as he'd got that second bottle with proof that it had come out of the bottle that Battle had confiscated, the inspector couldn't touch him. He wouldn't be hearing from the stewards this time but it had been a close shave and it wouldn't be the last time that Battle tried to pin him down. Danny knew he'd have to be even more careful from now on.

Connie, Danny, George and Sylvia were sitting round the large kitchen table, engrossed in the morning editions.

'Oooh! Danny! Listen to this!' Connie read out loud from her newspaper. 'Last night, Danny McCoy took the boxing world by storm. The first of McCoy's boxers opened his account with a knockout within the first few seconds of the fight.'

'Oh aye!' George was laughing. 'You'd better listen to this. Even McCoy's attractive fiancée…'

Connie preened herself.

'…admitted she didn't see the first fight at all. Connie Green, daughter of publicans George and Sylvia Green of the Wellington, said she had just bent down to pick up her programme, when she heard all the cheering. She looked up and Jarvis was lying on the canvas.'

Everyone was giggling except for Connie who was furious.

'Oh shut up Dad. Trust you to find that bit. Anyway, listen to this. George Green is backing McCoy in a new gym, which he's opened above the Wellington, in Chesterfield. McCoy is the nephew of the renowned orthopaedic surgeon, William McCoy, who practises at The Rotunda, Dublin.'

'They've got that wrong,' Danny cut in.

'What d'you mean. You told us your Uncle Willie's a surgeon.'

'Yes but he doesn't practise at The Rotunda.'

'Oh well. Never mind about that,' said Connie, impatiently, 'just listen to the rest. Danny McCoy says he's carrying on the family tradition by treating his boys when they get injured.'

'That should bring in plenty of business, Danny. At this rate, you'll be able to treat members of the public and charge 'em a fortune.' But George could see his joke had fallen on deaf ears. 'What's up?'

Danny was reading another paper and frowning. 'The McCoy family isn't new to boxing. Another uncle, Frankie McCoy, left his native Ireland thirty years ago, to set up a gym in New York. Will this new venture bring him over to England, to join his nephew?'

'Don't worry,' said Connie. 'They're only speculating.'

'So what's it matter if he does come over?' George asked.

'It doesn't matter,' Danny said, nonchalantly.

Connie hurriedly found another sports column to quote from. 'Guess what? There's a reference to your RAF days. Someone's found out you were the squadron champion.'

Just at that moment there was a knock on the back door and Father Murphy poked his head round the door. 'Sure an' t'is here you all are.' He walked over to the table and dropped a pile of fivers down. Then he started splitting them up.

Connie's and Sylvia's eyes widened whilst Danny and George looked sheepish.

'Right! Now let's see!' Father Murphy glanced at the scrap of paper in his hand. 'There's £850 for you George and the same for you, Danny. However, when your Uncle Frankie was over, he gave me another £40. Said I was to put £20 on each of your boys and give the winnings to yourself, so he did. You've got to use it to bring over a couple of Johnny's cousins.' He read the note more slowly, struggling a bit over the names of the boxers. 'Bloke called Katusha Latou and his sparring partner, Garfield Nabatoa.' He handed the bit of paper to Danny.

Connie had finally found her voice. 'You didn't tell me you were gambling money on your boys.'

'You don't want to know. What...'

'I know! I know! What I don't know about, I can't talk about.'

Sylvia held out her hand. 'Right George! This is going to cost you a new coat and I could do with a pair of new boots as well.'

'Ger on wi' you.' George tried to pocket the money.

Sylvia grabbed a handful of notes. 'This should do nicely.'

Danny was quicker. His winnings had already disappeared into his back pocket.

Anticipating more trouble from Connie, Father Murphy was backing out of the kitchen. 'So I'll be seeing you all at Mass on Sunday?'

'Aye Father but just remember. Let's conduct our business in the gym in future.'

Father Murphy was laughing as he left the kitchen.

Danny and Connie were still arguing about how to spend the money.

CHAPTER EIGHT

The months passed quickly. It was well into September and Danny was in the gym watching his boys train. There were some new additions. There was a young miner called John Clegg from Clay Cross and another boy who was from Worksop called Jim Roberts. Then there was David Davis, a Welsh boy from Matlock. They were all as keen as mustard.

The door opened and George peered round. 'Got a bit of a surprise for you.' He opened the door wide and the midget staggered in. He was very much the worse for wear and could hardly walk.

Danny jumped up, went over, picked him up and carried him to a bench. 'Mate! What the hell are you doing here?'

Everyone gathered round.

'You said, "get a decent job" so I've come to ask you for one.'

'How did you find me?'

'Got the address off that doctor.'

'How did you get here?'

'Walked here.'

'What? All the way from Newcastle?'

'More or less. Managed to get a few lifts, here and there. Anyway, don't bother about that. I've come to offer my services. I don't want paying. I'll work for free. I can sleep here on the floor. Not be any bother. Would be grateful for a bit of food. Please Boss. Give us a chance. I'll never let you down. I'll do owt. Any dirty job that no one else wants to do. Please sir!'

'Not bloody likely!'

The midget's face fell at Danny's outburst. But Danny's next words soon cheered him up.

'I'll certainly give you a job but you'll not be working for nowt. I'm not having anyone work for me for nowt. I'll give you a proper job. You'll get a proper wage like everyone else. And summat else. There's no sleeping on the floor. You can sleep in a bed like everyone else round here. God knows...'

Everyone crossed themselves.

'...we've got enough beds in this place. And you can eat down in the pub kitchen, like Johnny here does. What do you say, George?'

George slapped him on the back. 'I had a suspicion that you were a good man, Danny. You've got a heart of gold. Looks like we've got ourselves an odd jobber.'

Danny turned to the midget. 'Right! What's your name?'

'You won't be able to pronounce it. My parents were Hungarian. I was born over here when they were working in a circus. When they died that Bert Shaw said he'd look after me.'

'So what did that bully call you?' Danny wasn't ready for the answer. It was a hell of a shock.

'Frank.'

Danny tried to collect his thoughts because a picture of his old mate, Frank, had just popped into his mind. 'So is that short for your real name,' he mumbled.

'No. It's short for Frankenstein. He said I was a freak of nature.'

This statement drove all thoughts of Frank Turner out of Danny's mind as he and George exchanged horrified looks.

Johnny Halanara looked intrigued. 'Who dat Frankenstein?'

'Right lads!' Danny clapped his hands. 'Back to work boys. We can't stand around like this. Those muscles will be knotting up. Chop! Chop!'

Reluctantly, the boxers obeyed him.

Danny didn't know what to say to the midget. He tried to adopt a business-like attitude. 'Right well you can forget all that. From now on, your name is Nipper. George, can you take Nipper downstairs and ask Sylvia to give him a bite to eat? Then can you run him a nice hot bath full of Epsom Salts? That should take away some of those aches and pains. And then he can have a nice long sleep. Job doesn't start till tomorrow.'

George could see that Danny had struggled with the name Frank. He'd have to explain it to Nipper. 'Come on, mate. Our Sylvia will look after you. From now on, you're part of the team and if anyone asks, you tell 'em. You're one of Danny's boys.'

Left alone on the bench, Danny picked up his Boxing Times but it was hard to concentrate. He'd never understood what made bullies tick. He'd never come across any before, neither at school nor in the RAF. They'd all had nicknames but not cruel ones. And why Frank, of all names. He still vividly remembered the day Frank had died but he knew he'd got to put it out of his mind. Just as he was about to return to his favourite magazine, he remembered the letter in his pocket. 'Johnny! Mac! Over here a minute.'

They joined him on the bench.

'Got this letter today, from your cousin. You know I've been making arrangements for him to come over?'

'Yes Boss.'

'Well, he's flying into Britain in two week's time with that other bloke.'

'Garfield Nabatoa.'

'Aye that's the one.'

'Bet that cost you a bit, Boss.'

'You're not wrong, Mac. It's cost near to a bloody fortune what with a passage to New Zealand, another to Australia and then the airfares and hotels and food and I'm footing the bill. But it'll be worth it. The winnings I had up in Newcastle have gone a long way to paying for it so I'm not going to be too much out of pocket. Anyway, I'm going to pick them up at London Airport so I wondered if you two wanted to come along for the ride?'

'Yes please Boss. Bin looking forward to seeing Garfield and Katusha.'

Mac looked surprised at the invite. 'You sure you don't want me to stay here and look after things?'

'Nah! Nipper can do that. By the time we go down, I'll have him trained up. I want him to feel he's part of the team. My boys won't give him any trouble. Anyway, I was thinking of taking two cars. Won't get these big lads all in one car.'

Two weeks later, Danny, George, Johnny and Mac were standing inside the airport, with their noses pressed up against the window.

'What the bloody hell do they think they're doing?'

'Dat der is Garfield with dem beautiful girls,' giggled Johnny.

Garfield Nabatoa was posing, like a film star, at the top of the steps, surrounded by adoring air hostesses. Katusha Latou was taking a photo.

'Looks like he's made a hit,' sniggered Mac.

'Dat sure is Garfield. He sure do tink a lot of himself.'

Garfield skipped down the steps and the two men strolled casually across the tarmac to the customs gate. Now the waiting party could see them much clearer.

'Bloody Hell!' Mac exclaimed. 'I thought you was getting a boxer no' a fancy effort like him.'

'Don't worry,' said Danny. 'If he can't box, we'll get him a part in a film.'

'You'll hiv tae put a chain aroon his neck, Boss.'

Johnny Halanara burst out laughing. 'You'll need a big heavy chain for Garfield. He crazy about women.'

He's right, thought Danny, as they watched the air hostesses throwing their arms around Garfield and kissing him goodbye.

It was only later, in a transport café, that Danny realised the full implications of Johnny's remarks. As soon as they got sat down, Garfield started ogling every woman in sight. He turned his big dark brown eyes on the waitress and she melted. She spilt tea when she put the teapot down. Then the sugar cascaded over Danny's jacket and he just caught the buttered teacake as it slithered off the plate. He breathed a sigh of relief when she tripped reluctantly back to the kitchens. But then Garfield lifted his eyebrows and two girls, sitting at the next table, dissolved into giggles.

'What you looking at, Garfield?' Johnny asked, fanning the flames deliberately.

'Dem lovely girls over there.'

Mac burst out laughing.

Danny glared at him. It wasn't funny. This Garfield Nabatoa was going to be a real handful. He'd be glad when he got him back to the Wellington so he could keep him under lock and key.

But when they finally did get back, Danny found his problems had multiplied. As soon as he introduced Garfield, it was the same thing all over again. 'Connie. Sylvia. This is Katusha Latou and Garfield Nabatoa.'

'Nice to meet you, boys.' Sylvia shook hands with them both and then she turned her full attention on Garfield. 'Now, I know you're a long way from home but we'll look after you. I'll show you to your room and when you need your washing done, just drop it in with ours. Danny'll show you where the laundry room is.'

'No!' Connie cut in, simpering. 'It's all right Mam. I'll show him.'

'Well, show him after we've all had summat to eat. You must be hungry, Garfield.' Sylvia tucked her arm through his and led him off towards the kitchen. Connie followed.

The other men had watched this performance in silence.

Danny raised his eyebrows at Johnny. 'Is it always like this?'

Johnny laughed. 'Oh yes. Women adore him. You'll get used to it. We have.'

CHAPTER NINE

Danny had decided to transfer his pigs to the Wellington. It had been George's suggestion.

'Wouldn't it make more sense, now you're living here, to keep your pigs here? We've got those outbuildings that aren't in use. You know, the ones that back onto that paddock. Don't think I'm butting in, lad. I mean, I don't want to upset Kathleen and Dermot. I know they like to see you once in a while.'

'Don't worry George. They'll be glad to see the back of them pigs. They're a bit too close to the pub. Ma's always complaining that they smell. And they've had to feed them every day since I've not been around. I must admit I felt a bit guilty about that so it's good they're coming here. Anyway, I'll make sure I still go over to see the mammy and the daddy regularly. I'm not worried about them. Everything's running ok now I've put that manager in but I still want to keep an eye on them.'

'Yer a good son to them, Danny. I don't know how you find the time to do everything.'

'Got some good people I can rely on. That's how. You and Nipper for two.'

'So when are these pigs due to arrive?'

'In about half an hour. Lot and Eli were picking them up at eleven o'clock.'

Lot and Elijah Yates were local pig dealers from Worksop. As well as collecting Danny's pigs for slaughter, they also dealt in second-hand furniture. By the time they arrived with the pigs; Danny, George and Nipper were waiting to herd them into their new home.

'Right Nipper. I'm putting you in charge of these little buggers. Think you can manage 'em, do you?'

'Certainly can, Boss. Nothing to it.' Nipper bustled off with a bucket of water in one hand and a bucket of kitchen scraps in the other.

'He's a strong wee man,' said Mac, who had just come out to see the pigs arrive.

'Aye.' George watched Nipper. 'He loves living with us, you know and I don't know how we ever managed without him.'

Inside the living room of the Wellington, Connie, Sylvia and Kathleen were sitting round the large dining table. It was littered with bits of paper.

'Now Kate, are you sure you've remembered everyone?'

'I'm absolutely sure, so I am and it's awful sorry I am that we've got so many coming over.'

'I keep telling you: it doesn't matter how many we invite. We can get three hundred or more, up in that ballroom. I've waited a long time to see my daughter married. Too long in fact.'

'Eeh Mam! Don't say that! Danny's mam'll think there's summat wrong with me.'

'No she won't. I've already told her how many boyfriends you've had.'

'MAM! How can you say that?'

'Will you not be taking on so, lass? I can see with my very own eyes that any man would be pleased to be walking out with you, so he would. I'm just glad my Danny found you before anyone else snapped you up.'

Connie blushed with pleasure at the compliment. 'Well, Danny won't be so pleased if I don't get a decent wedding dress to walk down the aisle in.'

'Hey up! Who's taking my name in vain?' Danny was standing in the doorway.

'Connie thinks she needs a posh frock to walk down the aisle in, son.'

'Never! I'll marry you in a potato sack, my lovely.' He bent down to kiss her as he passed her chair.

Connie pulled away, wrinkling her nose in disgust. 'Pooh! What's that awful smell?'

'Pigs, my sweetheart. We've just moved 'em in. That's a good healthy country smell. That's the smell of commerce. Bacon! That's what everyone wants. Anyway, what's all this about a posh frock? I meant what I said. You don't need to go paying a fortune. You'll look good in…'

'Forget it!' Connie snapped. 'I'm not walking up the aisle in any old frock. I want a dress as nice as our Queen's dress.'

'What for?' George came through the door. 'What d'ya want a dress like that for?'

'For the wedding, Dad.'

'You're getting' above yer station, my girl! You ain't havin' a coronation.'

Connie's voice rose by several octaves. 'I'm not talking about her coronation dress. I'm talking about her wedding dress. Mam!' She appealed to Sylvia. 'Mam! Tell him! Tell him! I'm having a proper wedding dress.'

'It's no good you trying to get her on your side. I'm the one who's going to be payin' for all this lot and I'm telling you: I'm not forking out that sort of money for a dress you're only going to be wearing for a few hours.'

Connie was crying by this time. 'Mam! Tell him!'

'Now see here George. I'm not letting my only daughter get married in any old rag.'

'Don't be ridiculous. Who said anything about rags? Just listen will you? You'll have to get that sewing machine out. You've been making clothes for her ever since the war started and she's always looked like one of those Paris models. A wedding dress can't be much harder. Anyway, you know how difficult it's going to be getting enough food...'

'Will you be letting me do my share, George? It will be a pleasure to be contributing, so it will.'

'I won't hear of it Kate. As far as the food goes: it's not the money that's the problem. It's all this damn rationing that's still going on. Sylvia's going to have a hard time getting sugar and butter for the cake. In fact, we might have to do with margarine.'

'MAM! I'm not having my cake made with margarine.' Connie was screaming with indignation.

Danny was keeping out of it. He edged nearer the door, hoping to get away.

George ignored his daughter. 'God knows...'

Everyone crossed themselves.

'...how we're going to decorate the ballroom. Just because the war's over, it don't mean there's a free market.' He glared at Connie. 'You're lucky that you don't have to produce coupons for a dress. Let me remind you, my girl, when our

Queen got married, back in 1947, she needed three hundred coupons.'

There was a few minutes silence at this amazing piece of information, made all the more amazing by the fact that George knew anything at all about the Queen's wedding dress.

Then Connie found her voice again. 'Why should my cake be rationed? It's not fair. It's very convenient for you isn't it? Your petrol's not rationed anymore.'

'Now then, dear. Don't cheek your father. He's had a lot of expense lately. He's got to be a bit careful. That's why we all went up to Newcastle on the train. Now don't take on. We'll sort something out. Go and wash those tears away like a good girl.'

Danny and Nipper were standing in a warehouse on the outskirts of Worksop. It belonged to Lot and Eli. Danny was after a second-hand physio couch and he'd had a call from Lot to say that they'd finally managed to get their hands on one. It was six foot long and two foot high with a black leather padded top. It was just what Danny needed. The second-hand dealers had got two heat-lamps as well.

'This treatment couch is more or less what I'm looking for. How much are you asking for that and one of those lamps?'

'We'll take a pony,' said Lot. He was stout and rosy-cheeked.

Eli, on the other hand, was much thinner and sharp-nosed, like a ferret. He'd always been a schemer. 'We'll take a pig,' he cut in. 'I noticed yours were looking very nice when we moved them, the other day. We'll take one of those for the bed and the lamp. Tell you what: we'll throw in the second lamp for free.'

Danny weighed it up. 'I'll have to think about it.' He strolled the length of the warehouse to where the two dealers couldn't hear him. They reached the door.

Nipper perched on a bale. 'What d'ya reckon, Boss?'

'To buy that bed and those two lamps would cost the best part of fifty quid. There's not a mark on that leather and the wood is good solid oak. It'll last me a lifetime. Hey! What's that?'

'What's what?'

'That. That what you're sittin' on?'

'Dunno, Boss. Let's have a look.' He jumped down.

Danny could see some material sticking out and he ripped the brown paper a bit more. 'Just as I thought. Would recognise this a mile away. It's parachute silk. That's handy.'

'What you thinking, Boss?'

'I'm thinking. Wedding! I'm thinking. Ballroom! I'm thinking about all those decorations we're going to need to tart that ballroom up and this stuff would make a fantastic wedding dress.'

'Oh no, Boss! What you're thinking is cheap and nasty.' Nipper had already bonded with the two women. 'Your girlfriend'll kill you and so will Mrs Sylvia.'

'Not if we don't tell them where we've got it from or how we've paid for it.' Danny fingered his chin absentmindedly, as he figured it out.

'What do they usually pay you for a pig?'

'Between thirty and forty, depending on the size. Come on.' Danny had made up his mind. He marched back to where Lot and Eli were stacking chairs. 'Ok you two. You've got yourself a deal but I want that roll of parachute silk thrown in for good measure.'

'Bloody hell, Danny! That's worth a fortune.' Lot might be easy-going but he wasn't daft. 'People are crying out for silk.'

'Yeah but there's no one crying out for an old physio couch. You could have that on your hands for years. And actually I only need one lamp not two.'

'A spare lamp's always handy.' Eli was quite crafty. 'You can put a bad back on the couch and a bad shoulder on a chair and treat two of your boys at the same time.'

'Well, I still reckon I'm doing you a favour, takin' that old couch off your hands. You can call the silk a sweetener and if you take my best pig, you'll be doing even better. Everyone knows. I do the best bacon in Derbyshire.'

'Can I pick my own pig?' Eli was as sharp as a knife.

Danny turned to Nipper. 'What d'you say?' He turned back to Lot and Eli. 'Nipper's in charge of me pigs now. What he says, goes.'

'Makes no odds to me, Boss. They're both fine specimens.'

Lot could see they were close to getting their hands on some prime bacon, which he could sell on for a fortune. He was keen to close the deal. 'Tell you what. We'll put the silk in for your best pig and we'll take the other one and slaughter it for your wedding breakfast: for a small butchering fee. We'll cut it up into nice joints and the bride's mother can cook it for all the guests.'

'Providing we get an invite to the wedding,' Eli slipped in.

'You cheeky bastard.' But Danny was laughing as he said it. 'Right! You've got yourself a deal. But I'm taking the silk with me today. And you don't tell any of my lot that I got it from you or how much...'

Lot cut him dead. 'There's nowt illegal about selling parachute silk.' Lot was furious at the suggestion of a crooked deal. 'We got it at a government auction. It's all above board.'

'Calm down. It's not the authorities I'm bothered about. I just don't want them two women knowing I got it here or how much I've paid for that matter.'

'Ah! Ha! So we have let it go too cheap!'

'Give over. We've all done very nicely out of this so let's keep it between the four of us. Give us a hand to load it into the van. I borrowed that van because I thought I'd be taking a couch back but you can bring the couch over when you pick up those pigs.'

CHAPTER TEN

The following week, Sylvia arrived at the Green Archer, with the roll of silk. Kathleen was just dragging out her dolly-tubs. 'T'is a good job I kept these old t'ings.'

'I can't argue with that, Kate. We'd have never got all this lot in my new-fangled washing machine.'

'No! And t'ink of the mess they'd have made on your lovely floor. Sure, an' how many colours have you brought?'

'Five. I've got a lovely pastel blue, a peppermint green, a rose pink and a very pale shade of lilac. I've also got this pale ivory for the wedding dress material. I think this white silk looks a bit dull especially for a wedding dress so I'm hoping this ivory dye will improve it. Connie is quite keen on ivory silk. My dress was ivory but the mice got to it.'

'That's an awful shame. It would have been nice to pass it on.'

'Yes. I would have liked to but maybe it would have looked a bit too old-fashioned. Anyway we'll need to pick the best part of the silk for the dress. We don't want any snags or marks on it. We'd better cut a length for the dress first before we start the dyeing. Perhaps we'd better cut twice as much as we need, just in case we do something wrong. Here's the pattern she's picked.'

'T'is a lovely dress. She's going to make a lovely bride. Danny is a lucky boy and t'is wonderful that he's taking her to Ireland for her honeymoon.'

'It's kind of your brother Willie to pay for two weeks at The Gresham. Danny says it's the most famous hotel in Ireland. He says they're having Paulette Goddard's suite of rooms.'

'T'will be on account of our Danny being a famous boxing manager. They've heard all about him over there, so the owner of The Gresham wanted to give him the best rooms in the hotel. They will have a lovely time in Ireland.'

'I'm looking forward to this wedding but there's so much to do.'

'So I'm thinking we should get started,' said Kathleen, rolling up her sleeves.

'It's good of you to help and it's nice that I can come over and use one of your bedrooms. At least I'll get some peace while I'm sewing.'

'So you will and it'll be nice company for me. If you need a hand with the sewing, I'll be happy to help. The auld eyes may not be up to any fine stitching though. I'm not as young as yourself.'

'We'll manage fine between us,' replied Sylvia, as they got to work.

Marriage had never been part of Danny's great scheme of things but when the chips were down, he knew which side his bread was buttered on. He spent his last night as a free man under the roof of the Green Archer. His mother took this opportunity to give him a good talking to. 'Sure an' she's the prettiest lass in England. You've found yourself a beautiful girl. She'll be an asset to you an' her mammy and daddy t'ink the world of you.'

So on Saturday the nineteenth of September 1953, Daniel James Dermot McCoy was finally hooked and landed by Constance Cecilia Green. The ballroom walls were hung with parachute silk in pretty pastel shades. The bride was radiant in her pure silk wedding dress. There were nowhere near as many Greens as there were McCoys and O'Clerys at the reception but that didn't bother George. He was so happy that his daughter was at last settling down. In the end, he'd spent a fortune on the day, as he always knew he would.

Some of Danny's family was staying at the Wellington and some at the Green Archer. The rest were spending two nights in whatever small boarding houses they could find. There were supposed to be thirty McCoys, five McCabes and six Kellys from Leitrim and Galway. Then there were at least forty O'Clerys from Cavan. There could have been more but no one was counting. Added to that were all Danny's RAF pals. Then there were the locals from both pubs.

'Well, to be sure! There must be two hundred guests, George!'
    'More like three hundred, Father.'
    'You and Sylvia have done a fine job, pulling this jamboree together.'
    'We had a lot of help.'
    'And when are the lucky couple departing for the honeymoon?'
    'I'm running them to the station in about half an hour.'
    'I expect all this lot will want to see them off.'

'Aye Father and this party's going to last into next week. Don't count on a full church in the morning.'

'This is a fine spread you've put on, George.' Danny had wandered over while he was waiting for Connie to change into her going-away outfit. 'It reminds me of some of the lovely parties we used to have over in Leitrim, before the war. Doesn't it just, Uncle Patrick?'

'It does, so it does. An' I well remember a little boy, who didn't know what a ceili was,' laughed his uncle.

'I must have only been about six when I went to me first ceili. I couldn't believe how many turned up to that one in the barn. An' they didn't come in cars, George. Oh no! They came by pony and trap.'

'Aye lad. An' they'd be coming from miles away as soon as word got out.'

Out of the corner of his eye, George could see one or two of the wedding guests drawing closer so they could listen to the crack.

'Course, we were giving that lovely party so everyone could come and meet our Dermot's boy, all the way from England. They loved your funny little accent.'

'Do you remember that lovely motor car that our Patsy came in from Fenagh, Danny?'

'Who is it talking about me?' Patsy joined the group of men.

'We were talking about that lovely motor car you brought over from America, Cousin Patsy,' said John. 'Mind you, I don't think our Danny was that impressed. He'd seen plenty of cars in Sheffield but it was something of a wonder to us.'

'He was too shy to say anything,' said Patrick.

Danny grinned. 'I remember being amazed when that ceili was still going on at two o'clock in the morning. And I remember all that dancing when that fella started playing his fiddle. What a party! Nobody wanted to go home. Never saw parties like that in Sheffield. And I was terrified in case the mammy got to know I'd been allowed to stay up and then sleep in till dinnertime the next day. That would never have been allowed in Sheffield. The mammy was a right tartar. I remember the grandmammy telling me I should get up when I felt like it. Phew! It was another world over there.'

'Do you remember when the mammy took you to Cavan? You didn't want to go.'

'Well that was because I was having to cut short the time I could spend with you lot. I needn't have worried. It was just as good at the mammy's home.'

'You had a good time with all of us,' said John.

'Aye! Right enough! So I did. It was good to get away from our Molly an' Mary an' Jane. They were always trying to make me toe the line.'

'What's that, our Danny?' The youngest of his three sisters joined them.

'I was just saying: what wi' you being ten years older, you were a right bully.'

'Oh aye! Just because we made you put your toys away for the mammy's sake?'

'You were all a right pain an' I was the rose amongst the thorns.'

'That'll be the day, our Danny!'

'I think I'll go and see if my bride is ready to leave for the station before you all start pickin' on me again,' laughed Danny.

CHAPTER ELEVEN

Danny put his arm round Connie as he scanned the horizon. 'I'm not sure I should be away for two weeks. I can't afford the time, with that big fight coming up.'

'Oooh! Danny! That's a bit mean! This is our honeymoon!'

'Aye! I know. An' I'm here, ain't I?'

'I don't know what you're bothering about. Mac and Nipper will keep everything ticking over and Dad'll be watching out for you. They'll all keep your boys training hard.'

'It's not the training I'm worried about. It's that Nosy Parker, Billy Battle. He knows I'm going away an' he'll be sniffin' round. He's itching to pin summat on me.'

'Well he won't, so forget him. See! Isn't that the coastline over there?'

They'd only been in Dublin a few days when Danny disappeared. It was three hours before he reappeared.

Connie was furious. 'Where the hell have you been?'

'I've been to hire a car.'

Connie looked surprised. This was a first: Danny McCoy spending money on a luxury. 'How come?'

'I want to take you to see the mammy's place in Cavan.'

'What about your father's farm?'

'Aye! That too but that'll be next week – just before we go back. Save the best till last, so to speak.'

So here they were in Cavan and Connie could now see why Danny's childhood had been so idyllic. 'It's very beautiful here. How many times did you come?'

'A good few. Mind you, the first time I came, it was under protest.'

'What do you mean? Under protest?'

'Well, the mammy was dragging me away from Leitrim. I didn't want to come. Didn't want to leave me pony and I didn't think Cavan would be half as good as Leitrim.'

'And was it?'

'Oh aye! It was great. Everyone was so pleased to see us. There was plenty to do. We went to the cattle fair in Kingscourt. That was fascinating. Second Tuesday of every month. The farmers from miles around would have driven those cattle all along the roads to get there. Maybe starting off at three o'clock in the morning. Actually heard 'em passing me bedroom window during the night. We watched the farmers buying and selling. An' then they'd go and celebrate a good sale with a few Guinness in the local pub. Dunno if they ever went home in profit.'

'Sounds like you got to enjoy it in the end.'

'Oh aye! It didn't take me very long to realise that life in Cavan was as laid-back as life in Leitrim. See this field. This is where we used to help the mammy's daddy, Granddaddy O'Clery, with the haymaking: well not so much help as watch. T'is a wonderful t'ing to watch the hay being tossed in the air on a warm summer's afternoon.'

'Why did they toss it?'

'To dry it out.'

'And I suppose you used to have a picnic?'

'Oh aye! The food my Auntie Nora used to put in that basket. There'd be lovely farm cheese to go with the home-made bread. And we had potato cakes and hard-boiled eggs from Auntie Nora's hens. And there was fresh farm milk to drink: thick and creamy. 'Course, we were lucky. We weren't rich but at least the granddaddy owned the farm. In those days there was a terrible lot of poverty. Consumption was rife in the streets of Dublin, so it was. Uncle Willie used to talk about it all the time. It fair broke his heart.'

'How long did you stay in Cavan?'

'Usually about two weeks. It'd be the last two weeks of summer before the mammy carted me back to Sheffield. She loved coming home. Used to go on about those mountains over there.' Danny pointed. 'Those are the Mountains of Mourne. You know? Like in the song.' He broke into song, 'Where the Mountains of Mou-ourne sweep down to the sea. She used to cry when she wasn't here and then when she got here she'd be crying again. Used to say she was so full of happiness to be back. I could never understand why she was crying when she was supposed to be happy but I can now.' There was silence for a few moments. 'See that pile of rocks in the distance? That's one of the duns. They're all that's left of our ancient forts. I remember me and a few of my cousins hiding behind those very rocks. There was me and Ronan and Patrick and Michael. It was all because I didn't want to go back home. The mammy had been packing the day before. I was detesting it. So my cousins decided to hide me till the bus had gone.'

'What did your mother say?'

'She went mad. She was screaming and shouting my name all over the place. We stayed hidden all day. We'd taken a bit of bread and cheese and summat to drink so we didn't go

101

hungry. The bus went without us and that meant we'd missed all our connections. We had to stay another week.'

'Didn't she smack you?'

'Not likely.' Danny laughed. 'She didn't dare lay a finger on me over here: not wi' all me aunts and the grandmammy looking on. And they didn't join in the search for me. They didn't want her to find me and they didn't want me to go home. They all adored me. Mind you, I didn't try it on again. I knew I wouldn't get away with it a second time. She used to watch me like a hawk when it was nearly time to go back to Sheffield.'

The second week of the honeymoon, Danny hired the car again and took Connie to Leitrim, to see the place where he had spent most of his childhood. The farm buildings were just a pile of stones. The wild grasses had steadily invaded the ruins and now they tumbled disconsolate though the farmyard, mangled and flattened by the autumnal rain and the onset of winter. Danny stared across the open countryside. The distant hills were a faint purple shadow, a barrier on the edge of time itself. The well was still there. Danny dropped a stone into the darkness and heard it plop softly into the water far below. 'See! This is where we used to get our water: wonderful, clean, pure water. Cold as ice. Tasted better than champagne.' His voice trembled and he was glad that for once, his normally talkative wife was silent. 'Come on girl. I'll take you to see where Tommy's buried.' He strode off down the lane towards the lakeside.

The lake was just as he remembered it. Its crystalline surface reflected the pale apricot sunset. Danny's thoughts skipped back in time. 'I used to ride Tommy down that lane into the farmyard. I'd miss that post by a hair's breadth. Tommy knew just how near to go. The mammy used to go mad. It took the daddy's mammy all morning to calm her down. What a performance!' He stared at the tree. 'See! That's where Tommy's buried. Under that tree.'

Connie put her arm round his waist. 'I think we should be getting back to the car. The sun's sinking behind that hill and it's getting cold.'

'Aye, all right but give us a kiss before we go.'

CHAPTER TWELVE

Danny didn't realise how quickly the months were passing. In what seemed like no time at all, he was a father. The twins were born on the fifteenth of November 1954 but Danny wasn't at the hospital. He was in South Africa, at a boxing match. Of course, he did have a jolly good excuse. Katusha Latou was fighting Johnny Arthur.

'We can't get a price on your boys, anymore,' was the constant complaint from the locals at the Wellington and it was true. Whenever Danny's boxers fought, they were nearly always odds-on.

By 1956 Connie was pregnant again and Katusha was training for a very special contest. He was in the gym, sparring with his cousin Garfield Nabatoa. Danny was on the sidelines, watching with George and Mac. 'This'll be a very important fight for all of us,' said Danny.

'D'you think he's ready?' George asked him.

'Oh aye! He's ready, all right. We'll show that Don Cockell a thing or two. If we beat him, it'll make my boy, at the very least, the uncrowned Empire Champion and then I want a match with Rocky Marciano. It's summat Uncle Frankie wanted and couldn't get. But Cockell's no slouch. It'll not be a walkover. In his latest fight he took Marciano into the ninth round.'

'He's looking good, Boss,' said Mac.

Danny watched Garfield dancing round Katusha, trying to land a punch, without any success. He could see that Garfield had just about had enough. 'Right boys! That'll do for today. Go and get showered.'

Just as the two men from Tonga were climbing out of the ring, there was a slight commotion at the other end of the ballroom. Nipper came in with a man who looked about fifty. 'Got a fella here who wants to see you, Boss.'

'You'll have your work cut out with this one,' sniggered Mac.

'You Mr McCoy?' The man had a strong Welsh accent.

'Aye! That's me!' Danny shook his hand.

'So this is Danny's Place?'

'That's what they're calling it, apparently.' Someone had coined the name recently and it had caught on with the locals.

'Well, you've been recommended by a friend of mine. I've got two lads outside who want to join your boxing club, see.'

'Oh aye? Well, bring 'em in an' let's have a look at 'em.'

The fella went to the door and shouted, 'Come up here, lads.'

There was the sound of metal-tipped boots clattering up the wooden stairs and a couple of young miners came in. It was obvious they'd driven to Chesterfield straight from a nightshift because their faces were black with coal-dust. They were wearing old woollies and thick coats.

'Sorry about the state of 'em, mate but this was the only time they could get here. If they look a bit bleary-eyed, it's only because they've had forty winks on the way over, see.

'How far have you come?'

'Oh, only from Newcastle-under-Lyme. By the way, my name's Gareth Williams.' He pulled one of the young lads forward. 'This is my boy, Bryn and this,' he pulled the other one forward, 'is his friend Steve Riley. They've been doing a bit of boxing at a club over in Stoke but the word is: this is the best place outside London. They're a couple of good boys, see. I'd be glad if you could take them on.'

'Well, I'm always on the lookout for a bit o' talent. As long as they're keen. That's the important thing.'

'They're keen all right. Keen as mustard. Get those coats off lads and show Mr McCoy what you can do, see.'

'Mac, put these two boys through their paces,' said Danny. 'I'll watch from the sidelines.'

The boys did very nicely and by lunchtime, Danny had made up his mind about them. He'd drawn up the standard BBBC contract and they'd signed on the dotted line.

'Seems like news of your gym is spreading.' George was sitting in the bar with Danny. They were having a pre-lunch beer.

'Aye. It seems so.'

'What's the verdict on those new lads?'

'They're not bad. I reckon I can do a lot wi' 'em. One of 'em looks like he's got some promise.'

'Which one?'

'That Steve Riley. I reckon he's got the makings of a champion.'

'How can you tell wi' just that one look at him?'

'Me Uncle Frankie taught me to size up a sportsman. I can tell you what he's thinkin' and I can even tell if he's got a touch of stage fright.'

'Never!'

'Oh aye. I'm telling you. It's true.'

A couple of days later, Danny was watching George and Mac walk two greyhounds round and round, in front of the outbuildings at the back of the Washington. Nipper was busy sweeping up. Danny was concentrating his attention on the dogs but out of the corner of his eye, he caught a tiny movement. He turned his head and there was Billy Battle, sidling round the corner of the buildings. 'What d'you want?'

'I heard as how you was going into greyhound racing.'

'What's it to you?'

'I've got a few friends down at the track. I'm going to warn 'em about you an' your little scams.'

'I dunno what you're on about.'

'I'm referring to what you did up in Newcastle. I ain't forgotten.'

Mac and George had walked up behind him.

He turned to confront them. 'I hope you're not trying to harass me.'

'Wouldn't dream of it, Mr Battle,' said Mac.

'I don't know what you're going on about Newcastle for,' said Danny. 'That was three years ago and you had that bottle of adrenaline for testing. You didn't find anything wrong wi' it.'

'I don't know how you did it, McCoy, but that wasn't adrenaline you used on that eye and it's not the only time you've used it, either. Someone was talking about that fight down at Bermondsey Baths. Same thing happened there. They're not calling you the Eye Specialist for nothing.'

'So why didn't you stop the fight?' Danny sneered.

'Because I wasn't there, that's why. I was away on holiday an' I'll bet a million pounds that you knew I was going away.'

'Oh aye! Prove it!'

Battle was about to have another go at Danny but George, helped by Mac, was pushing him out of the yard. 'Go on! Clear off! Yer not welcome on my land if yer going to make accusations about my son-in-law.'

'All right! All right! I'm going but be warned. I'm watching you, McCoy. One of these days you're goin' to make a big mistake an' I'll have you! You see if I don't.' He marched over to his car, got in and drove off.

George looked at Danny. 'Has he got anything on you?'

'There's nowt to have. He's talking a load of rubbish.'

'So what did all that mean?'

'What?' Danny pretended not to understand.

'That stuff about people calling you the eye specialist?'

'Don't worry, George.' Danny spoke soothingly. 'They're only calling me that because I'm good wi' the adrenaline. It works better because I keep it in the fridge.' Danny was making this up. Anything to keep George from knowing the truth. 'It'll be all right. Visiting times are Tuesdays and Thursdays.' He could see his little joke had fallen on stony ground but at least George didn't ask anymore questions.

It was the night of the big fight. They were down in the dressing rooms under Wembley Stadium. Danny was bandaging Katusha Latou's hands. Nipper was hovering with the sticky tape and scissors. Everyone was looking very nervous, everyone except Danny.

'Apparently there's eighteen thousand out there, tonight.'

When Katusha heard George say that, he rolled his eyes in mental torment and looked even more nervous.

'I don't know what you're looking so nervous about,' Danny said to the boxer, as he took the slivers of tape from Nipper and placed them between Katusha's fingers. 'It's no different to fighting in New York.'

'Not ever fought in front of eighteen thousand, Boss.'

'Well, you can forget about the eighteen thousand out there. What you want to remember is: this match is being broadcast over the airwaves. Your lot in the South Pacific will be listening to it.'

On hearing this, Katusha looked like he was going to pass out.

'What d'ya want to tell him that for?' Mac asked.

'It'll keep him on his toes.'

There was a knock at the door. 'Telegram for Mr McCoy!'

George opened the door. 'What's that lad? What you got there?'

The boy in the navy-blue uniform touched his gold-braided cap. 'Telegram for Mr McCoy, sir!'

George took it and gave him a tip.

'Thank you, sir.' He touched his cap again and was gone.

George shut the door and handed it to Danny. 'Who's it from?'

'Well! Well! Well! Talk of the devil!' It was the wrong thing to say.

At the mention of the word "devil" the man from the Friendly Isles started quivering and rolling his eyes again.

Danny ignored this reaction. 'Listen to this, lad.' He read the telegram out loud. 'Remember. The ears of Tonga will be listening, Good luck. Signed Queen Salote.'

Katusha was now grinning like a Cheshire cat.

'You do well tonight, lad and she'll probably buy you a pineapple plantation.'

109

'Let's have a look at that, Danny,' said George.

'Not right now, George.' He folded it up and shoved it in his back pocket. 'We've got to go. Remind me to show you later.' He'd got Katusha's gloves on and he hustled everyone out of the dressing room. 'Come on. Let's go. They'll all be waiting out there. Best of luck to us all.'

Reporters and interviewers crowded round Danny. 'Were you expecting your boy to knock Cockell out?' This was the man from the BBC.

Danny was enjoying being in the limelight and happy to talk. 'Well, I did have a good feeling about this fight. My boy was ready for it but I was a bit surprised when it happened in the second round.'

'When's his next fight?'

'When he's had a nice little rest.'

'Who's he fighting next?'

'I'd like him matched with Marciano.'

There was a universal gasp from the reporters and photographers.

'We've heard that Harry Levene wants your boy to fight Joe Bygraves.'

'Well, I've not been approached yet. Now that's enough, lads. Off you go. My boy needs his beauty sleep.'

The media departed except for one bloke who hung back till everyone else had gone. 'Could you spare me a minute, Mr McCoy? I'm from ITV. I've got a proposition, which I'm sure will interest you.'

Danny turned to Mac. 'See to Katusha while I have a word with this fella.' He stepped outside the dressing room door, into the corridor and the man followed. 'Right. So what do you want?'

'Is it true that Frankie McCoy's your uncle.'

'Yes. What of it?'

'Oh nothing. It's just that you must have a lot of experience. We've got an idea for a new gimmick. We need someone to appear on "Sports Desk" to answer questions from viewers about boxing.'

'Questions?'

'Oh don't worry. It'll only be questions about boxing. And you'll get a chance to study them before the programme starts. It's not a quiz. It's really so we can help the boxing fans to understand the game better. Anyway, shall I send you a contract to look at? You'll find it very beneficial. You'll get plenty of exposure for your boxers and your gym. We'll pay all your expenses of course like for instance: top-drawer hotels and first-class travel. Train of course.'

'Aye all right. Send us the contract and I'll look at it.'

They were back at the Wellington. It was a few nights after the fight and Katusha Latou was still "the toast of the town" and the locals were still buying him drinks. George was having a drink with Danny. 'By the way, Danny, have you got that telegram from Queen Salote?'

Danny fiddled around in his pocket and then he paused. He watched as two young women fawned over Garfield Nabatoa. He finally located the telegram and he passed it to George. 'Aye! Here you are.'

'You want to get this framed.' Then his tone changed. 'Here! What the bloody hell's this?'

Danny started laughing. 'Keep your voice down.'

George read it out loud but not loud enough for anyone else to hear. 'Good luck for your first big fight. Frankie.'

'Just came at the right moment,' laughed Danny. 'He was getting a bit too wound up for my liking.'

George shook his head in exasperation.

Danny didn't notice. His attention had been caught again by Garfield who was still flirting with the girls. 'I'm going to have to nip that in the bud. He's spending far too much time chasing those lasses. He's never got his mind on the job. If I don't sort him out soon, he'll not be fit for anything.'

'So what you thinking of doing.'

'No idea but I'll think of summat. Don't you worry.'

CHAPTER THIRTEEN

Danny and Connie were sitting at the kitchen table. The twins were in their high chairs. Connie was busy spoon-feeding Patrick. Danny was feeding Michael.

'Will you tell me why we're having breakfast down here when we've got a perfectly adequate self-contained flat upstairs?'

'I told you last night,' snapped Connie, 'but as usual you weren't listening. You had your mind on those other boys of yours. Anyway, stop grumbling. It's only for today. I told Mam I'd keep an eye on the gasmen. They're supposed to be finished today and she doesn't want them leaving a mess behind.'

'Come on now, Micky, open yer mouth.'

'I wish you wouldn't call him that. You promised you wouldn't shorten his name. Danny! Are you listening?'

'It's only while he's a little'un. He'll not remember, anyway.' He changed the subject skilfully. 'When are them fellas supposed to be getting here?'

'Any minute now.' She wiped Patrick's face and lifted him out of his chair, onto the floor. 'Here, Danny, nip next door and put him in the playpen. Nipper brought it down last night. I'll just clean Michael's face. Be a good boy Patrick and go with Daddy.' She stretched up and leaned over, in an effort to ease the pain in her back. It wasn't easy being seven months pregnant.

'Come on then, Paddy, laddie.' Danny lifted up his son and carried him out of the kitchen.

Connie's screams followed him. 'His name's Patrick! Patrick! Patrick!'

Danny deposited the toddler in the playpen and muttered, sarcastically, 'Yer mammy's got a temper, so she has.' He imitated his wife's high-pitched voice. 'His name's Patrick! His name's Michael! It's Patrick! Michael! Patrick! Michael!'

'I can hear you. You cheeky pig.' Connie had walked in, carrying Michael. 'Here take him. He's getting heavier by the minute.'

'You shouldn't be carrying him in your condition.'

'Oh yes! Is that so? What do you care about my condition? You weren't even around when he was born. You were at some boxing match on the other side of the world.'

'Stop going on about it. It wasn't the other side of the world. It was in Johannesburg and that's in South Africa not Australia.'

'It was far enough and you know what I think about it. Anyway, let's get back to the present day. I'm ok if I don't carry him for too long. I won't be carrying either of them soon. They're putting on too much weight.'

'Aye! That's true. They're going to be a couple of heavyweights, all right.'

'I've told you till I'm blue in the face, Danny McCoy, I'm not having any of my children going into that game. Neither of them is following in your footsteps. You can forget it right now.'

'Oh aye! An' what happens if they want to? You won't be able to stop 'em.'

114

'They won't want to as long as you don't encourage them. Where are you going?'

'I've just remembered summat I need out of the kitchen.'

'Will you call me when those men arrive?'

'Aye, all right.' Danny went back into the kitchen. He had just picked something up off the floor, when there was a loud banging on the back door. He went through into the outer kitchen, which led to the bowling green. He unbolted the door. 'Morning boys. Come on in.' He ushered them into the kitchen. 'Be finished today, will youse?'

'Aye. More than likely,' said the boss, putting his tools down.

'Got an hammer I can borrow?'

'Aye.' The other man opened his tool bag and produced one. 'Not thinking of doing a bit of plumbing are you?'

'Not likely. I just want to flatten this.' He held up the spare bit of lead piping he'd picked up off the floor. 'I need a ruler. Gotta draw up some rules and regulations for my young boxers.' He put the pipe on the kitchen table and banged the hammer down on it, flattening it quite easily. 'Here. Job's a good 'en. Thanks for the loan.' Just the ticket, he thought to himself as he went to find Connie. 'Them gas fitters have arrived. They're getting stuck in. You can leave 'em to get on wi' it. By the way, you do remember, don't you? We're off to London, this afternoon.'

'What train are you catching?'

'The two-thirty.'

'It's all right for you,' Connie pouted. 'I never get to go anywhere with you, these days, Danny McCoy! You've got the best of everything. You're always going off somewhere nice and staying in the best hotels.'

'Give over girl! It's hard work having to take my boys up and down the country. I've got to look after them. Keep them out of trouble. Keep them in form. Practically wipe their noses for 'em an' all that malarkey. It's no bloody picnic. Anyway, you'd look nice, rattling up and down the country, in your condition. Look! I promise I'll take you for a holiday after you've had the baby, so I will.'

'You know that'll be months off.'

'Give over. You're due in two months.'

'Yes and I don't need telling! But it'll be longer than two months before I'm fit to get away and that's what you're banking on.'

'Give over. I'll prove you're wrong. I'll go and book us a holiday, tomorrow.'

'When for?'

'Just after Christmas. How's that?'

'CHRISTMAS!' Connie's voice was louder than a foghorn. 'That's miles away. That's six months if it's a day.'

'Yeah! I know! But it's the best I can do. We're booked to appear on "Sports Desk" right up to the end of November and you'll surely want to be here for Christmas and the New Year. Don't worry. Everything will work out.'

Danny had just arrived on the platform with Katusha, Johnny and Garfield in tow. He noticed that the Duke of Devonshire was there with his wife and daughter. Danny, being a local celebrity was quite well known. The Duke raised his trilby and Danny did the same.

'Good afternoon, Mr McCoy. How are you today?'

'Good afternoon, Your Grace. Quite well thank you. Good afternoon, M'Lady.' He raised his hat to the Duchess.

116

'Good afternoon, Danny. We listened to your last fight on the wireless. It was very exciting.'

'Thank you M'Lady. We did very well, I'm glad to say.'

'Are you off to another venue?'

Danny noticed Garfield was already ogling the Duke's daughter so he stood on his toe, hard! 'Oh sorry, Garfield.' He turned back to the Duke. 'No, Your Grace. Actually we've been invited to appear on "Sports Desk" for ITV.' Out of the corner of his eye, he noticed Garfield was hobbling away. Good!

'Oooo! How exciting!' The Duchess turned to her husband. 'See! I told you we should get one of those new televisions. We could watch Danny and his boxers on it.'

A distant toot announced the arrival of the Sheffield-to-London train. The Duke turned to kiss his wife and Danny took the opportunity to push his boxers further down the platform.

'Who dat beautiful girl, Boss?'

'She's the daughter of the Duke of Devonshire and she's well out of your league.'

'Why is she getting on dis train?'

'Her and her mother will be going to London to do a bit of shopping. Now I'm telling you, Garfield. YOU LEAVE HER ALONE!'

'No need to shout, Boss.'

'Oh yes there is need. You listening to me, are you? Keep away from her. I don't want you bothering her.'

Because the train was pretty full and owing to the fact that Danny and his boxers were travelling First Class, they ended up in the same carriage as the Duchess and her daughter. As soon as the train drew away from the platform, Garfield was at

117

it! There he was, as bold as brass, making eyes at the daughter of the Duke of Devonshire and Danny couldn't stand it any longer. He'd brought his favourite magazine with him, The Boxing Times and he now had it rolled up in his hand. No one seemed to be looking and quick as a wink, Danny cracked Garfield on the head with the magazine.

The boxer gasped in pain as a bump, the size of an egg, appeared on his forehead. 'Ooooh! Aaaah! Ooooh!' He bent forward and leaned against the window. He had his eyes closed and he was moaning and groaning.

Katusha and Johnny stared at Danny in horror.

Danny ignored them. He just stared out of the window, trying not to laugh.

By the time they pulled into Rugby everyone was reading a newspaper or magazine but Garfield was still leaning against the window, moaning. 'Ooooh! Aaaah! Ooooh!'

'What is it Garfield? What's the matter?' Danny leaned forward.

Garfield cowered and whimpered, 'When you were boxing, Boss, what weight did you box at?'

'Never above eleven stone, three pounds, Garfield! Middleweight Garfield! Middleweight! Why?'

Garfield was heavyweight. 'Ooooh! Dear me! I'm glad I never had to fight you, Boss.'

'Yes! Well! Think on! Don't you ever ogle another girl, like that, or you'll get some more of the same.'

Garfield rolled his eyes and leaned against the window, as the train pulled out. Danny surreptitiously transferred the lead pipe from the magazine to his overcoat pocket.

CHAPTER FOURTEEN

The twenty-eighth of August was a lovely sunny afternoon. Everyone was standing around watching the workmen put the finishing touches to the boxing ring. There was a huge tarpaulin covering the bowling green and tiered seating had been erected. They were all there. Danny, George, Nipper, Mac, Father Murphy and Irwin Goldberg. Every now and again, a few more interested passers-by would join the group.

'It's looking good,' remarked George.

'Aye! An' we've got Goldie here to thank for providing all this.'

'It wouldn't be much good without the right boxers, Danny, my boy. Your boxers have brought in four thousand punters. It's a good crowd. There's a nice little profit to be made for all of us. It's good for everyone if money goes round and round, Danny.'

'You've got some good names on the bill,' said Father Murphy to Danny.

'All laid on by my good friend Bruce Woodcock. He promised Uncle Frankie that he'd start me off with a bang. It's just a pity it's taken us three years to get this idea off the ground.'

'So tell me, Danny! You try! You do your best! It's not easy!' Irwin Goldberg sighed. 'Still, Danny, my boy! Everything comes to those who wait!'

'Aye! True enough, Goldie. We should do well tonight.'

'Tonight,' said George, 'will make up for all the waiting. And talking of waiting, when's that new grandchild of mine going to make an entrance?'

'Be another two weeks or so the doctor reckons. You still taking bets on the event?'

'Nope. I closed the book last week. I've taken too many bets on it being a boy. I tell you Danny, if it's not a girl, I'm done for. They'll be no new suite for our Sylvia. I won't even have enough for a single armchair.'

'You should worry,' said Irwin Goldberg. 'You haven't got the problem our Danny's got. He'll be worrying about the baby turning up tonight.'

'What! It'd better not be tonight. Not on my big night! An' all the seats sold out. Tonight is going to be the best night's fighting that anyone's seen outside of London. What with Randolph Turpin and Johnny Williams boxing as well as Katusha Latou and Johnny Halanara. This is going to be a feast fit for the gods. And I'm putting a few of my young boys on as well. Give 'em a bit of experience.'

'How are those young lads of yours?' Father Murphy asked.

'They're doing nicely, aren't they Mac?'

'Och! Aye! Especially that Ron Charleton. He's a cracker. He'll take some beating. I reckon we've got ourselves a light heavyweight champion as long as he can keep his weight down.'

'Aye! That weight of his takes some handling. The trouble is, he's such a nice little eater. It's always a problem if a boxer puts on too much weight, too quickly.'

'He only has to look at a piece of cake an' the scales go up by five pounds,' joked Mac.

'Well at least he's not as hard to handle as Hudson.'

'What's wrong with Hudson?' George was quick off the mark. He'd already got a bet on Hudson's next match. 'I thought you said he was world championship material?'

'So he is, on a good day. The trouble is, he gets so many bad ones. Even in the morning, even before he gets started, he's moaning that he's had a bad night and he's done in. He gets so low but I've got his dodge marked down. I know exactly how to deal with it.'

'So what do you do?' George was still concerned about his bet.

'Well,' said Mac, 'if you get yourself up to the gym at six o'clock tonight when Danny's giving them their pep talk, you'll see for yourself.'

Sylvia rubbed Connie's back as her daughter leaned forwards, her hands resting on the edge of the table. 'Are you sure you're all right? Do you want Danny to run you to the hospital?'

'No Mam! Honestly! I'm all right. I'm not due for another two weeks. I've just got a bit of backache and I feel like a beached whale but I'm ok.'

'Where is Danny, anyway?'

'He's in his office giving them the usual pep talk. Him an' his boys. He thinks about now't else.'

Danny was sitting behind his desk. All his boys were there. Johnny Halanara. Katusha Latou. Carlo Santini. Bryn

121

Williams. Steve Riley and a very nervous Jackie Hudson. They were perched on chairs and stools. George, Mac and Nipper were hanging around at the back.

'Right then. How's everyone feeling? Anyone got any twinges? Speak up now. I don't want anyone fighting tonight if they're not one hundred and ten per cent fit.'

There was silence for a few moments.

Then a lone voice piped up. 'Well, as a matter of fact, I don't feel absolutely spot on.'

It could only be! It was! Jackie Hudson! The hoots and jeers were deafening.

'Now then, boys. Quieten down. There's no need for all that. We all know our Jackie's a sensitive soul. What's up, Jackie?'

'Well,' Jackie groaned, 'I had a terrible night last night. I'm done in.'

'Well, that's a pity Jackie, because…' Danny opened his newspaper, '…it says here, you're going to have a good day. You are Virgo, aren't you?'

'Mmmm!'

The whole room was silent, waiting for Danny's next words. If someone had dropped a pin it would have sounded like a bomb going off. Danny folded the newspaper so he could read from the horoscope column. 'That's good! It says here that this is your lucky day. Taurus is entering Virgo and consequently everything looks good.' Danny's voice dropped to a more dramatic level. 'Don't be afraid to take chances. You will reap a great success. By midnight, you will have achieved your heart's desire.' Hudson was already starting to look better as Danny slipped the newspaper into his drawer. 'Right! That's it lads. Off you go. Get yourselves down into the kitchen. You'll find a meal waiting.'

As soon as the office door shut behind the last boxer, Mac and Nipper burst out laughing.

George looked mystified. 'What's going on?'

Danny fished the newspaper out of the drawer and handed it to George. 'Here. Read it for yourself. There.' He stabbed the Virgo sign.

George read it. Then he looked up. 'It don't say owt here about Taurus entering Virgo. It says finances might need careful...' He stopped reading and looked up. 'You just made all that stuff up. You crafty bastard!'

'Well it worked, didn't it?'

Connie and Danny were just getting dressed for the big fight night. There were several extra-large cocktail dresses laid out on the bed because, as usual, Connie couldn't make up her mind what to wear. 'I'm fed up of having to wear a tent.' She held up a blue one.

'Don't be too long getting dressed, girl. You don't want to arrive in the middle of the first bout. It won't look good.' Danny was already decked out in a black dinner-suit and a bow tie. 'I've told you which one I like best. Anyway, I'm off. See you downstairs.' He shot out of the bedroom.

Connie held another dress up in front of the mirror then she doubled up in pain. Staggering to the bed, she collapsed and screamed, 'Danny! Danny! Come back!' Several minutes went by but despite her screams Danny didn't return. Luckily help was at hand.

Nipper poked his head round the door. 'Oooo! Mrs Connie. What's wrong?'

'Where have you left the twins?' Connie gasped.

'On the floor. In the nursery. Don't worry. They can't get out. We were playing when I heard you screaming. Whatever's the matter?'

'The baby's coming early. Go and fetch my mum, quick. Look after the boys won't you? That husband of mine is bloody, bloody useless,' she snarled through clenched teeth.

'Don't worry Mrs Connie. I'll go for Mrs Sylvia. Don't move.'

George and Sylvia were also getting ready in their part of the Wellington. It took Nipper a good few minutes to run down the stairs, through all the corridors and up some more stairs. He banged on the door. 'Mrs Sylvia! Mrs Sylvia! Come quick! The baby's started!'

Sylvia threw open the door. 'Mother of God. What are we going to do now? Quick, George! Run and tell Danny! Where is she?'

'She's in her bedroom.'

Connie was frantic with pain by the time Sylvia got there. 'Can you hang on till Danny gets you to the hospital?'

'Yes. I think so,' gasped Connie between waves of pain.

Danny arrived on the scene. 'What's up now. Oh my God! Jesus, Mary and Joseph! What the hell have you done now?'

'It's nothing I've done,' screamed Connie. 'It's more what you've done. Your baby's arriving early, that's what! Just get me to the hospital!'

'I can't take you to the hospital now, you silly cow! I'm just about to start the first bout. Everyone's waiting for me.'

'Then get downstairs,' snapped Sylvia, 'and see if one of the regulars will take us.' Her lips were white with fury.

'I'll never forgive you for this, Danny McCoy,' Connie screamed as Danny disappeared out of the door. 'Go on! Get back to your stupid boxing match an' don't bother coming to the hospital at all. I never want to set eyes on you again.'

By midnight, Connie was sitting up in bed, holding her baby daughter, watched over by Sylvia and Father Murphy.

'I'm terribly sorry that you had to bring us, Father.'

'Don't take on, lass. Sure an' wasn't I glad to be here when this wee mite arrived. I can see a boxing match any old time but a miracle like this is not something I would ever like to miss. Sure an' what names will you both be thinking of for this perfect little angel?'

'I would like you to christen her, Bridget Kathleen, Father and don't bother consulting Danny. He couldn't be bothered to bring me to the hospital so it'll be me naming her.'

'That's a nice name, so it is. An' t'is a kind thought to be naming her after Danny's mother, so it is.'

'Well actually, Father,' said Connie, her eyes sparkling with anger, 'my own mother's second name is Kathleen.'

Father Murphy ignored the animosity behind the words. It was his job to keep peace between man and wife. 'Sure an' isn't that a lovely coincidence?'

He bent over the two women as they continued to exclaim with delight at Bridget Kathleen's tiny fingers and cute toes. He just hoped that Danny had the sense to bring a big bunch of flowers to the hospital. It wasn't that he was a bad man. He was just thoughtless. If only he spent as much time with his own family as he did with his boys.

CHAPTER FIFTEEN

'Now then, how's your weight, this morning, Ron?' Danny was on his way to Glasgow with Mac, Nipper and George. They were taking Ron Charleton to fight the Scottish Light Heavyweight, Willie Armstrong at the Kelvin Hall. They'd taken a sleeper from Sheffield, the previous evening. 'We'll soon be pulling into Glasgow.'

'Well, Boss, I don't know. I might just make it. On the other hand, I might be over.'

'Brilliant!' Danny exploded. 'Nice time to tell me you're overweight: nine o'clock on the morning of the fight!'

'Sorry Boss.' Ron was sheepish.

'We'll have to get you weighed as soon as we pull in.'

They were all standing on the platform. 'Right,' said Danny, 'where can we get weighed?'

'They'll have one of those big weighing machines in Woolworths, Boss.'

'Right! Good idea! Where's Woolworths?'

'Come wi' me, Boss. I know this city like the back o' me hand,' said Mac.

'Oh aye! Keep forgetting you were born here.'

Back at the Wellington, Connie had Bridget Kathleen on her knee. Sylvia was knitting a little matinee coat for the newest family member. The twins were messing about on the floor.

Sylvia frowned and stopped knitting. She looked up. 'I can't help you.'

'Well, Mam! I'm telling you! If you don't, I'll get one of the locals to help me an' then it'll be all round the pub.'

'What's the weight set at?' George asked.

They were all standing around the weighing machine, just inside the main doors of Woolworths.

'Twelve stone, four pounds,' replied Danny. 'Giv us yer jacket, Ron.'

Ron took off his heavy tweed jacket and gave it to Danny.

'Good God! Twelve stone, eight and three quarter pounds. 'You're nearly five pounds overweight. Can't have this. The contract for this fight stipulates that in the event of us not making the weight, the other side will be allowed to claim forfeit of one hundred pounds. That comes out of your purse, Ron.'

Ron gasped. 'Why didn't you warn me, Boss?'

'That's a hell of a lot of money.' George sounded worried.

'Let's weigh him wi' out his clothes on, Boss,' Mac suggested.

'Good idea! Get yer kit off, Ron.'

'I can't do that,' Ron protested. 'This is a public place.'

'Don't be soft, lad. You'll be standing up in front of about ten thousand punters tonight in nowt but a pair of shorts. Listen. Me and George'll hold our raincoats over you, while you get on the scales.' Danny took off his long coat, put it over his head and extended his arms to make a tent.

127

George followed suit and they stood over Ron.

Nipper split his sides. 'You look like a couple of Bedouins out of The Desert Song.'

'Never mind all that. Ron! Get on with it!'

Ron stripped off his shirt and trousers and a crowd of interested shoppers started gathering. 'Aye look! A stripper! What's going on?'

'He's fighting one of your lot tonight,' said Nipper, 'and he thinks he's a bit over the weight so we're just checking it out.'

'Who's he fightin' then?'

'Willie Armstrong.'

'Wullie Armstrong?'

Ron was now down to his underpants.

The manager appeared on the scene. 'What's going on here?'

'He's got a very important match tonight. He's got to weigh himself in case he's overweight.' The crowd tried to convince the manager that it was all kosher. 'He's fightin' the Pride o' Glasgow, oor man, Wullie Armstrong, tonight.'

On hearing this, the manager took off his own jacket and joined up the human tent while Ron jumped on the scales.

'Twelve stone, six pounds! Right! Get dressed Ron!

'What are we going to do, Boss?'

'Well, I don't know about you Ron but I'll tell you what I'm going to do. I'm going to have some breakfast in the cafeteria. Let's go.'

Father Murphy was just sitting down.

Sylvia poured him a cup of tea. 'Will you talk to her, Father. She won't listen to me.'

'It's no good Father. I've made up my mind. Nothing you say is going to make me change it. Anyway, it's only till he comes to his senses.' She got up and walked out of the room.

'Right! I'm having bacon, sausage, tomatoes, two fried eggs, toast an' a nice mug of tea. Same for you George? Nipper? Mac?'

'Aye Boss.'

'Aye Danny.'

'What about me?' Ron asked.

Danny turned back to the waitress. 'A glass of water for this lad here. He's fightin' tonight at the Kelvin Hall so he doesn't want anything to eat.'

Ron groaned. 'I can't sit here and watch you lot all tucking in.'

'Right, well, here you are.' Danny felt in his trouser pocket. 'Here's sixpence. Nip out and buy yersel' a Daily Express. If you put it up to your face to read, you won't be able to see us eating.'

Connie had just finished bungling her clothes into one of two boxes. She picked up the box and followed her mother into a bedroom several doors further down the corridor, 'Right! That's the lot! Now I'm telling you Mam. I'm sleeping in here till Danny takes me somewhere on holiday. If I don't make a stand now, I'll be pregnant again and he'll have another excuse not to take me anywhere.'

Danny and his companions had just emerged from Woolworth's. Danny hailed a cab. He bent down to speak to the driver. 'I need some good Turkish Baths for my fighter.'

'For a fighter! Och! Aye! A fighter! Who's he fightin' then?'

Danny mentioned their opponent's name.

'Och! Aye! Wullie Armstrong is it? Oor man'll kill him!'

That's handy, thought Danny as the driver opened the door and they all piled in.

He took them miles out of the centre to a place called Maryhill Baths.

Danny had never seen anything like it. 'I didn't know they had hot water in the Stone Age,' he quipped to the driver. 'Here!' He passed him a tenner through the window. 'I'll double that if you'll call back in an hour.'

'I don't need to do that. I've not got any other jobs booked and I need a break anyway. I'll pop into that café opposite and have a bite tae eat.'

After twenty minutes in the steam bath, poor Ron looked like a boiled lobster. There were some old-fashioned scales and Danny got him out and onto them. He had to do that a few times but gradually the weight came down. By the end of the session, they'd got it down to twelve stone, five pounds. 'Right! We'll have to throw ourselves on their mercy, Ron. I can't leave you in here any longer.' While Ron was dressing, Danny spoke to the others, on the quiet. 'Quite honestly, I can't see him making this fight. He looks all in.'

The driver took them back into Glasgow city centre, into Oxford Street, to Tommy Gilmore's place: a very nice little gym in the heart of The Gorbals. In they went, to be officially weighed. The taxi driver asked if he could come and watch.

'Aye. Course you can.'

Willie Armstrong jumped on the scales.

'Twelve stone, four pounds exactly. And your man?'

'Aye! Here's here. He's had a terrible time trying to make this weight. He's weak and drawn.' Danny was piling on the agony hoping they wouldn't be too hard on his boy.

Ron got on the scales.

'Twelve stone, five and a quarter pounds.'

'We're claiming forfeit!'

Oh dear. Danny turned pale. Those scales at Maryhill Baths mustn't have been accurate. Then Danny remembered something. 'Just one moment. There's a clause in the contract that states, in the event of a boxer not making the weight at the first attempt, he's allowed one hour to get it off.' Even as he spoke, Danny knew he was clutching at straws.

There was a few minutes consternation and they consulted the document but there it was, in black and white. 'And how are you goin' to get it off him: cut it off?' Armstrong and his men burst into raucous laughter.

Danny ignored them. 'Come on, Ron.'

'Where are we going?'

'Back to Maryhill Baths.'

'Oh no!'

'Good job you're still here mate. Fancy another job?'

'Och Aye! No' a problem.'

Danny turned to the officials. 'Can I borrow a blanket please?'

They handed him one.

Danny wrapped Ron in the blanket, picked him up and carried out to the cab.

'Need any help Boss?'

'No thanks. Just hold the doors open.' He bungled the half-conscious Ron back into the cab and off they went: back to Maryhill Baths. Danny carried Ron in. He was nearly dead. He

131

was absolutely on his knees. 'What a performance!' Danny muttered.

After another session in the steam, Danny wrapped Ron in the blanket again and carried him back outside to the waiting taxi.

'I dunno where you gets your strength from,' said George, admiringly.

'Bin a sportsman all me life and I still keeps mesel' fit.'

They got to Tommy Gilmore's just in time. Danny carried Ron in and put him on the scales.

'Twelve stone, four pounds, two ounces!'

'You're never going to claim forfeit over two ounces surely.' Danny was quick to appeal. 'The poor lad can hardly stand up.'

'Oh all right.'

'WEIGHED IN!'

'Give us some water,' gasped Ron. He sounded like someone who'd walked a hundred miles across the Sahara Desert. One of the officials fetched a glass and Ron downed the contents in two seconds flat.

'Right! Let's get him dressed and then we can get out of here.'

Out they went into the hurly-burly of Glasgow city centre. Right opposite was a café with a Kiaora dispenser in the window. It had the usual luscious-looking plastic oranges floating round a large bowl.

'That's it!' Ron gasped. He looked like he was about to snuff it. 'Get me over to that café, quick!' He staggered across the road and into the café.

'Can you give me a glass of that?' Danny asked the girl behind the counter.

'No! No!' Ron shook his head. 'I don't want a glass. Just give us a jug of it.'

Before Danny had even got his money out to pay, Ron had downed the lot and was asking for another. 'Go easy,' said Danny. He could see Ron visibly blowing up before their eyes.

'A bit thirsty, is he?' the girl asked, in an interested voice.

'Something like that,' replied Danny as he paid her for both jugs.

They all sat down and watched Ron drink the second jug more slowly.

'Now I'm going to pay for a room in a nice hotel so you can have a sleep before tonight.'

'How about something to eat?'

Typical thought Danny. 'That's exactly what got you into this mess in the first place.' He watched Ron's face fall. 'Don't worry lad. I'm only kidding you. As a matter of fact we've got to get a few steaks inside you: build up your strength now.'

'Surely not,' said George, 'not after he's already weighed in.'

'Oh yes,' said Mac. 'He's allowed to eat and drink any amount now. That's why they have the weigh-in so early. It gives the boxers time to get themselves ready.'

They found an excellent hotel where they had a large sirloin steak. Ron had two. Then Danny insisted that Ron should get himself to bed.

Later in the bar Danny talked to the others. 'I'm a bit concerned about this fight,'

'Why's that?' George asked him.

'Well, I know it means a lot to him. He wants to win but he's seriously weakened himself by all that weight loss. It's taken a lot out of him. You didn't see him in the bedroom. I literally had to undress him and he'd no sooner crept under the sheets than he was flat out. Absolutely dead to the world.'

'He's just tired,' said Mac. 'He'll be all right once he's had a sleep.'

'That's not what's bothering you, is it, Boss?' Nipper asked.

'You've got a sharp eye. No! You're right. There is summat else. We're facing a dangerous opponent. This Willie Armstrong, he's a very popular fighter. He's known for his left hook. He's fought the best and won. And on top of that, the whole of Glasgow will be cheering him on.'

'Well, so what,' said Mac. 'Oor boy's just beaten the British Empire Champion.'

'Well, we'll just have to see if he recovers. It's all in the lap of the gods now. At least we don't have to report in till eight o'clock.'

Glasgow was a "fight-crazy" city. The dressing rooms at the Kelvin Hall were underneath the tiered seats. It was just like being under a bullring. There was a constant stamping of feet on the boards above their heads. It was deafening and the atmosphere was electric. Eventually Danny's team was called out and they climbed into the ring. Ron looked quite cool. He was an intelligent boxer: a good ABA champion: knew his way around.

SECONDS AWAY! ROUND ONE! DING! DING!

Next thing Danny knew, almost before he'd got to his seat, there was such a gasp from the crowd. He looked round and there was poor Ron, flat on his back. Danny's brain was working like a railway engine. The thoughts were steaming through at sixty miles an hour. This was a desperate situation after all they'd been through. A knockout in the first round would look very bad on Ron's record. Right! I'll get him disqualified, thought Danny. Quick as a flash, he dashed round to where Ron was laid on the floor and shouted as loud as he could, 'RON! GET UP! GET UP LAD!' Danny knew that by doing this he was breaking all the rules because as Ron's manager and chief second he wasn't, under any consideration, allowed to take part in the proceedings. But he didn't care. Even if he himself got warned off, it would be worth it, just to get Ron disqualified. A disqualification would look much better on his record than a knockout. However, his plan backfired, to a certain extent because, to Danny's great surprise, Ron seemed to hear him, opened his eyes and scrambled to his feet just before the referee could count him out. And by a stroke of good luck, Danny's indiscretion had gone unnoticed and the fight continued.

There were nine more gruelling rounds. The two boxers were well matched and the crowd never stopped screaming encouragement. The outcome was a draw, announced by the referee, which Danny was quite pleased to accept. A draw was an unusual hometown decision. He was just about to start cheering when he felt a tap on his shoulder.

'Right! Got you this time, McCoy!' Billy Battle was standing right behind him. 'Right! I'll be reporting this to the authorities. I'm going to get you banned. You wait and see. Told you I'd be watching your every move.'

There wasn't a great deal of cheer on the train back to Sheffield. 'We tried to warn you but you weren't listening,' said George.

There was even less cheer back at the Wellington, when, for the first time in his marriage, Danny found himself sleeping on his own.

'I'll come back to your bed when we return from our holidays,' yelled Connie, at the top of her voice, as she disappeared into her new bedroom.

'What holidays?'

'The holidays we're going on before I get back in your bed.' She slammed the door.

CHAPTER SIXTEEN

'This isn't quite what I had in mind, Mam.'

'Well, beggars can't be chosers. At least he *has* brought you on holiday. Anyway, you wouldn't have wanted to leave the children behind, now would you?' Sylvia was sharing a bedroom with Connie and they had nine-month-old Bridget Katie with them.

'You're right, Mam. I wouldn't leave any of the children, not even for a day.'

'Then isn't it a good thing that I'm here to help you with them?'

'Of course it is. Eeh! Mam! I didn't mean it to sound like I don't want you here.' Connie hugged her mother. 'I'm right glad you've come.'

'And surely you wouldn't begrudge Danny's parents their first trip back in twenty years?'

'You know I wouldn't, Mam. What I meant was: I really fancied sunning myself on a beach in Spain. The one thing I am mad about is the fact that Danny's using this so-called holiday as a business trip.'

'What d'ya mean? Business trip?' Sylvia was onto this piece of information like a terrier onto a rat. 'Business! I hope you don't mean he's going to a boxing match. I've not come all the way to Dublin to baby-sit while Danny goes off to a boxing match.'

'Oh no he's not going to a boxing match, he's planning a trip to Leitrim.'

'Well? Isn't that where Dermot comes from? I wouldn't mind going there, myself.'

'Danny's meeting up with his Uncle Peter.'

'What's wrong with that? They'll all be wanting to see him now he's a famous boxing manager.'

'Being famous has got nowt to do with it. He's going to look at a boxer that his Uncle Peter's been training. Uncle Willie's told Danny that he's got to see him. He's a "promising" young boxer, you know the sort of thing?' Connie was scathing about it.

'Oh well. That doesn't sound too bad. It shouldn't take up too much of his time.'

'Who knows how much time it's going to take,' said Connie, gloomily. 'I mean, Mam, just look at what's happened today.' Her voice rose ominously. 'We've only been here a day and here we are: looking after two toddlers and a baby while he's pissed off for a few pints of Guinness!'

'CONNIE! You know I don't like you using bad language.'

'Sorry Mam but he brings out the worst in me. He makes me see red. He's got such a cavalier attitude. He always puts them damn boxers first. Sorry Mam! I know! I know! But you can see how it is. It's "my boys this" and "my boys that" and I'm fed up of it!'

'I don't think he does it on purpose.' Sylvia poured oil on the troubled waters. 'You know he's a good man, at heart. Even your dad likes him and that's something of a miracle. He's never looked at another woman. He loves you and the twins and he worships Bridget.'

138

Danny was sitting in the bar of the hotel with Kathleen, Dermot, and Willie. They were all drinking Guinness.

'I'm still cut up about youse staying in this hotel instead of with me.'

'Don't be daft,' said Kathleen. 'We'd never have fitted into your house.'

'I suppose not. Still, never mind. What time are we setting off tomorrow?'

'Soon as we've had breakfast. Is that all right?'

'Certainly.'

'It's glad I am that you're coming with us,' said Dermot.

'As soon as I knew that the man himself was coming back, I arranged some time off. Anyway, I only go in three days a week now.'

'Our Danny's hired one of those shooting brakes so we can all be together. I can't believe I'll be seeing our Peter tomorrow. T'is such a shame that your Uncle Frankie couldn't get over from America, Danny.'

'Well,' said Danny, 'there's always someone who has to stay behind and keep things ticking over. I feel sorry that George couldn't come and Mac and Nipper. They'd have loved it over here, so they would.'

'You can't leave a pub without someone at the helm. T'is a good job the daddy and I have retired, or we couldn't have come. And t'is good that you have people like Mac and Nipper to keep an eye on your boys, Danny.'

Danny was driving the station wagon and his Uncle Willie was sitting beside him, navigating. The countryside was absolutely deserted and they'd been driving for what seemed like hours.

'Are you sure we're on the right road, Uncle? We haven't seen a soul for hours.'

'I am sure we're right for haven't I been on this road more times than I can count? See! Look at that will youse?' There's the sign. See! Sure as I'm telling youse! There it is now! Our Peter's bar. Pull over.'

Danny pulled over and parked. Everyone got out. It was more a shop than a bar.

"McCOY'S GENERAL SUPPLIES"

The door was just opening. Peter McCoy ran to the car and Kate McCoy fell into his arms. There was so much shouting and laughter and hugging and kissing that Connie felt quite overwhelmed by it. There seemed to be hundreds of Irish McCoys all over the road. God knows where they'd all come from. It was the wedding all over again.

Then they were all inside the shop. The door opened again and a big fella stepped inside. 'Oh! Oh! Patsy! T'is the man himself,' exclaimed Kathleen as he darted over, threw his arms around her and smothered her with kisses.

'The blessings of God be upon you. Sure an' haven't I come all the way from Fenagh to see you, Kathleen. An' where is this famous boxing manager that everyone is talking about?'

Kathleen McCoy pulled her son into the centre of the gathering. 'Here he is.'

'For sure an' t'is the boy himself.' He hugged Danny.

Danny turned round to his children. 'This is my mammy's cousin Patsy who we haven't seen since our wedding. These are my twins, Patrick and Michael and this little'n is Bridget Kathleen.'

Patsy kissed everyone and stroked the baby's head. 'Sure an' you have a lovely family. An' I can see the baby is taking after the two most beautiful girls in the world.'

Sylvia and Connie both blushed with pleasure.

The door opened again and three men came rushing in. 'We're looking for a cousin of ours from England. Danny McCoy. Where is he?'

'Bejasus! T'is Tom and Colm and Hugo.' The four men embraced.

Another door opened at the back of the shop and Maggie McCoy bustled out with a young man and a teenage boy in tow.

Peter dragged them forward. 'Here we are now, boys. You remembers your Uncle Danny from his wedding in England. Sure, an' here's his two little lads who've been named after yourselves, so they have, have they not Danny?'

'Aye they have that.'

'Michael's twenty-five now and Patrick is just coming up to his seventeenth.'

'See,' said Maggie, 'find some seats for our Kate and Sylvia and Connie.'

Peter pulled three of the upturned barrels over to a table and the three women sat down. Connie lifted Bridget Kathleen on to her knee.

Every now and again, the street door opened and more people streamed in.

'Go and fetch the fiddle, Michael,' someone begged. Michael went out while his father got behind the counter and started pulling pints of Guinness from a barrel.

'Who are all these people and where have they come from?' Sylvia asked Kate.

'Sure an' aren't they all distant cousins of ours?'

'But when we were driving here, we didn't see a single person. The place was deserted. So did you write to them all?'

'Jesus, Mary an' Joseph!' Kathleen crossed herself. 'Sure an' I did not at all. Sure, it would take me a whole year to write to all this lot. I only wrote to Dermot's brother, Peter, so I did. But it'll have got round, so it will. They'll be popping in all day to see the famous boxing manager, Danny McCoy, so they will. See! Now! Will you look at that? T'is Michael with the fiddle. Now the party can get started.'

'Here,' said Peter to Maggie, passing her two bottles of Irish. 'I've opened these but I'm just taking Danny into the back room for a bit of the crack. Keep the drinks flowing, will youse?' He wriggled through the crush round the bar and shouted, 'Danny! Danny! Over here. Come into the back room.'

Back in Chesterfield, Father Murphy and Sammy Clark were sitting at the side of the gym, watching Mac. He was giving some pointers to Jim and Len Clark. Joe and Ray Clark were watching Katusha sparring in the ring with Garfield. 'So are you pleased with the way your lads are coming along?'

'I am that, Father. It's like a miracle, Danny McCoy setting up like this. Three years ago they were just four little ragamuffins, scrapping in the gutters. After their mam died I thought I'd never get them on the straight and narrow. I thought as how they were on their way to reform school, especially the eldest two lads.'

'Jim and Len?'

'Aye. They were a real handful.'

'Joseph and Raymond could easily have followed the same path but look at them now: all four keen and raring to go. I hear Jim's got his first amateur fight next month.' Father Murphy watched Jim trying out the moves he'd just learnt.

'Aye an' it's about time an' all. Won't be long before he's off to do his National Service. Thanks to Danny, he did better than expected at school. It's like this boxing lark has given him something to aim for. He got a good job when he left school and now he's talking about going into the RAF like Danny.

Mac suddenly turned round and shouted, 'Father, do you know where Nipper is?'

'No. Sorry. I haven't seen him for a couple of hours.'

'I thought he was going to be giving me a hand.'

'Maybe he's seeing to Danny's greyhounds.'

'Aye! Maybe! He hates it when Danny's away. Hope he's not gone to join him.'

'That's not very likely. Danny's relying on him to look after those dogs. He won't let him down.'

'Now Paddy. Show us how they've been bandaging your hands.' Paddy had followed them into the back room. Peter turned to Danny. 'I t'ink it's being done wrong. He's joined an amateur club in Jamestown but I don't t'ink the coach knows much about the game.'

They were in a makeshift gym at the back of the shop. Danny looked around. He felt a wave of sadness at what he saw. It wasn't a patch on the gym at the Wellington. There was a homemade punch-bag hanging from an exposed oak beam. There were a couple of rickety tables and an old first-aid box on one table and that was it. And it was dusty and dilapidated. 'Well that's no good at all. It's one of the most important things, is that. Right, lad, let's have a look.'

143

The boy showed him, as best he could, how they were doing it.

'Yer daddy's right. On no account must you put those bandages between the fingers, like that.' Danny unwound the bandage. 'You make a figure of eight, like this. Around the thumb, around the wrist and across the four fingers.' He nodded towards the first-aid kit. 'Now if yer daddy will get me some thin strips of tape.' He waited for Peter to cut the sticking plaster and hand him a strip. Danny placed it between Patrick's fingers, securing the bandage on each side. 'When this is done, This hand should be like a little walnut. Let's see you do it, Peter.'

Peter did the other hand.

Danny picked up the boxing gloves from the table. 'Now then Paddy, let's get these gloves of yours on.' He pushed them on and tied the strings. 'Now can you feel how those hands are curled up inside the gloves?'

'Sure, Danny. They feel great, so they do.'

'Well, that's exactly how they should feel. See, once the hands are bandaged the right way, the hand grips the inside of that glove quite naturally, as it curls into a little fist. Now, we'll have a little go to see how it feels. What weight are you, lad?'

'Nine stone.'

'Mmmm! Featherweight are you? I thought you looked about that, so I did. Right! Come on lad. I'll get behind this punch-bag and hold it.'

Paddy followed Danny to the centre of the room.

'Right! Now, throw two left hands and follow with the right. Hard as you can.'

Paddy did exactly what Danny had told him to do. When his right hand hit the punch-bag it broke away from the beam and was hurled across the room. The trouble was, Danny went with it.

Peter was shouting, 'Danny! Danny! Are you all right?'

'Danny! Danny! I'm sorry. Mother of God! Is he all right Daddy? I didn't mean to hit it that hard.'

'Jesus, Mary an' Joseph!' Peter crossed himself. 'I should have been telling you, he has a good strong punch.' He bent down to help Danny.

Danny panted, trying to get the oxygen to his starved lungs because he'd been very badly winded. When he could finally speak he said, 'He's got a hell of a punch for a featherweight. I've got middleweights in training that can't punch as hard as this lad. This is the promising young boxer you were telling me about on the phone, isn't it? I don't suppose you'll be letting me take *this* young fella back to Chesterfield.' There was a wistful note of longing in Danny's voice because he knew Peter wouldn't want to lose his son.

'Well as a matter of fact, Danny, I was hoping and praying that you *would* want to take him on. The lad deserves a proper chance. He won't get one here. And you're the only one I would trust with my lad.'

'I can't believe it.' Danny was close to tears. 'There's nowt better than working with a member of yer own family. You won't need to worry about him. We'll look after him.' He draped his arm round Paddy's shoulders. 'I've got some fellas over from Tonga and they've never been homesick. Aye! I wonder what they're all getting up to.'

Bert Shaw's caravan was near the generators that fed the fairground with its power. They were horrendously noisy and it was difficult to be heard. He had to shout. 'Thanks boys.' He pulled a wad of notes out of his pocket and gave each of the two men a fiver. 'Have a drink on me.' He turned round to shake a fist at Nipper. 'That'll teach you to steal the take and run off with it.' He turned back to the men. 'Like I said, that little bastard nearly sent me bankrupt. He stole two weeks takings from me at the end of that stint in Newcastle.'

Nipper was screaming from inside the cage. 'Don't believe him. He's lying. I've never pinched a penny in my life. Let me out! Let me out!'

'Don't worry, I'm only going to keep him in that cage till he's told me where he's stashed the money. I borrowed it from a lion tamer I know.' He laughed as though he'd made a joke. 'I'll just teach him a lesson.'

'Don't matter to us, Boss, how long you keep him there. Never could stand them bloody goblins or whatever they call them. Creepy little bastards. Anyway, we'll get off.' The men walked away, towards the road: off to the pub to spend their money.

Bert Shaw walked over to the cage and poked Nipper in the belly with a long stick

Nipper grabbed it.

'Ooh! Vicious little bugger aren't you. Well. We'll soon knock that out of you. An' yer can shut yer mouth Frankenstein. No one's goin' to hear you at this end of the fairground. An' no one's goin' to see you either.' He pulled the tarpaulin cover over the cage. Then he disappeared into his van, banging the door behind him.

A small clown was standing behind the caravan. He waited five minutes till he was sure the coast was clear and then he slipped under the tarpaulin that covered the cage.

A week later, the same clown was climbing out of a taxi, outside the Wellington. He cut a comical figure because although he was in ordinary clothes, he still had his circus face on. He leaned into the cab and spoke to the driver. 'Wait here. I won't be long. I've got to see someone in there.'

When he walked into the gym, the Tongan boxers looked at him in astonishment.

'Is this Danny's Place?'

'Yes,' said Garfield. 'Who are you?'

The clown ignored the question. 'Which one of you is Mac?'

'None of us. Who wants him.'

'One of his mates. Bloke called Nipper.'

The three boxers gathered round the clown.

'What's happened to him?' Johnny asked.

'Where is he?' Garfield growled.

'Come on. Tell us now and don't mess about,' said Katusha, looking angry.

The clown looked a bit bothered. 'I've come as a favour to Nipper. It's not my fault where he is. Don't shoot the messenger.'

'What you on about?'

The clown could see his last words were beyond their comprehension. 'Bloke called Bert Shaw's got him locked in a lion's cage.'

'With a lion?' Johnny gasped, panic-stricken.

'No. The cage is an empty one.'

'Why didn't you let him out?'

'Because I ain't got the key. In any case, I don't want to end up with two broken legs. That Bert Shaw's a real vicious bastard. And it wouldn't have done any good if I had let him out. He couldn't have made a run for it. He's in a bad way. He can't stand up anymore. I'd have come sooner but it took me this long to worm out of him where he'd come from. I guess he

147

didn't trust me. Maybe he thought his friend Danny was going to get a pasting.'

'Right mister. Can you take us there?'

'Yeah! I've got a taxi waiting outside. I haven't got any money for it, by the way.'

'Don't worry about dat,' said Garfield. 'We'll take care of dat. Come on lads. Get changed and then we're off.'

'Shouldn't we wait for Mac?' Johnny was a bit more cautious.

'No. He won't be back till late. He's checking all the hospitals in Sheffield.'

'Don't leave it too long. He's in a bad way.' The clown looked anxious.

By the time they reached the fairground, the clown had filled them in on what had happened to Nipper and where he was. 'Listen, don't forget what I've told you. When we get there, you follow me but no closer than a hundred yards. When I bend down to tie my shoelace, you'll know that's the one and then you're on your own.' It was clear he was scared.

'Don't worry mate.' Johnny put his hand in his pocket and produced a wad of notes. He pressed twenty pounds into the clown's hand. 'Don't bloody argue, mate.' Then he leaned forward and gave the driver twenty pounds. 'There'll be another pile like this if you're still here when we get back. We shouldn't be more than twenty minutes and we'll be wanting a quick get away.'

'Aye! I'll be waiting for you. Don't matter how long it takes.' Forty pounds was a hell of a lot of money. It was a week's work.

They all got out of the cab. The taxi driver watched in amazement. He hadn't realised how big they were. They'd all piled in so fast. Now he knew why the engine had struggled up those hills. How in hell had they all got fitted in? That bloody clown must have been sitting on the floor. He watched the clown stroll casually down the street. The three massive black men followed.

As soon as the clown finished tying his laces, he disappeared so fast Johnny Halanara wondered if he'd really been there at all. 'Quick lads. Over here. It must be that one. Keep quiet. Let's check and see if there's anyone at home before we go round the back of the van.' He looked round to see if anyone was watching. The alley between the vans was deserted. They could hear the generator the clown had told them about. Johnny sidled up to the door of the van, followed by Garfield and Katusha. Considering their average weight was fourteen stone, they were surprisingly light on their feet, probably due to Danny's strict training regime. Johnny tried the door. It opened. He peered in. 'No one here.'

'Right,' said Garfield. 'Dat little man said dat cage was round the back. Let's go.'

'Careful. Might be someone there.'

There was someone there. Bert Shaw and his two mates were having a game of cards right in front of the cage. All that could be seen of Nipper was a lump of rags on the floor of the cage.

'There's Nipper: inside that cage, just like that clown said.'

The three fellas looked up in surprise as the boxers erupted onto the scene. None of them got a chance to call for help.

Danny's boys pounced like the lions that had previously occupied the cage. They beat the three fairground men absolutely senseless. There was blood all over the place. Their faces were unrecognisable: reduced to a pulp.

Johnny searched Shaw's pockets and found some keys.

Garfield peered into the cage and gasped in fear and disgust. Nipper was absolutely filthy. What looked like his own excreta was splattered all over the floor. His legs were bent under him in a funny sort of way. 'Man! He dead!' Garfield whispered.

'No! No! Oh no! He can't be.' Johnny unlocked the door and jumped in. He felt for a pulse. 'He's alive.' He lifted him up and passed him to Katusha. Then he jumped down. 'Come on lads. Let's go. We've got to get him to a hospital quickly.'

'He not going to make it,' Garfield was crying.

The driver had other ideas. 'Hospital's at least thirty miles. I know a good doctor. We'll take him back to your place. It's the nearest. I'll stop at the first telephone box we see and call the doctor. Get him to meet us at the Wellington.'

All Danny's boxers, as well as Mac and George, were standing round the bed, watching the doctor dress Nipper's wounds.

'I've done the best I can, for the moment. Can one of you go and look for that ambulance. I've given him a shot of morphine. Don't want him waking up. Those broken legs are giving him a hell of a lot of pain. Can't tell how long he's been like this. That's the trouble. He might lose both legs.'

There were tears streaming down Garfield's face and the others looked like they weren't far off joining him.

'I want you to send me a bill for this,' said Mac.

'Oh no. I don't intend charging for this.'

'Well I'm sorry but you'll have to. I've got to have some proof of how badly this little bloke's been injured. Got to protect my boxers. What they've done is entirely illegal. For a boxer to use his fists outside the ring is punishable by a spell in jail.'

'Oh dear! I didn't know that. Well, in that case. I'll send you a detailed medical report but you won't need to pay for it. Give my name to your solicitors and I'll be glad to stand up in court, on your behalf. I'll tell them how your boys saved this man's life.'

'Thanks doctor. I'm still hoping the police won't get to hear of it. Them fairground types don't like to get involved with the authorities.'

The boxers knew what Mac was talking about and they looked extremely anxious. None of them was keen on spending time in jail.

CHAPTER SEVENTEEN

'Well, you dozy buggers!' Danny was back and he could be heard shouting at the other end of the Wellington. 'We're in a hell of a lot of trouble now. And how the hell did this happen?' He shook the newspaper under their noses. 'Bloody hell! I can't believe it!'

'Well, they didn't get it from us,' said Mac, biting his lip.

'Well, someone must have told them,' shouted Danny. 'Christ this is a bloody nice welcome home. I knew I shouldn't have left you. Come on! Which one of you has taken a back-hander to spill the beans?' Danny was spitting feathers.

'Not me, Boss.'

'It not us, Boss.'

'Don't accuse the boys, Danny. I warned them about keeping their gobs shut. I told them they could go to jail.'

'COULD go to jail? COULD go to jail?' Danny screamed at Mac. 'There's no could about it. They WILL go to jail. I'm telling you. The next knock on that door. It'll be the police. They ARE going to jail: no COULD about it.' He had to stop to take a breath.

'I not want to go to jail, Boss.' Garfield rolled his eyes in fear.

'Listen Danny, it could only have been the taxi driver. He might have thought he was doing us a favour.'

'Oh aye! More likely he thought he was going to get rich quick,' snapped Danny.

'Taxi driver nice man, Boss. He help us carry little Nipper in.'

'Shut up Garfield and let me think.'

There was silence for a while.

'Summat's got to be done before that Board of Control swings into action.'

'D'you really think they will?' Mac asked. 'I mean, let's face it, that little fella's got two broken legs and the doctors say he won't walk again. This article hails your boys as heroes. Even the public is baying for blood and Bert Shaw has fled the country.'

'I couldn't give a shit about Bert Shaw. It's Billy Battle that's going to be baying for blood now. Mine! He won't let the Board falter just because the public's fallen soft. You lot have played right into his hands. I know for certain. He'll be down at the police station right now. It's absolutely forbidden for boxers to use their fists outside the ring.' Danny was shouting at the top of his voice and the big giants from Tonga cringed away like beaten dogs. Suddenly Danny collapsed into his chair. He banged his head down on the desk and muttered, 'I'm finished. I'm done for.'

'So the boys should have left Nipper in that cage to die, ay?' Mac's voice was dangerously low.

Danny looked up and sighed. 'No! No! They did exactly what I would have done but at least if I'd been the one to do it, the boys wouldn't be losing their licences.'

'Well you weren't here to do it.'

'We think we might have the answer,' Johnny Halanara volunteered in a shaky voice.

Everyone could see he was terrified that Danny was going to start shouting again.

'We've been talking, Boss. We want to go home.'

'Home! Home! What the hell d'ya mean? Home?'

'Home, Boss. Home to Tonga. Listen, Boss. It makes sense. We've done well over here. We've got all that money in dem bank accounts you made us open. We can all go back to Tonga, rich men. Be able to buy a pineapple plantation, each,' he grinned, trying to make a joke of it, 'thanks to you, Boss. Anyway, we've been feeling homesick ever since we went to London.'

'Oh Jesus!' Mac muttered, under his breath.

'You what? Since we were down in London? It's ages since we were down in London. You've never mentioned you were homesick before today.'

'No! We went while you were away. We got a special invite from dat Harry bloke,' said Garfield. 'You know. Harry. Dat big man in boxing.'

Danny leapt to his feet. 'Which Harry?' He was shouting again. He turned to Mac. 'Who's he talking about?'

'Harry Levene. Wants to take 'em under his wing. Says he can get them some world title fights.'

'Not bloody likely! Not under any consideration! I've already told Harry he can bugger off! Anyhow, what d'ya mean: an invitation? What bloody invitation? If they've been appearing anywhere for Harry Levene while I've been away, you're fired.'

'Calm down, Boss. It's nothing like that. While you were in Ireland, Harry Levene invited them down to London to see an exhibition of...'

'What bloody exhibition? I ain't heard of any boxing exhibition and nothing goes off without I read about it in my Boxing Times.'

'Not a boxing exhibition, Boss. It was just an exhibition about Captain Cook at Greenwich Naval College. The Navy was keen to get your boys there for some publicity.'

'It was beautiful, Boss. Dere was all dem photos of Tonga, Boss,' said Garfield.

Mac cut in, 'They've got a replica of that ship. You know the one. The Endeavour. They've made it look like it's at anchor in Tahiti. All them blue seas and green palm trees. It made your boys as homesick as parrots!'

'Tonga, man! Not Tahiti.' Katusha corrected Mac.

'Well, actually, it was Tahiti that Cook sailed to in the Endeavour. Tonga came later when he was travelling in a different ship. Anyway, it's all the same, ain't it?' Mac got a filthy look from all three boxers but before anyone could have a go at him…

'For God's sake,' shouted Danny. 'Tonga! Tahiti! What's it matter? Are you telling me that just because you've seen a few pictures of palm trees an' a bit of sand, you wanna go home?'

There was a united chorus.

'Yes, Boss!'

'Yes please, Boss!'

'Dat is what we want, Boss.'

'That bastard Levene!' Then Danny started to laugh. 'Well it looks like the tables have been turned on that bastard. I'll bet this isn't quite the result he was aiming for. I'll bet he only invited you down to London so he could give you a taste for the high life. He'll be expecting you to snatch his hand off when he offers to look after you. He won't be expecting you to disappear to the other side of the world.'

155

'It rather solves our problem, don't you think?' Mac asked quietly.

'Providing we can get 'em out of the country before the police come looking for 'em,' replied Danny. 'Right. Better get moving then. All right, boys. You're going home. I'll pay for your passage. It'll be a pleasure. You've been good to me, my boys.'

They crowded round him.

Garfield was crying. 'We'll miss you, Boss.'

Danny was close to tears himself as he thought about letting them go. 'Aye lads an' I'll miss you. We've had some good times. Don't you forget 'em.'

'I'm telling you, we've got all the proof we need here…' Billy Battle waved the newspaper like a flag on VE Day, '…in this article. I propose we lodge a complaint at the main police station in Chesterfield. Get the local boys in blue involved. Our complaint should lead to all three of those boxers being arrested. I'll handle everything. We don't want McCoy to slip off the hook again like he did after that debacle up in Glasgow, do we? This is a much more serious misdemeanour. Are we taking a vote on this?'

'It's not necessary,' said the chairman of the Extraordinary General Meeting that Billy Battle had called, down in London. 'This is, as you so rightly point out, a matter for the police. You'd better get on with it. Meeting closed.' He stood up.

Billy Battle nearly danced out of the committee rooms. As he closed the door he executed a jig down the corridor. 'Right! Got you this time, McCoy! Whoopee! Once your boys are in jail we can see about getting you banned for life. Whoopee!' He darted into the lift. The lift operator looked at him as though he was bonkers.

'Yes? What can I do for you, Inspector?'

'It's Constable, sir.'

'Well Constable. What is it you want?'

'I'd like to interview...' he looked in his notebook, '...Katusha Latou, Johnny Halanara and Garfield Nabatoa.'

'They aren't here, Inspector.'

'Constable!'

'Sorry. They aren't here, Constable. They left last night. Went to Southampton to catch a boat to New Zealand.'

'Don't believe him,' screamed Billy Battle. 'Search the place! Search the place!'

'Sir! If you don't stop shouting at me, I shall be forced to arrest you.'

'Search the place by all means, Inspector...'

'CONSTABLE!'

'Sorry! Keep forgetting. Anyway, like I was saying, you are welcome to search the whole of the Wellington. Course, you'll have to ask the landlord's permission but I don't expect Mr Green will have any objections. We've nothing to hide.'

'He's lying! I insist you search the place.' Billy Battle was apoplectic.

'I assure you, Constable, I'm not lying. Search by all means. Be my guest but you'll be wasting your time. They were sailing at eleven o'clock, this morning, for New Zealand.' Danny turned to Billy Battle. 'If you hurry, you might just catch them. They'll be just passing Falmouth.' He turned back to the policeman. His face was a picture of innocence. 'Of course, you do realise, if that boat has to stop, it'll take it about ten miles to grind to a halt. By that time, they'll be out of your jurisdiction, won't they? Constable?'

The policeman stared at Danny. He was obviously at a loss what to do next.

Danny rammed home his final punch. 'Anyway, surely you've seen that little fella? You must have seen how bad he is? My boys couldn't stand by and do nowt. They only did what they did on an impulse. And it was only after them three louts attacked them.'

'So you're saying that your boxers didn't start it?'

'No! They didn't start anything. They just asked for the key to that cage.'

'Mmmm! It said in the newspaper article, someone was locked in a cage. I thought that was an exaggeration on the side of the newspaper.'

'Oh no! Constable. That was absolutely true. He was in a terrible state. You wouldn't treat an animal like that. A couple more days and he'd have been dead. He's got cracked ribs, a ruptured spleen, fractured wrists and two badly broken legs that were left too long without treatment. The doctors say he won't walk again.'

All four policemen looked decidedly disturbed by all this information. It was as though they knew they were looking for the wrong people and they didn't like it.

Billy Battle was stalking round the gym. His face was as black as thunder.

The constable shut his notebook. 'I think we'll have to leave the matter, Mr Battle. As you can see, those Tongans won't be fighting in Britain again so that seems to solve both your problem and mine as well.' He put his notebook away.

All four policemen took their leave.

'I can't believe you've wriggled out of this one,' hissed Billy Battle.

'Get off my premises,' said Danny. 'Just looking at you makes me want to spew.'

'Good riddance,' said Mac, as he watched Billy Battle slink out of the gym. 'You've beaten him again. Feel like a drink to celebrate?'

'Not really. There's bin no pleasure in this victory, this time. I can't stop thinking about Nipper. It's breaking my heart, so it is.'

Nipper was in hospital for six months and then he came back to the Wellington. The doctors told Danny, in private, that Nipper would never walk again. So everywhere the little fella wanted to go, someone carried him. Either George or Danny or one of his boys. Even the locals helped. He was never left on his own for a minute.

But Danny was the only one who refused to accept what the doctors had said. He gave him hours of physiotherapy. He nagged him. He cajoled him. He took him swimming at the public baths. And eventually, Nipper walked. All the regulars were amazed and told anyone who would listen that it was thanks entirely to that man McCoy. And as soon as Nipper was well enough, George and Sylvia threw the biggest party Chesterfield had ever seen.

CHAPTER EIGHTEEN

'I dunno what you're makin' such a fuss about. It's only a bit o' fun.' Danny tried to pacify Connie as the twins paraded round the gym; both of them wearing a red and gold boxing robe each. They were exactly the same as the ones Danny's boxers wore. He'd had them made especially for today. Today, Patrick and Michael were eight. Time flies, thought Danny as he watched them. Bridget Katie was nearly six. Daniel Dermot was four. Thankfully, Jack was still in his high chair. One less to chase around, thought Danny to himself. Not be long though before he'd be walking. He'd been born in 1961.

'He's right, lass.' George put his arm round his daughter. 'You've no need to worry about them little lads at this stage. They're not interested in boxing at all. In fact, yer mam's bought them a football an' two little goal posts, aye, nets an' all. You watch. Give 'em ten minutes and they'll be off outside, kicking that ball around on my lovely bowling green.' He rolled his eyes, pretending to be horrified at the thought. 'Stop frettin' lass. See! Look at all the pleasure Danny's boys are getting, fussin' round 'em.'

'Oh for goodness sake, George, stop molly-codling her. She knows very well that by the time those two little boys are of an age to box, I'll have retired and she knows full well, I wouldn't trust anyone else to manage them so that'll be that. End of an era.'

'Never!' George was shocked. 'You can't be thinking of retiring. Good God, man! You're only forty-two.'

'Aye an' by the time them lads are twenty, I'll be fifty-five. I'm not talking about retiring now but I'm telling you George, this game is a dirty profession and it's getting dirtier all the time. Give me another ten years and I won't want to stay in the game. There's some very funny people coming into it now: people that know nowt about boxing as a real sport. All they wanna do is make money and they don't care how they do it. For a start off, there's too many of these mis-matches being put on for my liking. It won't be long before the only people running things will be jumped-up millionaires. I'm fed up wi' it.'

'I don't understand why you're saying all this. Your lads are flying at the moment. Young Paddy's won thirty-seven fights out of forty and three of them were championship contests. He's British, European and WBA Featherweight Champion. He can't go much higher. Your Uncle Peter's over the moon.'

'Hmmm!'

'What d'ya mean? Hmmm? What about Carlo Santini? He's got a European title tucked under his belt and Ron Charleton's won forty-four contests out of forty-nine. He's finally made it this year. British and British Empire, Light Heavyweight Champion and it's all thanks to you.'

Mac was listening to George and now he chipped in, 'Aye, Boss. He's right. You must be the first trainer, in living history, to have four boxers in the Top Ten, all at the same time. You're riding high on the crest of a wave.'

'Hmmm! That was two years ago,'

161

'What the bloody hell's the matter with you?' George was losing patience with him. 'That Gareth Williams and Steve Riley are turning out to be very useful and then there's the Clark brothers. And what about Bert Longthorn? Already a British and British Empire Heavyweight Champion. They're talking about Danny's boys all over the world.'

'Yeah? So what! It's not what I've done. It's all about the stuff I haven't done.'

'So what little ambition haven't you realised so far?' George's voice took on a more sarcastic tone. 'Preferred to have been a jockey, would you?'

Danny glared at him. 'I could have done better for them boys from Tonga. That Katusha Latou would have been a world champion if he'd stayed wi' me.'

'It wasn't your fault that they got homesick.'

'Hmmm!'

'Patrick! Michael! Come on now. Time for that party of yours,' Sylvia shouted through the open door of the gym. 'Everything's ready and Nipper's already entertaining some of your school chums.'

Everyone followed her downstairs to the kitchen at the back of the pub.

A month later, nothing had changed. Danny was sitting at his office desk with his chin in his hands. He stared at the calendar on the wall. Sixteenth of July and the year was 1962. He'd been in the game nine years. Where had all those years gone? The door opened. 'Aye! Aye! Come in, Abe. Sit down. What's coming off then?' Danny tried to sound more hopeful than he was feeling and looking.

'They said I'd find you up here. I'm glad I've caught you. You're first on my list, Danny. I've come up with this fantastic idea. It's going to make us a fortune apiece.'

'Oh aye! So who's turned you down so far?'

'Danny! Danny!' Abe put on a hurt voice. 'Who would I be thinking of seeing before you? I just thought to myself, who's the one person in the world that I should be sharing a bit of good fortune with? Yours was the first name that popped into my head. In fact, it was the only name.'

'Oh aye! So what's this good fortune then?' Danny was still suspicious.

Abe ignored his sarcastic tone of voice. 'I'm planning the biggest tournament of boxing that Britain has ever seen. Everyone who is someone will want to come. Honestly Danny! The tickets will sell like hot cakes. We'll be able to charge whatever we like. They'll be queuing up to buy them.'

'And where are you goin' to stage it? Buckingham Palace?'

'Don't get cocky, McCoy. Just because you've had a few boxers in the Top Ten. Don't think that'll last forever. You might need a diversion like the one I'm offering you. Don't forget, you lost those fellas from Tonga within four years of 'em coming over.'

'That was over five years ago and I haven't lost anymore of my boys, in spite of Harry Levene trying to poach 'em. Anyway I didn't lose 'em. They got homesick. They all went back to the South Pacific.'

'That's not how I heard it. Word was that they beetled off because the police was after 'em for brawling in public. Anyway, never mind all that. Concentrate on this boxing tournament. Just hear what I've got to say.'

'Go on then. Let's hear it.'

'I want to stage it here.'

'HERE?' What d'ya mean? Here?'

'Here at the Wellington.'

'What the hell are you talking about? There ain't room here.'

'There's plenty of room here, outside. I'm talking about an open-air tournament.'

'Don't be ridiculous. How many punters are you expecting because this place will only take about four thousand? Anyway, it's all been done before. What's new about an open-air boxing match? We've been putting 'em on for the last few years.'

'I know all that. Will you listen for a minute? I'm going to hire that field across the road. We can get everyone to park their cars in there. Then we can extend the seats right down to those outbuildings of yours. What d'you think, Danny?'

Suddenly Danny heard the voice of his Uncle Frankie, calling to him through the mists of time, "Watch out for that Abe Rosen. He's a devious bastard." And as he listened to his uncle's voice he made his mind up to get everything written down and signed in blood: preferably Abe Rosen's blood.

'Danny! Danny! Have you heard what I've been saying?'

'Yes. I've heard everything.' Danny stroked his chin. 'It'll take a hell of a lot of organising. Anyway, I reckon we've reached saturation point with the punters from round here. They've been coming from all over Derbyshire and South Yorkshire. There's only a limited number of fans in the Midlands. If you wanna draw such big crowds, why don't you hire Wembley Stadium?'

'Don't be ridiculous. I want to make money, not lose it. Anyway, it won't be just folk from round here that'll come. The bill I'm putting on will attract fans from all over the country, Scotland and Wales included. I'm going to put six bouts on in one night but the thing is, they are all going to be heavyweight bouts. And they're all going to be champion boxers fighting.' He sat back in his chair, trying to gauge Danny's reaction.

'What's in it for me?'

'Plenty. We share the profits, fifty fifty.'

'Oh aye? And how much money are you expecting me to put in?'

'Nothing! Not a penny! Not a brass farthing! I just need your expertise.'

'Come off it, Abe. You're never going to pay me fifty per cent of the profits just for my expertise.'

'Well I thought you could provide free accommodation for all the boxers I'm bringing. Got one coming over from California. You'll have to stoke up the fires for him.' He grinned. 'And I want you to provide all the facilities free of charge. You know the sort of thing. The gym, toilets and showers for the boxers and them mobile toilets for the punters. And I'm talking about net profit of course. I'll have to take out all my expenses first. Listen. I've put it all down on paper...'

'That's a first then.'

'Cheeky! Anyway, like I was saying, it's all here. You can get George to look at it or you can get a solicitor to cast an eye over it. Waste of money, in my opinion. You'll be able to see at a glance, it's all above board.'

'Go on then. I'll have a look at it.'

'Well George, what d'ya think? You've been going over it all morning and I spent all last night pouring over it as well. It looks sound enough but maybe we ought to get your solicitor to look at it.'

'Nope. It's straightforward. Mind you, he's a crafty bugger. You'll have to make sure he doesn't bump up his own expenses. You'd better get him on the blower and tell him we're in.'

'You won't regret this.' Abe Rosen was just signing the contract. 'It's going to be a great night for the sport. I've been in touch with King's manager. Soon as we've fixed up a date, they'll sign up. That contest between King and your boy will be the most important fight of the night. It'll be the jewel in the crown. This is going to an exhibition of boxing like no one has ever seen in the history of the sport. That'll make them bigwigs down in London sit up and take notice. So what day is it going to be? Any ideas?'

Danny lifted his calendar off the wall. 'Favourite night for summat like this is always a Monday night. We need at least four weeks to get ready so what about this one? The second Monday in the month.' He stabbed the page with his finger.

Abe Rosen looked over his shoulder. 'No! I'm not having that. Can't have that, under no circumstances!'

'Why?'

'Because, Dumbo, that's the thirteenth. I'm not risking it. This is my biggest promotion ever. I'm not having it on Monday the thirteenth. We'll go for the Tuesday.'

George was listening and he took out his diary. 'Right! Tuesday the fourteenth of August it is.'

Connie was having a drink with George and Danny. She was quizzing Danny. 'Aren't you even a little bit excited? There's only two weeks to go. Everyone's talking about it. I heard someone saying that Jack Solomons and Harry Levene are furious that Abe Rosen's staging it. He's got the cream of the

166

world's boxers fighting on the same bill. He's got all six contests arranged already. Will there be time for six?'

'Well, he might be cutting it a bit fine but it's starting at six o'clock and as far as I'm concerned it can go on till midnight, but it won't.'

'Why not?' Connie stared at him. Danny's voice had the usual "know-it-all" ring that she ought to have been used to by now.

'Well for one thing, that Eric Hope will be no match for Bob Walsh. Should be over in twenty minutes including all the razzmatazz and Honeyboy King won't last more than three rounds against my boy.'

'Who's that?'

'Howard "Honeyboy" King. Boxer that's coming over from California.'

'Why do you call him honey boy?'

'Because that's what they call him over in America.'

'Why? Because he's nice?'

Danny frowned then he realised what Connie meant and he laughed. 'Oh No! He's no honey. In fact he's a real big bruiser. They call him Honeyboy, all one word, because he's a beautiful shade of honey brown. Anyway, you'll see for yourself. He's arriving tomorrow. Got to get him acclimatised.'

'By the way, they're saying we're sold out,' said George. 'Someone put an advert in last night's Evening News offering a hundred pounds for a ticket.'

'Yeah?' Danny sounded surprised. 'As much as that, ay? Well maybe we should have priced them at a hundred pounds ourselves instead of five guineas. We'd have bin able to retire to Bermuda.' Danny's dreams of retiring to Bermuda were rudely interrupted as the street door opened.

Tony Whiteside burst in. He looked round, spotted Danny and headed over. 'Evening you lot. Hoped I might find you in here.'

'Hi Tony,' said Connie. 'If you're going to be talking business, I'm off.'

'I'm all right for pies, Tony,' said George. 'I gave your lad my usual monthly order over the phone yesterday.'

Tony Whiteside was the local pork pie manufacturer and supplier to most of the pubs in the area. 'I've not come about that. I'm here to see Danny.'

'What can I do you for, Tony?'

'Well, it's more what I can do for you.'

'Oh aye? How's that then?'

'Can you use a bit of influence?'

'Why? What for?'

'I want to get into this jamboree you lot are puttin' on. I want to do the catering.'

'Oh no!'

'No! Hang on a minute! I'm not talking about pies and stuff like that. I just happen to know where there's a big consignment of frozen chicken legs going begging. I can cook 'em at my kitchens, hire some portable bain-maries to…'

'What?'

'Bain-marie. Them French pans, full of hot water. Keeps stuff hot for ages. You can get these catering vans fitted up with 'em now. Anyway, if I have a few of those stashed around the grounds, I can supply chicken-in-the-basket. It's all the rage in them posh pubs down in London. Everybody's doing it.' Tony could see Danny looked interested. 'Listen. It'll go down a treat. Anyway, don't decide now. Talk it over with Abe Rosen. You've got more pull than I have. See! If you think about it; everybody will be coming straight from work. They'll need summat to eat. You're gonna have to do food.'

'Now Honeyboy, this is Danny McCoy.'

Howard King was carrying a suitcase.

'He'll be looking after you. You'll be staying here at the Wellington, till after the tournament. With a bit of luck we'll get some publicity from this.'

'Right lad, go with Mac. He'll show you the ropes an' where you're sleeping. You'll like it here. My mother-in-law will feed you up. You're looking a bit peaky after that long flight.' Howard King went off with Mac.

Danny turned back to Abe. 'Don't disappear. I want a word with you.'

'Why? What's up?'

'Nowt's up. Don't go jumpin' to conclusions. I just wanted to talk to you about the catering.'

'What catering? We ain't doing any catering.'

'Well, that's the problem. We ain't given any thought to it. Them folk are coming straight from work. They'll need feeding or they'll be off as soon as them fish an' chip shops open an' we don't want that. Do we?'

'I take it you've got something in mind, Danny my boy?'

'Tony Whiteside wants to do "chicken-in-the-basket" for us.'

'How much does he want to pay for the franchise?'

'Well. I expect he'll pay whatever you ask.'

'All right. Tell him to come and see me.'

The day before the tournament was the hottest day of the year. The seating had all been built and the ring was up. Danny, George and Mac were surveying the scene.

'Looks grand, doesn't it?' George was cock-a-hoop.

'Aye, it's not bad,' Danny agreed.

Connie came wandering out, wearing a sleeveless dress. 'Are you keeping your eyes on the boys, Danny?'

'Aye! Stop fretting. Everybody's watching them. You got your dress sorted out for tomorrow night?'

'Well, as a matter of fact…'

'Forget it! I'm not shelling out on another new outfit. That wardrobe is packed to bursting. It's bulging at the seams. I've seen you trying to close the door and you can't.'

'Do you know something, Danny? If I'd have known, all those years ago, how mean you were, I'd never have married you.' She stalked off towards the pub.

'Well? What?' Danny glared at George and Mac. 'It's all true. She has got too many clothes. She's cost me a fortune over the years.'

Next morning Danny was standing with Tony Whiteside and Abe Rosen. He looked up at the clouds that hung menacingly on the horizon, blotting out the sun. 'I told you we should have held it last night, Abe. Last night was warm and balmy. Now look at it.'

'It'll be all right. We don't want it as hot as it was last night or those boxers'll be fainting. You got all them chickens ready, Tony?'

'Yeah! It's all in hand. They've all been defrosted ready for going onto them spits. Tonight will make us all millionaires.'

'Is that so? Maybe I'm not charging you enough for that franchise.'

'Get lost. I've paid you plenty. You should be glad to be sharing your good fortunes with me.'

Danny thought he'd better change the subject. 'How many are we expecting?'

'About ten thousand. How many of them chicken legs are you expecting to sell?'

'Plenty and you can forget about any percentages. The contract's already been drawn up by you and signed by me. The profit's all mine.'

It was eight o'clock and the second fight was already in progress. On the front row were all the honoured guests. There was the Duke of Devonshire and his wife. Various local dignitaries were there sporting their gold chains of officialdom. Famous boxers like Bruce Woodcock, Ronnie Crookes and Randolph Turpin had accepted an invitation. All the men were in black ties and dinner suits. The women were decked out in fancy cocktail dresses and diamonds. They'd all come in mink coats; showing off like, which was a good job because a cold breeze had sprung up.

George looked up in fright. 'Was that a drop of rain?' He'd no sooner spoken than the "drop" turned into something more than a "drop" and there were cries of alarm from the women in the audience.

'Oh my God,' said Danny, 'we can do without this.'

'Don't worry, lad. They've all got popped into their seats. None of 'em are going anywhere now 'cos they can't get out.'

There were cheers from the ten-thousand-strong crowd as the referee announced the winner of the fight.

Five minutes later and the rain was lashing down. It was raining stair-rods. The third fight had started but now the ring was swimming with water. The boxers were slipping about all over the place. A newspaperman was parading up and down

171

the aisles and doing a roaring trade. 'Evening News, sir. Perfect for keeping the rain off your head. That'll be a pound, sir and cheap at the price.' The entire crowd had newspapers on their heads. The fella selling them was in seventh heaven.

Over at one of the chicken barbecue stands the rain was pouring off the canvass awning. Tony Whiteside, his overcoat slung over his head, was talking to the man behind the counter. 'I can't believe you. What d'you mean? You've hardly sold any? What happened when they all came in?'

'They were in too much of a hurry to get into their seats, Boss. And it looks like most of them had paper bags, probably with sandwiches in. I distantly saw some fellas carrying bottles of beer. I thought it might pick up when they smelt the chicken cooking but with all this rain it's hopeless.'

Then the fight between Bert Longthorn and Howard King started. The boxers could hardly stand up. The wind had started blowing harder and it was just like a tornado. It swept straight across the wide-open fields that surrounded the Wellington. There was nothing to check its progress.

The referee beckoned Danny and Abe Rosen over. 'Listen! I'm going to have to stop this fight. It's ridiculous asking them to box in this.'

'So who's won?'

'On points, your man. Longthorn.'

A fella in the crowd had heard them. The news spread round like wildfire. 'They're going to stop the fight. Boo! Boo! We want our money back!'

Longthorn marched over, followed by King. 'You're not thinking of stopping the fight, are you?'

Danny turned to the big black American, who was shaking with cold. 'What do you want to do, Honeyboy?'

'I'd rather fight on.'

Danny turned back to the referee. 'How about if both men box in bare feet?'

'Good idea, Boss,' said Longthorn, marching back to his corner and sitting down. Nipper ran over and started unlacing his boots for him.

'You can't be serious,' said the referee.

'Suits me,' said King. 'Can someone give me a hand?'

'Listen,' said Danny, to the referee, 'while they're taking their boots off, let's see if we can make the conditions a bit better.'

'What you got in mind?'

'See those outbuildings over there.' He pointed to his pig huts. 'There are some barrels of sawdust in there. If we get a bit of sawdust down in the ring, it'll stop 'em slipping around.'

'Ok. I'm willing to give it a try,' said the referee, who wasn't keen on telling ten thousand punters that the contest AND the tournament was off. 'Send a few fellas to get it.'

'Will you organise it, George?'

'Aye. I'll round up a few of your boys to help. Won't be a tick.'

Danny went over to Bert Longthorn. He was dancing around, trying to keep warm. 'You sure you want to carry on? You've already won on points. Referee's just told me.'

'Well if it's all the same to you I'd rather carry on. I can knock him out if he'll just stop slipping all over the place. I'm ok apart from my feet. They're like blocks of ice.'

'Don't worry about your feet because they can't be as bad as his.' He pointed at Honeyboy. 'His are like choc-ice.' As

Danny walked away, Bert Longthorn collapsed onto his stool, absolutely in stitches, tears of laughter running down his face.

George and Danny's boxers arrived with the sawdust. 'Right boys. Let's get this stuff down before that crowd lynches us.'

'Leave it to us,' said Ron Charleton, one of the lads who wasn't fighting that night. 'Come on, Carlo. We'll start over there.' He pointed to the side of the ring that was right in front of the Duke of Devonshire's party. They staggered over, carrying a barrel between them. Putting it down, they prised off the lid. 'Right, Carlo!' Ron shouted as loud as he could, hoping to be heard over the wind. 'Lift it up again. On the count of three, just like we said, we do it. Ready! One! Two!

'No!' Danny screamed at them but the ninety-mile-per-hour wind blew his words back in his face and it was too late anyway…

'Three!' Ron shouted and they flung the sawdust up in the air and over the canvas. The ninety-mile-per-hour wind caught it and in a split second all the lovely people in their beautiful furs and dinner suits, looked like they'd been dropped in the flour bin. There they were, opening and closing their mouths like fish and blinking like owls.

'Shit! Danny said under his breath. 'Bloody hell!' He ran over. 'You bloody fools.' He was shouting now. 'You stupid bastards! You're supposed to sprinkle it, like this.'

Eventually Danny was able to get round to the distinguished guests and he tried to get them cleaned up, as best he could. Everyone was furious: everyone except for the Duchess. She was in stitches.

'Danny! Danny!' She shouted in his ear. 'I've never laughed so much in all my life. I've never enjoyed a boxing

174

match so much in all my life. When are you putting on another tournament?'

The fight resumed at last. But the wet sawdust made things worse. It was like an ice-rink. Honeyboy still couldn't keep his footing. He was a big, handsome, coloured fella but he was more used to temperatures in the nineties not winds in the nineties. The referee kept both boxers on their feet, as best he could, but now the American was facing the wrong way. Bert Longthorn turned him round so they were face to face and then he hit him hard. Honeyboy went down and the referee counted him out, rather quickly.

Tony Whiteside never heard the cheers of the crowd. He was sitting on the back steps of the Wellington, with his head in his hands. 'What's up, Tony?' Sylvia was on her way to look in on the children.

'I'm ruined! Skint! Bankrupt!' Tony moaned, without lifting his head.

Back in the ring, the referee had declared that conditions were too bad to carry on. The huge crowd was now keen to get away as quickly as possible but most of the cars were stuck in a quagmire. People were getting madder by the minute and when it looked like there was going to be a riot, Danny called the police. It was five o'clock in the morning before the last car was towed away. There had been several threats of legal action and promises of retribution. There was no point in going to bed, thought Danny as he walked slowly back to the Wellington to seek the sanctuary of his office.

175

Breakfast time and Danny was still sitting behind his desk. A blue haze surrounded him from the cigarettes that he'd been chain-smoking. His hopes, that the debacle had missed the morning paper, were dashed when Mac brought one in. There it was on the front page. "BATTLE IN BARE FEET" screamed the headlines.

'Well at least there aren't any pictures. Maybe it was too dark.'

'What? With them floodlights beaming out. It was like daylight!'

'Well they haven't bothered printing any.'

At six o'clock, Nipper arrived with the evening paper, 'There's a full spread inside,' he said gloomily. 'They've really gone to town.' He opened it at the centre page and sure enough there were more big black headlines. Danny's head was spinning and his eyes could hardly focus but he had no problem reading the words. They were big and bold and black.

"BOXING FARCE" "QUAGMIRE" "BAREFOOT BOXERS"

And even worse, the pages were filled with pictures. And there was plenty of room for pictures. The Evening News was a broadsheet. There was a picture of all the people sitting with newspapers on their heads. There was one of Danny's boxers throwing the sawdust up in the air. There was one of the Mayor of some town or other covered in sawdust. Maybe the editorials weren't as bad. He read the opening line of one of them. "Last night, boxing returned to the days of bare-fist fights. It was a travesty. What promised to be a spectacular night turned into a glorified mud-wrestling match with the boxers fighting in their bare feet." Danny closed his eyes. He felt sick.

'D'ya know what that Abe Rosen's gone and done?'

'I don't want to know,' mumbled Danny.

'He's given an interview and listen to this. "I wanted to stage this promotion on the Monday night but my partner wouldn't hear of it because it was the thirteenth." How can he say that? It was him that made us have it on the Tuesday night.' Mac was blazing mad.

Danny looked up. 'I'll kill him. The rotten bastard. Uncle Frankie warned me about him. I'll sue him. I'll make him retract that.' By now Danny was shouting so hard he could be heard down in the bar.

His boxers slunk away. They'd no intention of letting Danny take his fury out on them.

'Er! I think I'll go and see if Mam wants anything doing.' Connie slipped away. She flung herself into the kitchen, 'I've left him to his own devises. I can't stand it up there. It's like a battleground. I've left Patrick and Michael watching over the other three. Those boys are so good with the children. It's so nice…' Her voice trailed away as she noticed her parents weren't listening to a word she was saying.

Sylvia and George were sitting morosely at the kitchen table. George had a letter in his hand.

'What's up? What's that? Oh God! Is that a writ already? Is someone suing Danny already? It can't be. It's too soon, surely?'

'This is much worse than someone suing Danny. That farce last night was a kid's tea party compared with this. We had no idea this had arrived. Someone must have picked it up with all the mail this morning and put it on the mantelpiece. This here's a letter from the council offices. Somebody in Sheffield

Town Hall has thought up a scheme to build a "satellite town" out on the edges of Chesterfield. Here! Bastards!'

'What's a satellite town, Dad?'

'It's one of them bloody high-rise schemes where they can dump a load of people from Sheffield, out into the country, on someone else's doorstep.'

'What d'you mean dump? Where from?'

'From all those back-to-backs they're pulling down. Slum clearance, it's called.'

'But they can't do that. Sheffield comes under Yorkshire. We're in Derbyshire.'

'They're talking about moving the boundaries.'

'They can't do that.'

'They can if they can get a vote through on it.'

'The Borough Council would never agree to that.'

'They would if enough of them got back-handers.'

'What will happen to the Wellington?'

'There's talk of pulling it down. It'll be right in the path of this ring road. See look here. There's an artist's impression.'

'But you own this pub.'

'So what? They'll make me an offer.'

'Who will?'

'Government, I suppose.'

'Well, that's all right then. You can refuse to sell.'

'Yes. And then they'll compulsory purchase it for peanuts. Bastards!'

Danny had spent all week deflecting writs. 'Go ahead! Sue! It won't get you anywhere. It was a referee's decision. Nowt to do wi' me mate.' He slammed the phone down. It rang again immediately. He stared at it. What was the point in answering it? It would only be another irate punter. The ringing was intensifying his headache. Whoever it was had no intention of ringing off. He grasped the receiver. 'Hello! Who is it?'

'Sure an isn't it your Uncle Frankie speaking to you all the way from New York!'

Danny sighed. He'd been dreading this. 'Oh. Hello Uncle Frankie.'

'I'm just phoning to ask how your big night went.'

'Which do you want first, Uncle? The bad news or the really bad news?'

'Why, whatever's up, Danny boy? Did no one turn up?'

'I don't know where to start. It was an absolute fiasco. It was in all the newspapers. Honestly, Uncle, I'm finished. I'm ruined.'

'What do you mean? A fiasco?'

'There was a torrential downpour. It was like something out of the tropics. The boxers ended up in their bare feet. I'm a laughing stock. I'll never be able to go in a boxing ring again.'

'Tell me what happened, from the very beginning.'

Danny spent half an hour telling his uncle all that had happened and it was the most depressing story that he'd ever had to tell. Frankie knew Danny wouldn't want to go over the telling of it again so he offered to phone his uncles in Ireland and put them in the picture.

Danny kept to his office, leaving Mac and Nipper to run everything. A couple of his top lads had asked him if they could accept an offer from Harry Levene.

'He says you're going to have to pack it in. He says you're finished.'

Danny exploded. Then he tore up their contracts and told them to bugger off.

'No! We can't leave you like this.'

'I'm sorry, boys. I didn't mean to take it out on you. It's true enough. I am finished. You'll do yourselves no favours by staying. I want you to go out into that wide world and show 'em what Danny's boys are made of. I'll keep my eye on your progress. Good luck.'

He watched them go with tears in his eyes. It wouldn't be long before the rest of them came to see him. He couldn't really blame them. He knew it was all his fault. He should never have got himself involved with Abe Rosen. This was the result. Danny knew he was watching the demise of his empire.

CHAPTER NINETEEN

'Stop crying, Connie. You know yer mam and me will fight it every inch of the way. We're going to get a petition up.'

'You can't fight the government, Dad. They can do what they like. Anyway, it's not just you that's going to be affected. What about me and the kids? Danny's finished. Everyone's deserting him. That Abe Rosen's made him a laughing stock. An' once he's got no boxers, we'll be done for. We'll be out on the streets.' Connie was getting to the hysterical stage.

'Don't be ridiculous!' George snapped. 'I'll not see you out on the streets.'

'Come on,' said Sylvia, putting her arm round Connie. 'We'll all stick together.'

Two days later, Danny got a phone call from his Uncle Willie. 'Now don't you be worrying, lad. Your Uncle Frankie's told me all about it and we've already come up with a solution.'

'Oh aye!' Danny said, wearily. He didn't really have the energy to listen to any hair-brained schemes. Only that very morning he'd had Billy Battle crowing over his predicament. 'I've got you now, McCoy. Did you know? We're holding an enquiry into that boxing tournament of yours, if you can call it that. It's a week on Wednesday. Keep that day free. You'll be getting a request to appear in front of the committee.' Danny was hardly listening to his uncle.

'…and so what you need is an entirely new start.'

'No! No! Uncle! I'm finished with boxing.'

'Haven't you been listening to a word I've been saying. I said football not boxing.'

'What?'

'I've been speaking to the manager of Blackpool Football Club and…'

'Please don't start wi' your Irish fairy tales. I'm not in the mood. I know you're just trying to cheer me up but it's not…'

'Will you keep quiet for a moment. This isn't a joke. You obviously weren't listening. The chairman is a good friend of mine and…'

'Listen Uncle. Football isn't my game and in case you've forgotten I'm far too old to be…'

'Well t'is not a footballer they'll be wanting. T'is a physiotherapist an' I've given you a glowing report. Told 'em how good you've been with those boxers and how I've taught you all about injuries. They're dead keen. Whoops! Shouldn't have said that. Their present physio has just dropped dead on that European tour. Heart attack! Haven't you heard? Anyway, you'll be getting a phone call about now so I'm ringing off.

Not five minutes after Danny had put the phone down, it rang again.

'Hello!'

'Hello! Can I speak to Danny McCoy?'

'Speaking!'

'This is John Peters, chairman of Blackpool Football Club. Your Uncle Willie's just been on the phone. Very good friend of mine. Says you might be able to help us out. Have you spoken to him yet?'

'Yes. He's told me you've lost your physiotherapist. I'm very sorry to hear about it. Terrible things, heart attacks.'

'You're right about that. It's been a dreadful time. His poor wife's distraught. The team was in Sardinia at the time. Anyway, to get back to the point, can you come over to Blackpool so we can have a little chat? Your uncle said you were looking for a career move and you could be just what we need.'

Thinking of a new career? That's putting it mildly, thought Danny.

'Hello! Hello! Are you still there?'

'Yes Mr Peters. I'm just thinking.'

'We'll make it worth your while. Tell you what. Pop over and I'll put something down on paper. We'll pay your expenses and I'll put you up in a nice little hotel while you have a look around the club and the town.'

'Oh all right!' Danny kept his tone casual: mustn't give the impression he was too eager. 'What did my uncle say, as a matter of interest?'

'Oh! Hmmm! Let me think. Oh yes! He said you were pulling out of boxing for personal reasons: something about your wife wanting to move to a better environment. Said she was worried about your children. Listen! This seaside air is much better for you than the smoke down there. Do your kids a power of good.'

'Aye. That's it in a nutshell. The wife's been going on about wanting to live at Skegness. Can't stand the place myself but I fancy Blackpool.'

'You'll like Blackpool. How soon can you nip over?'

'Is next Monday all right?'

'Perfect! Come on the train. See if you can get one that comes into Central Station. Then get a taxi to the club. It's only ten minutes away. If you can get here for lunchtime I can treat you to a meal and we can talk then. Give us a bell when you've had a look at the timetable for the trains.'

Danny wrote the number down. 'Thanks Mr Peters. I look forward to seeing you.'

'Me too. We're quite desperate. Good physios are thin on the ground. We're lucky we heard about you. See you soon.' The phone went dead.

Danny stayed in his office to consider the recent events. He wasn't sure whether to tell Connie now or wait till he'd been over to Blackpool. If it materialised, this offer could be the answer to his prayers. He could hand his licence in to the BBBC before they had time to take any action. That'd spoil the party for Billy Battle! Only thing was, he didn't like the idea of leaving George in the lurch. He went to the door and opened it, shouting at the top of his voice. 'Nipper! Nipper!'

Nipper came running. 'Yes, Boss. Here I am. I was just tidying up after that last session, Boss. Did you want something?'

'Yeah! Can you beetle down to the bar and see if you can find George? If you spot him, ask him to come up here. But listen! Don't let them women hear you and tell George to keep it quiet. I only want to see him.'

'Right, Boss.'

'So what's up Danny? What's all the secrecy about?'
    'Come in and shut the door. I wanna talk to you.'
    George closed the door and sat down. 'Got another writ?'
    'No thank God. What I have got is the offer of a new job.'
    'Grab it! Who's it from?'

184

'Blackpool Football Club.'

'Never! What do they want with a boxing manager?'

'They don't. They want a physiotherapist to replace one who's just dropped dead.'

'Job's as bad as that is it?'

Danny laughed for the first time in a week. 'Trust you to think of that.'

'Only joking. So what you going to do?'

'Well, the thing is, I don't like leaving you and Sylvia in the lurch.'

'Give over! What's me and Sylvia got to do wi' it?'

'Well, you took me in and gave me a chance. Without you I couldn't have done anything in the game. I'd still be a pig man. And Sylvia, she's stuck by me and looked after me like my own mother. Now you lot are in the shit over this government thing. It'd be like a rat leaving a sinking ship and I don't want to do it.'

'Don't talk soft. What they offering you anyway?'

'Well, I don't know. I've got to go over on Monday to see the chairman but it sounds like they intend being quite generous. They're pretty desperate.'

'How the hell did they hear about you?'

'My Uncle Willie's a friend of the chairman.'

'Well, you go and see them and find out what they're proposing. It might be the best thing all round. Blackpool would be good for the kids. And I reckon me and Sylvia could take the offer on this pub, follow you over and buy a small boarding house to run.'

'That would be fantastic. I can't think of a more perfect ending to what has been the worst week of my life. But are you sure you could swap Chesterfield for Blackpool?'

'Are you kidding? A nice bracing sea breeze! Good for the constitution.'

'Right, well, just one more thing. Don't say owt to anyone yet: not even Connie or Sylvia. Better see how this interview goes first. Might not like the salary they're offering or the place. Anyway, I'd rather tell Connie when it's all cut and dried. Then she can't argue.'

'What's going on, Dad? Where did Danny disappear to, this morning? He'd gone by the time I got back from the hairdressers.'

'No idea, love. Maybe he's gone to get some new gear for the gym.'

'No! He's up to something. I can tell. He's been looking shifty all weekend.'

'What's going on, George?' Sylvia sounded anxious. 'I've got enough on my plate, worrying about this pub.'

'I haven't got any idea. I wish you'd stop asking me summat I don't know the answer to. I'm not his keeper, you know.'

'No but whenever Danny is up to something, you're always in on it.'

'Not this time, I'm not.'

'Right then Danny. I'm glad we've been able to work something out, beneficial to us both. So you'll be with us a week next Thursday?'

'As long as you think you can manage till then.'

'We'll muddle along somehow. Our trainer can keep his eye on things. Now, don't forget, bring the wife and kids and we'll put you in a nice hotel till you can find something suitable to buy. You'll find something easy enough. House prices aren't too bad in this neck of the woods.'

All the way back to Chesterfield, Danny was composing his letter to the BBBC. The deed was done. He'd been offered a very tempting salary to look after the health and welfare of the players at Bloomfield Road and he'd signed on the dotted line. He'd no idea what Connie would say but he didn't care. She could come with him or stay with her mum and dad till they moved. Danny hadn't the slightest doubt that George and Sylvia would follow him to Blackpool. Connie could rant all she liked. End result would be the same.

Danny, Connie, George and Sylvia were all in the living room at the back of the bar. Danny had told them he'd got some news.

'What have you gone and done now, Danny McCoy?' Connie's voice went up by a couple of decibels. 'I knew you were up to something when you disappeared so quickly, yesterday morning and what the hell do you mean by staying out all night?'

'I told you on the phone, I was conducting a bit of business and now you're about to find out what it is. So shut up and listen! As you know, I've been thinking of quitting boxing and…'

'Well thank God. At last I'm going to have a man about the house.'

'…and I've just had this marvellous offer.'

'What offer? You never told me about any offer.' Connie was red with temper.

'I'm telling you now. I didn't want to tell you till it was all settled.'

'All settled? What d'ya mean? All settled?' She was shouting now. 'How can you settle something without discussing it first?'

Danny knew he was tackling this all wrong. Too late now. Better get it over and done with. 'I've signed up with Blackpool Football Club.'

'Blackpool Football Club? A football club?' Connie screamed. 'You can't play football! They must be bonkers!'

'Not to play,' Danny shouted back. 'They want me to be their physiotherapist and I've accepted.'

'Connie. Will you calm down?' Sylvia looked worried.

Her daughter collapsed into a chair, in tears. 'See what he's like, Mam? He's pissed off and signed up without even telling me.'

'I wanted it to be a surprise.'

'Surprise!' Connie's screams could have shattered the iceberg that sunk the Titanic. 'Since when have you ever wanted to give me a surprise?' Her voice rose even further. 'I'll give you a surprise. It'll be a surprise to you that we're married because you've forgotten every anniversary. And since we're talking about surprises, well, guess what Danny: I've had five babies. All yours but that'll be a surprise won't it because you were never, ever around when I was giving birth.' She was beginning to lose her voice. 'You've never, ever been at the hospital. Oh no! It's become a standing joke amongst the regulars. Who's going to run Mrs McCoy to the hospital this time?'

'Oh well, if you're going to take this attitude, I'm off.' Danny slammed the door behind him.

'Mam! Mam!' Connie gasped. 'Come and help me. I'm moving into my own room and I'll need help. That bastard is never sleeping in the same bed as me ever again.'

The following morning Danny borrowed George's van and drove over to Halesowen. He shoved an envelope through the door of the secretary for the Midland Area of the BBBC. Inside the envelope was his trainer's licence and a covering letter. Then he went to see the mammy and daddy. Now retired, the daddy was suffering with arthritis: left over from when he'd broken his leg but the mammy was as sprightly as ever, even at seventy-two. They were both pleased as Punch that he was getting a new job.

'Don't you be worrying about us, son. Your sisters will keep an eye out for us. T'is grand you can begin again, in a new town, far away from Abe Rosen. And we'll be able to go to the seaside now and again, for our holidays. That'll be nice, so it will.'

Next day, it was time to tell his two best friends. 'Nipper! Mac! Can you give us a minute in the office? Got a bit of news.' They followed him in.

'Not bad news, is it, Boss?' Mac asked.

'Depends how you looks at it. I've had an offer I can't refuse from Blackpool Football Club. They need a physiotherapist. I've accepted. Got no choice with the BBBC gunning for me. I've already handed me licence in so tomorrow I'm going to have to break the news to the boys that are left.'

'Well! I'm flabbergasted,' said Mac, 'but I'm pleased for you.'

'Congratulations Boss,' said Nipper, his voice trembling.

'What you looking so down in the mouth for? You're coming with us unless you don't fancy it.'

Nipper's face coloured up with joy. 'Course I fancy it. And even if I didn't I'd still come with you. I'd follow you into the black hole of Calcutta, Boss.'

'What about you, Mac? I might be able to offer you a job.'

'Well, I've been meaning to talk to you. My brother-in-law's not well and my sister is having to run that hotel of hers on her own. It would be a help if I could go and live up there. In any case, I'll be due for my pension in three years. It's time I gave up.'

'Bloody hell, I'd forgotten you were that old.'

'I'd rather you didn't remember. I can't understand where the years have gone.'

'You got enough of the readies to tide you over?'

'Aye Boss. Been saving a bit for a rainy day and I'll be living in at the hotel. My sister will be so thankful if I can go.'

'Right. Well that's that. End's come quicker than I thought. I'm going to miss you.'

'Me too Boss. What you going to do about your boys?'

'I've been in touch with Bruce Woodcock. He's given me a few names. Ex-boxers. Friends of his who are just getting into the training game. They'll be glad to take 'em on.'

'What about Mrs Connie?' Nipper looked worried.

'She's kicking up a fuss but she'll come round, especially when she knows you're going with her.'

'So she's no' keen then?'

'Nope but she ain't got a choice, particularly seeing as George and Sylvia are going to accept that offer from the government so they can…'

The door burst open.

'What the bloody hell?'

'What d'ya mean by this, McCoy?' Billy Battle was waving Danny's letter and he was purple with rage. 'What d'ya mean by handing in yer licence?'

'Can't you read, Billy? That letter says I'm quitting the boxing game.'

'You can't do that. You've got a disciplinary hearing to go to next Wednesday.'

Danny thought Billy Battle was going to have a heart attack. 'Well, unfortunately,' he could hardly keep a straight face, 'I've got a train to catch, a week tomorrow. That's the day after your kangaroo court. I'll have too much packing to be there in person.'

'It'll go ahead without you, you know.'

'So!'

'They're going to ban you.'

'Oh aye? An' how are they going to do that if I ain't got a licence?'

'They can fine you. Anyway, I've got your licence here an' I won't be handing it in till after a decision's been reached. I'm going to make sure you never train or manage another boxer again, as long as you live. Anyway, wherever you're going, I'll be waiting for you when you come back.'

'I ain't coming back. See them packing cases over there, Billy? I'm leaving. I'm going away. Leaving Chesterfield for good. So you'll have a long wait. But I'll tell you what. If you get onto that platform at ten o'clock next Thursday morning you can tell me what them men at the BBBC have decided.'

'I'll be on that platform all right. And I'll have some policemen wi' me. You're not getting away with this.'

'Well until you've got news from that hearing, you can shove off.' He pushed Billy out of the office. 'Go on! Get lost!'

191

They watched him stamp across the gym and out of the door.

As the last of his footsteps faded away, Danny grinned at Nipper and Mac. 'That's the last we'll see of him, I reckon.'

'What if he's on the platform?'

'Well, I've already thought of that and I've got a little surprise planned for him.'

'You're not going to bash him?' Nipper said, looking worried.

'What? And give him the opportunity to get me sent to jail? Not likely! No! I've just got a little present for him. Summat to remember me by. Summat he's been dying to get his hands on for ages.'

No matter how hard Nipper tried he couldn't get anything further out of Danny.

Sylvia, George and Mac went to the station with them. Connie was in tears and Sylvia tried to comfort her. 'Don't worry. It won't be long before we'll be over. Now, Patrick, you look after your little sister and Michael, keep an eye on Daniel. You'll be all right with baby Jack, will you?'

'Yes Mam! I've got Nipper to help me.'

'And Danny.'

'Poof!' Connie snapped. 'Fat lot of good he is.'

'Now then. Don't keep on at him. You'll be all right. See! Get in the carriage. The train's about to leave.'

'What's the matter, Danny?' George asked him.

'Nothing.'

'Are you looking for someone?'

'Nope!'

'Well, everyone's on the train except for you. You'd best get aboard.'

Danny got on the train and banged the door, pulled down the window and stuck his head out. Then he saw him.

Billy Battle was scurrying on to the platform. He saw Danny and started waving a piece of paper. 'See! Here it is! You've been banned for good,' he shouted.

'What?' The train was moving.

Billy Battle ran alongside the window. 'You've been banned McCoy. This bit of paper prohibits you from taking part in the game. Forever. You've been accused of; and found guilty of; bringing the game into disrepute.'

The train picked up a bit of speed. Danny reached inside his pocket and pulled out his little farewell present. Holding it up in the air, he shouted, 'See Billy. Here's summat you've wanted for ages.'

Suddenly a ray of sunshine caught Danny's hand and a tiny rainbow burst from the little bottle he was holding up.

'What's that McCoy?' Billy was still running alongside the train.

'Them Steel Drops that you've been trying to get hold of.' He had to shout even louder. 'You know! The stuff I used up in Newcastle. Catch!' Danny threw the bottle towards the receding figure of Billy. 'Oh dear! Butterfingers!'

Billy had fumbled the catch. The tiny glass phial slipped through his fingers, fell to the ground and smashed.

The last thing Danny saw as he steamed away to a new life was the satisfying sight of Billy Battle scrabbling about on his knees. And Danny was still laughing when they trundled into Manchester.

CHAPTER TWENTY

'Hello, Uncle Willie! It's me! Danny!'

'And the top of the morning to you! And how are you liking the new job? Settling in are you?'

'Give over, Uncle! You say that every time I phone you. You know it's over a year since I moved here!'

'Good God! Is it that long? Anyway lad, it takes longer than a year to settle into a new place, so it does. Any problems with the job?'

'Well, that's what I'm ringing about. There is one problem I need your advice about.'

'Only too happy to help. I'm bored with retirement already.'

'Well, I'm speaking from the club. One of my players, Tony Grey, has had a bad accident on the training field. Only just happened. Before I ring for the ambulance, I thought I'd speak to you. I'm not too keen on him going to the local hospital. I reckon he's damaged the Achilles Tendon.' Danny went on to describe Tony's symptoms.

'Well, if it's as bad as you say it is, you're right. It does sound like the Achilles Tendon that's been damaged and there's only one man in the world that can help you.'

'An' who's that, Uncle?'

'Hayden Barnes at Wrightington.'

'An' where's Wrightington?'

'It's in the very same county that you're speaking from but I warn you now, before we go any further, t'is easier to get an audience with the Pope than it is to get an appointment with Hayden. Stop laughing, Danny. I'm deadly serious.'

'Well! What am I going to do then?'

'Leave this to me. I'll see what I can do. He's a great friend of mine. I'll speak to him myself this very day, so I will. I'll see if I can get him to see you. By the way, how good is this player?'

'He's our star striker.'

'Hmmm! Well at least we're not asking the great man to see a duffer. That's something then. I'll get in touch with you as soon as I've talked to him. Make your boy as comfortable as you can and wait by that phone.'

'Don't worry Uncle, I've already done what I can for him.'

A few days later, Danny put the injured Tony Grey into his car and took him to Wrightington where Mr Barnes was waiting to welcome them.

'I know your Uncle Willie very well. Most renowned orthopaedic surgeon in Dublin. He's earned a lot of respect in my circles for the work he's done. I'm rather sorry to hear he's retired. Sad loss to the bone world. Anyway he did the right thing, sending you here. I'd like to examine this boy of yours before I pronounce judgement on him.'

A couple of hours later, Danny and Tony were in the office of Mr Barnes waiting for the verdict 'Well, it is the Achilles Tendon and it's very bad. There's no two ways about it. This injury can only be repaired by an operation but before I agree to do it, I've got to tell you what it entails. The recovery period will be very long and someone is going to have to virtually live with this chap for the next twelve months.' He looked enquiringly at Danny. 'Are you willing to do that? He's going to need hours and hours of treatment for months and months.'

Danny thought about what Mr Barnes had just said. Having brought Tony all this way, to the best orthopaedic surgeon in the world, what could he say? He looked at Tony's face. He was waiting anxiously for Danny's answer. He was clearly worried that his career in football was coming to a premature end. 'Well, I'll give it my best shot.'

'The wife'll help,' Tony chipped in.

'And the club will be keen to do everything they can, as well.' said Danny. 'They paid a fortune for this boy, last year.'

'In that case, I'll give you both a run-down on what I'm going to attempt, which, I might add, has never been done before. Then you can have a cup of coffee and weigh up the situation. When I open up, I intend to cut away the damaged parts of the tendon and replace them with man-made plastic fibres. I'll insert them into each end of the remaining tendons, making a bridge for the new tendons to climb across. I'm telling you all this in the simplest of lay-man's terms, you understand?'

'Yes, Mr Barnes,' murmured the spellbound physiotherapist.

'Yes, Mr Barnes,' whispered the petrified Tony Grey.

'You don't need to worry, lad. You won't know a thing about it. You'll go to sleep and wake up a couple of minutes later, a new man. One more thing: I need to do this operation tomorrow before the ankle deteriorates any further. I've rescheduled all my other operations so I can fit you in.'

When Tony eventually woke up he found the operation had taken six hours. Danny had stayed at the hospital the whole time. Tony's wife, Denise, had joined him. Luckily she had a mother who was more than willing to look after their two little children. Danny phoned Blackpool Football Club to make sure no one needed him.

'You stay there, Danny,' said the manager, Bob Singleton. 'We all appreciate what you're doing for Tony. We've been discussing whether or not to get you an assistant for times such as these.'

'You don't need to do that, Bob. Just have a word with Nipper. He knows all my little dodges.'

'Will you give me a ring when the operation's over?'

'Yes! Certainly, Bob!'

'Does your wife know where you are?'

'Well, she knew I was bringing Tony to see Mr Barnes but she doesn't know I'm staying for a few days. I haven't had time to ring her. Do you think you could speak to her?' Connie had already muttered something about him being back for a slap-up meal she was planning. She wasn't too pleased that he was heading off down the motorway on the eighteenth of September. It was their tenth anniversary on the nineteenth. She would have been even more suspicious if she'd seen his overnight bag in the boot of the car.

'I'll do just that, Danny,' said Bob. 'In fact, I'll go and see her. Don't you worry about a thing. We can't thank you enough.'

Good! That would save him a fair bit of earache on the phone. Let Bob do the dirty deed. She couldn't have a go at Bob.

Mr Barnes came to see them after the operation. 'I think the operation's been a success but he'll be in bed for at least four weeks. I'll keep him here, under my close supervision. Then he'll be on crutches for a long time and he'll have a plaster from his hip to his toe. I'll want to talk to you, Danny, before he goes home. He'll need some specialised nursing even after he gets home and I'll have some specific instructions for you. I'll give you a bell. By the way, it'll be a long time before he's playing again and I can't guarantee that he'll be world cup material. Still, if he can walk and run, I'll count it as one of my major successes. This operation's never been done before. Anyway, listen! He'll be asleep for a few hours. Why don't you go and have a nice meal? There's a pub at Parbold I can recommend.'

It was the following morning when Danny got back to Bloomfield Road. He'd left Denise behind. The club had told him to sort out some temporary accommodation for her, so she could be on hand. The little pub at Parbold turned out to be just the right place. Good food. Nice clean bedrooms. And near enough for her to drive over to the hospital in her Mini.

'You're in hot water,' was Nipper's greeting. 'Mrs Connie is spitting mad.'

'Too bad,' said Danny. 'Can't dictate to a man like Mr Barnes when he schedules an operation like that.'

'Well done, Danny McCoy! You've managed to miss another anniversary!'

'Don't start. It's not my fault. It wasn't me who fixed the date.'

'Sometimes Danny, I wonder if you do things on purpose,' Connie continued, ignoring his denial.

'On purpose?' Danny shouted. 'How the hell d'ya think I could do owt like this on purpose?'

'I wouldn't put it past you to have bribed that surgeon into choosing that particular date.'

'Don't be bloody ridiculous.' Danny tried changing the subject. 'Where's them kids, anyway?'

'Michael, Patrick and Bridget are at school. Where the hell d'you expect them to be on a Friday? Forgotten the days of the week as well as our anniversary, have you?'

'Well I wouldn't be surprised to find that posh school gives 'em Friday off.'

'What d'you mean? Posh school?' Connie screamed. 'It's just a nice private school that's promised to get them into a grammar school. It's not costing that much and since it's only just up the road, you should be grateful. You'd have something to grumble about if you had to drive them all the way to St John Vianney's.'

'What d'ya mean?' Danny was glad to have her up against the ropes instead of getting at him. 'All the way where?'

'St John Vianney's out at Marton.'

'Give over. Don't try and pull the wool over my eyes. There's a perfectly good Catholic primary and junior school just down the road.'

'What on earth are you talking about?'

Danny knew Connie was pretending not to know about the nearest school. He'd got her on the run now. 'St Kentigern's! That's what!'

'Never heard of it. Anyway, our kids need pushing and that posh school, as you call it, will push them.'

'How can any school push 'em into a grammar school? If they're too thick, they won't pass that eleven-plus and that'll be that.'

'You listen to me, Danny McCoy.' Connie lowered her voice, ominously. 'You'd better pray that this school gives

199

them a good grounding because I'm telling you now, even if they fail that eleven-plus, they're still going to a good Catholic grammar school. I want them to go to a school where the teachers are good and strict.'

'Oh aye! How you going to manage that then, if they fail that exam?'

'Well, as a matter of fact, I've been making some enquiries.' Connie's voice was quivering with triumph. 'St Joseph's will take Patrick and Michael even if they fail the eleven-plus. They've got some private places. They'll just have to pass an entrance exam. An' it's the same for girls an' all. The Convent will take Bridget as a paying pupil.'

'I'm not bloody well paying for 'em to go to a grammar school. Now! Excuse me while I go and get changed.'

'Well if you don't, I'll ask Mam and Dad to help and that won't put you in a good light, will it?' She raised her voice and yelled, 'And don't slam that door on your way out!'

He slammed the door as hard as he could.

Danny was still blazing mad by the time he reached Bloomfield Road. As fast as he was making money, she was spending it. He tried to calm down. He'd got to concentrate on his boys. They'd got a match tomorrow.

Bob Singleton was waiting for him. 'Thanks for all you're doing for Tony. It's going to be a long job, I take it?'

'Aye! He could be in that hospital for weeks. An' when he's well enough to come home, he'll still be in a plaster for months. He's going to need hours and hours of physio.'

'D'you think you can manage?'

'Aye. I think so.'

'I don't want you to worry about a thing, Danny. The insurance company will cover all the hospital bills and the club will pay you overtime whenever necessary.'

'I'm not bothered about the overtime money. I just want to be on hand to help the poor lad. He's already depressed and he'll be a hundred times more depressed after he's been in a plaster for months on end. I'm telling you this, Bob, we've got a long haul on our hands. Anyway, is everybody else all right?'

'Aye and they're all ready for tomorrow's match.'

CHAPTER TWENTY-ONE

It seemed to Danny that for the first time in a long time everything was coming right for him. He had a well-paid job in a sport that he loved nearly as much as boxing. They had a big house, on the outskirts of Blackpool, with an outlook over the countryside. What was even better was the fact that he'd paid cash for it. And he was making friends as fast as Blackpool Football Club was scoring goals.

He missed his Chesterfield cronies like Mac, Father Murphy and Irwin Goldberg. He even missed Lot and Ely Yates. But on the whole, life was good. The best thing of all was the fact that there was no one dogging his footsteps. There was no horrible Billy Battle waiting round every corner for him.

Blackpool had even been good for his in-laws. In fact, Sylvia and George were doing so well they'd booked an end-of-season holiday in Majorca, flying from Squires Gate Airport on what was known as the "Landlady's Special" and that was when Connie had started on Danny.

'Even Mam and Dad can go away on holiday,' she screamed at him, during another of their many arguments.

'If you want to go on the "Landlady's Special" you can go on yer own. It won't bother me. Go on! Go! Good riddance!

Take the kids an' all! I'm not going thousands of miles to look at some sand an' slot machines. I can see all that here. Anyway, I can't take time off yet. I'm only just finding my feet.'

'I'll give you one more chance, Danny McCoy. Either you take me somewhere proper or the kids and me are going with Mam and Dad. An' it won't be cheap either.'

Threatening Danny hadn't made any difference so Connie had taken the kids and flown off to Majorca for what she called "the holiday of a lifetime" in the most expensive hotel she could find. '…and what's more, Danny McCoy,' she screamed, 'I'm treating Mam and Dad to the same hotel, seeing as I can't be on my own with the kids.' However, George had come to Danny's rescue, telling him they could and would pay for themselves. So Danny was on his own for two weeks. The house was strangely peaceful and he was enjoying this unexpected term of isolation.

It was true that he couldn't take any time off. He needed to keep his finger on the pulse at Bloomfield Road. And anyway, he wanted to get his feet further under the table before he started taking holidays abroad. Two weeks away was a hell of a lot different to an occasional day at the races. And then there was Tony Grey. He was coming home today, in an ambulance, all the way from Wrightington. Mr Barnes had already phoned Danny.

'I'm sending Tony home next Thursday. Now remember. He'll be in plaster for at least two months, so he'll be on crutches. He'll need a lot of help keeping the rest of his body toned up. He'll be very depressed but I know I can rely on you to lift his spirits. If you have any problems, I'm just at the end of this phone.'

Danny was down at Tony's house, with Denise. As soon as the ambulance pulled up, they hurried out to welcome him home.

'Don't worry, everyone,' said the ambulance men to Danny and Denise. 'Leave it to us. We'll carry him into the house. We know best how to do it. Just point us in the direction of the bedroom.'

Luckily Tony and Denise lived in a large bungalow. There was plenty of room and no awkward stairs to climb. It was a blessing to have the bedrooms and bathroom on the ground floor. 'This way, boys,' said Danny to the ambulance men. 'Don't worry, Tony. You're home now. We'll soon have you settled in then Denise can make you a cup of tea.'

'I'd love a beer…'

'TEA!' Danny said, firmly.

'TEA!' Denise echoed, just as firmly. 'You won't be getting any beer yet. What you really need is a good sleep.'

'You were right about that,' whispered Danny when Denise brought the tea in only to find Tony had fallen asleep already. 'He's dead to the world. Better leave him to sleep.' They went into the lounge.

'Are you sure he's all right, Danny?' Denise was even paler than Tony.

'Don't you be worrying. He's fine. He's just tired, that's all. It's a long journey from Wrightington, so it is and an ambulance isn't at all comfortable, you know. Now you listen. He's got to be supervised twenty-four hours a day but you're not on your own with this job. Like I said, I'm going to share this with you. So, tomorrow morning, I'll be here at eight-thirty, to help you get him washed and dressed. Then I'll take him down to the club for some physio. Someone will fetch him home and I'll come round again about four o'clock and we'll get him into bed. Now listen. Should anything happen that you can't cope with, you ring me at the club or at home. It doesn't matter what time of day or night it is: I'll be round straight away to help.'

As Danny drove towards Bloomfield Road, he knew it was going to be a very long business. He was going to have a hell of a job stopping the rest of Tony's body from wasting away, whilst he was in that plaster. But if there was one thing that Danny relished: it was a challenge and this was the biggest challenge of his life, so far.

'Did he get home all right?' The Chairman was waiting for him in the staff car park. He'd obviously seen Danny driving up and hurried down, eager for good news.

'Aye. He's safely in bed, having a nice sleep. He was exhausted from the journey. It's a long way from Wrightington for an invalid.'

'Come into my office, Danny. I want to talk to you.'

Oh aye! Danny thought to himself. Wonder what's up now.

'Sit down, Danny. I've got a bit of news. I've had a reporter from the Evening Gazette, wanting to interview you.'

'Why? What's he want to do that for?'

'Well, he's heard we've got a boxing champion down here at Bloomfield Road...'

Danny started laughing. 'Typical!'

'You've nothing to hide, have you?'

'Nowt much. Nowt as'll bring you lot into disrepute anyway.' Danny laughed. If only John Peters knew the half of it.

205

'So how do you feel about it?'

'Well as long as you and the directors don't mind.'

'Well, I've had a word and they seem to think it'll get us a nice bit of publicity. But I wanted to leave the decision to you. Might get your family into the spotlight, you know.'

'Don't worry about that, John. I know exactly how to deal with these Press boys. Been doing it most of my working life. You've just got to make sure they stay on track. Stick to the facts, like. Anyway, is there anybody waiting for physio today?'

'No Danny. For once the whole team's injury-free. I suggest you take advantage of it and have the afternoon off. You're bringing Tony in tomorrow, aren't you?'

'Yes.'

'Well, you go home and relax. I'll be in tomorrow myself. You bring Tony in and I'll take him home. Most of your boys will be here. They're keen to see him and he'll need cheering up.'

Danny was glad to get home. He went to look for Nipper. Danny had provided Nipper with a self-contained flat above the garage. 'This is so you can get some peace and quiet from those kids of mine. You do know they regard you as their own personal playmate. Don't you let them take advantage of you. When you want to get away from them, you get in that flat and bolt the door. We all need our own space sometimes.'

'Is that why you're always down at the Catholic Club?' Nipper had quipped, sarcastically. 'To get away from Mrs Connie?'

'Cheeky! Anyway, whatever gave you that idea?'

'Mrs Connie!'

'She's got a bloody cheek! Here I am bringing home good money so she can live like a duchess and all she does is complain that I'm not here. Anyway, mind what I say. This flat is yours to do with what you want.'

But the self-contained flat might just as well have been attached to the house. The kids were never away from it and that was the way Nipper liked it. He adored them and the feeling was obviously mutual. In fact, Nipper was the only one they listened to. His word was law.

The next morning, Danny put Tony in the back of the car, to take him down to Bloomfield Road. 'You have a good night's sleep, Tony?'

'Aye! I was out like a light. It was better than sleeping in them hospital beds but I still feel exhausted.'

'You do look a bit peaky, I must say but the sea air will soon perk you up. You can leave that back window open.'

Tony was just in the process of winding it up. He wound it back down again. 'Don't you think it's a bit nippy, Danny?'

'You're just not used to it, coming from hospital. I opened the window on purpose so you can have a nice breeze on your face. Wake you up a bit, so it will.'

Tony was welcomed with open arms. And as soon as he started talking football to the rest of his team-mates he began to look a lot more cheerful.

'Just give us a hand, Alan. We'll get that tracksuit bottom off.' Denise had cut one leg off all his tracksuit bottoms to accommodate the plaster. 'I'll give those muscles a massage then I'll show you some exercises you can do to get that leg back to normal.'

'Doesn't look much like a footballer's leg,' said Tony, starting to sound depressed.

'Don't you worry. I'll soon have you fit again and while I'm working on this leg, I'll tell you about my childhood in Ireland.'

'Can I stay and listen, Danny?' Alan asked.

'No fear. You get yourself out onto that field and get some training done. Anyway, you've heard all my stories before.'

No sooner had Alan Scott gone than George Wallis came wandering in. 'Can you just show me one more time, how to put these contact lenses in? Oh hello Tony. Nice to see you back. God! You do look thin!'

Danny sighed. 'Thank you George! That will be enough of that. Where's them contact lenses?' Sometimes it seemed that looking after footballers was harder than looking after boxers.

'Danny! Danny!'

'Who's that? Come in! Oh it's you Des!' Des McClure was the club secretary.

'There's a bloke here from the Evening Gazette. Says he's been promised an interview.'

'Correct but I don't want him in here, eyeing up Tony. Take him into the boardroom and ply him with coffee and biscuits. Keep him talking but for Christ's sake, watch what you say. Tell him I'll be about twenty minutes. Right Tony. Let's try these exercises. We'll only do five minutes, this first time. Next time, we'll do ten minutes and so on.'

'Can I have a day off, tomorrow?'

'Aye lad. I was planning on resting you tomorrow.' Poor Tony looked knackered already and in any case, the team was playing away, at Wolverhampton.

The interview with the newspaper reporter went quite well. It was going in The Green the following night. The Green was a newspaper that came out every Saturday night, round about six o'clock, just after the Evening Gazette, which came out at five o'clock. This late edition was printed on pale green paper and contained all the sports results; rugby, football, boxing, cricket, everything. Every sports game from all round the world got a mention, as did all the amateur games from all over the Fylde. After the interview, Danny had a bit of lunch and then it was time to get the players in for their pre-match check-up.

Monday morning and Danny had just arrived with Tony Grey. The team was all waiting.

'What a fabulous write-up you got in The Green on Saturday,' said Dave Lennox. 'You never told us you were a boxing champion.'

'That was only in the RAF.'

'You never told us you had all those boxers from Tonga,' said Steve Harris. 'Crikey! It said one of 'em fought Don Cockell at Wembley.'

'Why have you only told us about your childhood in Ireland?'

'Why did you leave boxing?'

The questions were coming thick and fast and Danny wondered if he'd made a big mistake, giving the interview.

'Come on, Danny,' said Tony, 'while you're giving me my treatment you can tell us all about your boxers. It'll take my mind off everything.'

'Yeah! Good idea!' Steve Harris chimed in. 'My ankle was giving me a bit of trouble on Saturday so, if it's all right by you, Danny, I'll hang on.'

Danny sighed. He could see that physiotherapy was becoming quite popular with the lads. 'And how's your leg, Brian?'

'Bad! Very bad!' Brian Watts sat down on the bench. 'I'll hang on as well. I don't mind waiting. Let's hear about that place – you know – that gym? The reporter said you had a gym called Danny's Place.'

The session seemed to go on for ages. At last Danny got to Brian Watts. 'Right Brian! Get on the treatment couch.' He poured some olive oil out and started to massage Brian's leg. Danny still used the "hands-on" techniques that were fast disappearing from his profession. You could tell much better, if the muscles were starting to heal, when you were in direct contact with them. He had a little trick of tapping the injured area with the tips of his fingers, to see if he could detect any stress. It was just like playing a piano.

'Come on. Tell us some more about your boxers.'

He'd just finished telling them all about the "Steel Drops" debacle and everyone was killing themselves laughing when…

'By the way,' Brian Watts panted, 'you're doing the wrong leg, Danny. It's the other one that I've injured.'

Everybody exploded with laughter.

'Bloody Hell, Brian! Why the hell didn't you tell me?'

'Because I was engrossed in your tale, Danny and I only noticed what you were doing when you stopped speaking.'

The chairman came trundling down the corridor and popped his head round the door. 'I can hear you lot right down in the boardroom,' Someone told him the joke and he joined in the uproar. 'Never mind, Danny. You can always tell Brian another tale while you're doing the right leg.'

'No! It's the left leg,' Brian wasn't too bright.

John Peters shook his head at Danny and raised his eyebrows in exasperation then he smiled. 'I might stay and listen myself, if that's ok.'

Danny certainly had his work cut out, looking after Tony. The worst part was trying to keep his spirits up. All through December, he'd had him down at Bloomfield Road for intensive physiotherapy. The treatment took anything from two to three hours a day, as Danny tried to stop Tony's body from wasting away. Even when he wasn't at the club, Danny was always on call.

Denise would phone him when Tony looked like he couldn't cope any more. 'Please come quickly, Danny. He's terrible. He's talking about doing away with himself!'

'What's up Tony,' Danny said, having driven like the clappers.

'I can't stand this any more. I feel like I'm never going to walk again.'

Danny could see he was in the depths of despair. 'Don't be silly, lad. We haven't come this far to give up now. That plaster will soon be off.'

In fact – the plaster came off a lot sooner than anyone expected. Danny was just supervising Tony's exercise regime when the plaster fell off in his arms.

'Oh my God! Danny! What do we do now?' Tony looked terrified.

'George!' George Wallis was hanging around in the gym. 'Go and fetch Bob Singleton in here, quick! Or failing that, get John Peters. Quick! Now! On the double! Don't hang about, George!'

211

Bob Singleton came running in. 'Oh my God! What's happened?'

'Don't panic, Bob. His leg's shrunk that much, this bloody plaster's just fallen off. Will you stay with him? Don't let him move. Now listen to me, Tony. Whatever you do you must lie still. Don't you dare put that foot down on the floor or you'll be a cripple for the rest of your life. I'm going to phone Mr Barnes.'

'Bring him over to Wrightington, straight away. As long as he doesn't put any weight on that ankle, he'll be all right.'

'I'll drive you there,' said John Peters. 'We'll be able to get him in the back of my car easier.'

So Danny, Bob and a couple more of the team carried him out to the chairman's car.

It was a nice smooth ride for Tony, in the back of the chairman's Rolls Royce.

'You all right, Tony?'

'Yes. I'm all right.'

'Don't you move a muscle.'

There was a stretcher waiting at the hospital and Tony soon had a brand new plaster on, except this time it just stretched from his knee to his toes.

'Good! We can work on those thigh muscles now.'

'Where the hell have you been?' Connie was in a really bad mood. It was nearly midnight.

'We had an emergency at the club. I had to race over to Wrightington with Tony in the back of the chairman's car.'

Connie calmed down a bit. 'What's gone wrong?'

'The plaster fell off. His leg's shrunk. We needed to get another plaster put on as soon as possible. Thank God he was at the club when it happened.'

'There's such a thing as a phone, you know.' Her voice returned to its previous caustic tone once she realised that it wasn't a matter of life and death and Tony was ok.

'How the hell could I phone from the chairman's car?'

'Couldn't you have phoned from the hospital?'

'I forgot.'

'You forgot! How could you forget, knowing how late it was and how I might be worrying about you? I phoned Des McClure and he hadn't any idea where you were. Even Nipper didn't know. He's been worried sick.'

'Oh aye! I forgot. I sent him home early.'

'Well you'd better go and put him out of his misery.'

'Yes! All right! You can stop going on. I'm home now. Anyway, you should know by now, if you don't get a call from the police, I'm just out on an emergency.'

'Emergency! Emergency!' Connie started shouting. 'Who the hell d'you think you are? A bloody doctor? You've got a Walter Mitty complex! And I'm absolutely fed up of playing second fiddle to those footballers. I'm off to bed. And when you come up you can sleep in the spare room.'

'Hi Boss. Thought you were home. Could hear Mrs Connie yelling.'

'Yes well! She's in a bad mood at the moment. Probably been working too hard. She's been going down to the Briardene sewing those bloody curtains all day long.'

The Briardene was the boarding house in Osborne Road that George and Sylvia had bought. It was in a good position, being near to the Pleasure Beach and it had recently been re-decorated, ready for the start of the holiday season. Sylvia and Connie were making new curtains for all the bedrooms.

Eventually the day came that Danny had been looking forward to. He got a call from Mr Barnes. 'Now Danny, it's nearly time for that plaster to be coming off so I want you to listen carefully. I've got some very special instructions for you.'

Danny listened to everything the surgeon had to say and then he went down to Tony's house. 'Right, Denise. How is he today?'

'He's fed-up, as usual.'

'Right! Well, I've got some good news. Mr Barnes wants to see him on Monday. He's taking the plaster off. You can go and tell him in a minute but before you go, there's something I want you to do for me. I want you to get me the last pair of proper shoes that Tony wore before his accident. Don't tell him I'm here. I want to get away as soon as possible. This job is urgent.'

'Shouldn't we buy him some new ones?'

'Definitely not. That's the worst thing we can do. No! I want his old ones.'

She came back with them. 'What are you going to do with them?'

Danny was half way out of the door before she'd finished speaking.

'Where are you taking them?'

'To the cobblers,' he shouted from the gate.

'What for? He's hardly worn them.'

Danny opened the car door. 'You'll see when I come back. I won't be long.'

Danny was back at eleven o'clock and by then Tony was sitting at the kitchen table. Danny handed him the shoes. 'You'll be wearing these when your plaster comes off.'

'Good God! This heel is two inches higher than the other one. What on earth have you done?'

'I've done exactly what the great man himself has told me to do, on the phone, just this very morning, so I have. Now Denise, listen very carefully. When Tony comes back from Wrightington, he'll be wearing these shoes. And the last thing you do at night, before he gets into bed, is to take the shoes off. Similarly, when he swings his legs out of bed, each morning, the first thing you must do is put his socks on and then put these shoes on. In other words, he mustn't put that injured foot down until it's been raised two inches.'

'Oh God!' Tony wailed. 'I'm going to look like the Hunchback of Notre Dame for the rest of my life. I wish I'd died under that surgeon's knife.'

Danny thought he could see tears in his eyes and Denise was screwing her face up. 'Don't be bloody ridiculous, lad. It's only for sixteen weeks. That foot's got to go down ever so gradually. If your heel goes down too quickly, the whole thing will collapse and then you WILL be a cripple. If you do what I tell you, you'll be playing next season.'

'Honestly Danny?'

'Honestly Tony!'

'How am I going to get my foot down, then?'

'The heel on this shoe is made up of sixteen layers of thin leather. I've got to take the shoes back to the cobbler, every week and he's going to peel a layer off, equal to an eighth of an inch each week.'

'It's going to be a long job, Danny.'

'We always knew it would be but it'll be worth it when you can play again.'

But as Danny left Tony and Denise celebrating with a bottle of beer each, he wondered if he'd been too optimistic. Maybe Tony would walk again but playing again? That was a different thing altogether. Mr Barnes had only ever talked about him walking again. Still! Better not say that to Tony. It was hard enough keeping his spirits up, as it was. If he thought he'd never play again he might just do something silly. These bloody footballers! They were a pain in the arse! They'd got no other interests in life except playing football.

The next sixteen weeks seemed to last forever. Danny had never known anything like it. He massaged Tony's wasted muscles every morning, while he was seeing to the other team injuries. Then he'd shout to Nipper. 'Nipper! Fill that bath with hot water and shovel in them Epsom Salts.' This was an old trick that his Uncle Willie had told him about.

'You get them fellas in a good hot bath and put plenty of Epsom Salts in. Buckets of the stuff. That'll get rid of them aches and pains.'

And it did. Another trick was to use olive oil to massage their muscles with. Danny had always bought it in pint bottles but after Tony got injured he started buying it in great big Winchesters. Normally you would take the empty Winchester back and get it filled up but Danny had decided to keep the empty ones. He wanted to see how many he used on Tony. He thought he might use three or four.

When Tony was finally walking again, Danny took him to the storeroom. 'I've got something to show you, lad. Now you know how I always use the best gear?'

'Yes Danny. Nothing but the best for Danny McCoy.'

'That's why I always use Epsom Salts instead of ordinary salt.'

'Yes Danny.'

'Well, I also use the best and most expensive olive oil. I used to buy it in pint bottles but when I started treating you, I was getting through so much, I decided to buy it in Winchesters.' They'd reached the storeroom. Danny flung open the door. 'I saved the bottles. There they are: all fourteen of them.'

Tony gazed at the bottles. He was struck dumb for a few minutes then he said, in a shaky voice, 'I can't believe it. I'll never forget what you've done for me, Danny. I'll never be able to thank you.'

'Yes you will: by getting out on that field. You take that training carefully and ease yourself back into it. Don't do anything silly and when you're back in the team: that'll be my thanks and that's all the thanks I want.'

CHAPTER TWENTY-TWO

The twins would be ten in less than three months. It didn't seem like ten years since they'd been born but the calendar said it was August1964 and he'd been at Bloomfield Road for nearly two years. Still time for things to go wrong, he thought to himself, cynically. Not today though because today was Sunday. There was a charity match on at Stanley Park but Danny hadn't bothered to go because his physio gear was in such a mess and he was quite desperate to get it sorted out. In any case, he knew that the St John Ambulance Brigade was covering the event and he didn't want to spoil their fun. Someone knocked on the door. 'Hello! Who is it?'

An ambulance man peered round the door.

'Oh hell! What now?'

'Are you Danny McCoy?'

'Aye. How did you get in?'

'One of the groundsman unlocked the door for us. Said it was all right to come up. We've got a patient for you.'

'I can't believe it. I didn't think any of my boys were playing today.'

'Oh! It's not a footballer. It's a famous singer.'

'Well you can't bring him in here. You'll get us all the sack. Take him to Victoria Hospital.'

'We already have. He wouldn't let anyone treat him. We were supposed to be taking him back to his hotel then we thought of you. We saw that write-up about you in the Gazette and Herald.'

The local newspaper had followed up the short sports article in The Green with a more detailed one in their special weekend publication.

'So who've you brought?'

'Rico Chico from that show at the ABC. You know the one? Caribbean Carnival. Anyway, listen. My mate's standing outside with Rico perched on a chair. So can we bring him in or not?'

'Go on then but I'm going to have to clear it with our Chairman.'

The ambulance men carried Rico Chico in and carefully deposited him on the chair that Danny dragged forward. 'Is it ok if we go now?'

'Certainly boys. You get off. I'll take care of him now.' The men slipped out of the door and Danny turned to Rico. 'Right! Now! Can you sit there for a minute while I phone our Chairman?'

'Yes,' he moaned, 'but I'm in terrible pain.'

'I can see that. Don't worry. Everything will be all right.' He went to the wall-phone and dialled John Peter's home number. 'Thank God I've caught you, John. Got a bit of a problem.' Danny paused to listen.

'No! No! It's not one of the team. It's someone from one of the summer shows.' He listened again.

'Well apparently it's because the ambulance men who brought him here saw that article in the Gazette and…'

'Yes I know you said there might be repercussions but I didn't think this would be one of them.' He waited for John's reply.

'What's wrong? You might well ask. It seems the ambulance men thought I could do a better job than that lot up at Victoria Hospital.' Danny started laughing. 'You'd better not let them hear you say that. Anyway, is it all right if I help him out?' Rico Chico was watching Danny, anxiously.

'Thanks. That's very kind of you.' Danny gave Rico the thumbs-up. 'I'll let you know how it goes.' He put the phone back.. 'Right! Let's have a look. Can you tell me what's wrong?'

'I've hurt my knee.'

'How did you do that? What were you doing at the time?'

'I was playing in that charity match and I was just running for the ball and this enormous man stepped back and fell on my outstretched leg.'

'Who was it?' Danny asked, trying to take Rico's mind off the pain while he examined his knee.

'The drummer from "Freddie and the Dreamers" but I know it was an accident. He was absolutely gutted. Ooooooogh! Aaaaaagh! Oooooogh! It's killing me! I'm dying!'

Danny knew exactly who he was talking about. The bloke was about fifteen stone. 'And what did they tell you at the hospital?'

'They didn't tell me anything to my face. You know what they're like but I could hear them talking behind the curtains. They said it was crucial. I felt like telling them, I know it's crucial. It's killing me.'

'No! No! They didn't mean crucial. What you probably heard was a reference to the cruciate ligament, which is inside the knee joint. It's a very dodgy injury to the knee. It usually

220

means you have to have your leg in plaster for about three months.'

'Yes! Yes! That's it. They did say they wanted to put my knee in plaster. I told them. I'm not having my leg in plaster. How am I going to dance with my leg in plaster?'

'Mmmm! Aren't you appearing in that show: Caribbean Carnival?'

'Yes but I'm not just appearing in it. As well as singing and dancing, I'm producing it. In fact I've sunk a lot of my own money into it. If I can't appear, the whole thing will have to be cancelled. I'm the hub of the show and we're only half way through the season. I'll be ruined! Finished!' He was starting to sound hysterical.

'Now Rico, don't worry. Today's Sunday. You don't do Sundays, do you?'

'No.'

'Right! So we've got twenty-four hours to sort something out. Now, I've examined this knee and I don't quite agree with the diagnosis. And I don't think it should be put in plaster. I can give you some treatment and then I'll strap it up for you. But can you cut down on some of your dancing?'

'Well, I might be able to. I could have a word with my principal dancer. She helps me with the choreography.'

'Have you got her phone number on you?'

'Yes. What for?'

'Well, I want to get her down here so I can talk to her about your dance routines. We're going to have to work something out: a bit different like: something we can get away with while your leg's strapped up.' Danny knew Rico Chico was a well-known song and dance man. He'd had quite a number of hits in the Top Ten and he'd starred in over a dozen movies, mostly

221

musicals. 'You'll just have to do more singing and less dancing.'

'Ok.' He produced a business card. 'Here's the hotel where we're staying. Her name's Angelina Belaflores. She should be in her room. She didn't want to go and watch the football match.'

Danny picked up the phone and within a few moments was talking to Rico's principal dancer. 'Yes! Right now! As soon as possible. Any taxi driver will know where we are. I'm just going to start his treatment.' Danny hung up and went to drag his heat lamp over. 'Right Rico, you just sit back and relax and I'll get a bit of heat into that knee. While that's happening, I'll tell you about a boxer that had to strip off in Woolworths. That should keep your mind off your troubles.' Danny positioned the lamp above Rico's knee and switched it on. 'A few years ago I was managing a number of boxers who had been sent to me by my old friend Bruce Woodcock. He was the British and British Empire Heavyweight Champion. Is that knee starting to feel any better, Rico?'

'Just a fraction.'

Danny was leaning against the treatment couch. 'At the time he joined me, this boxer already had a contract to fulfil, that had been arranged by Bruce. If I'd known the problems this fighter was going to cause me, I'd never have taken him on. Poor old Ron Charleton. Now there's a coincidence Rico. He had the same initials as you.'

'What happened? Did he have an accident?' Rico was concentrating so much on Danny's tale: the lines of pain on his face were already starting to fade.

'No! He had weight problems. That boy was far too fond of his food.'

Rico started laughing.

'You ok Rico. Lamp's not too hot, is it?'

'No! It's just right!'

'Good!'

'Go on Danny. I can't wait to hear about this boxer of yours.'

Danny went over to a nearby stool and perched on it. 'We went up to Glasgow for the fight. We were on the train when he warned me he might not make the weight, great teacake that he was. So there we were, standing on the platform and…'

By the time Angelina arrived, Danny was plugging in the ultrasound and Rico was almost weeping with laughter.

'Watch that knee, Rico. Don't move it an inch.'

'I'm trying not to,' said Rico, between gasps of laughter.

'I told you not to play in that match, didn't I?' The elegant Latin-American dancer glided into the treatment room.

'Oh there you are. I know. I know. But you know how I love football…' Rico was from Brazil, originally. '…and it was for a good cause: a children's cancer ward and I just couldn't turn the invitation down.'

'Don't worry, Angelina, we're on top of the problem now. I'm just going to give Rico some ultrasound and then I'll strap this up. Now I've been thinking about this and I'm willing to come to the dressing room so I can give you a top-up between the first and second house.'

'That's very kind of you. I'll make it worth your while.'

'Well, I don't think that will be necessary. This little effort is courtesy of Blackpool Football Club. The Chairman made that clear when I spoke to him. He's a very nice chap. In fact, we've got a marvellous bunch of very helpful folk here at Bloomfield Road so I don't think we'll talk about money.'

'Right!' Rico grinned. 'In that case, you've got to let me treat you. Have you got any family?'

'Yes!' Danny sighed as he remembered he'd told Connie he'd be home for tea, three hours ago!

'Well. You let me know how many seats you can fill and what night you want to come down and I'll have some tickets waiting for you at the stage door.'

'Thank you very much.' Danny hoped the promise of a night out for all the family would get him a meal that night. He started to explain to Angelina that Rico would need some new dance routines.

She was quite hopeful that they could work something out to tide them over till Rico was fit to dance.

'I'll put this strapping on and tomorrow night, I'll pop up to your dressing room and re-do it. Don't want it falling down halfway through the act, do we?'

'Are you sure your wife won't mind you being out every night?'

'Don't you worry about that, Rico. I can always bring her along and prop her up in the bar with a couple of Guinness.'

CHAPTER TWENTY-THREE

'Right lads! Got a little surprise for you, this morning.' It was 1968 and Danny had been at Blackpool Football Club six years. 'I've been a bit worried lately that some of your aches and pains have been dragging on a bit so I've devised a new type of exercise.'

Some of the footballers looked a bit apprehensive,

'What sort of exercise, Danny?' Dave Lennox asked.

'Well, as you all know, the person I turn to these days, when we've got any problems here at Bloomfield Road, is Mr Barnes. This time he's given me an idea that might just work on you lot.'

Danny's Uncle Willie had died suddenly, in 1966. It had been a great shock to all the family because he'd always been a robust fellow. A mild cold went on to his chest, swiftly turned to pneumonia and that was that. The funeral in Dublin was attended by a great many notable figures from the world of orthopaedic surgery, including Mr Barnes.

Danny thanked him for going. 'My mother and father couldn't come. They haven't been in the best of health lately.'

'I'm sorry to hear that, Danny. Old age! Comes to us all, you know. Your father must be very sad to lose a dear brother so soon and you will miss him for all his advice.'

'Aye! Whenever I had a problem he was just a phone call away.'

'Well, you know you can always call on me. Whatever I can do, I will do. You must ring me whenever you or any of your boys are in trouble.'

So when Danny noticed that that it was taking a certain footballer longer than usual to recover from a strained tendon, he picked up the phone and dialled the number. It was just like calling his uncle but out of a deep respect for the surgeon he still called him Mr Barnes. 'I've got a slight problem with a boy of mine. I can't seem to get him fit. He's doing all the exercises I've prescribed but every time he's ready to play, something else goes wrong. He's not putting it on because he's desperate to play.'

'Well Danny. I'll give you a bit of advice.'

'Don't you want to see him first?'

'Not yet. Only if this fails. Now, living in Blackpool puts you right on the doorstep of the best orthopaedic clinic you could ever wish for.'

Danny was amazed. Was this a place that had just opened? Mr Barnes told him where it was and Danny promised to try it.

'Go on then. Tell us Danny. What does Mr Barnes say we've got to do?'

'We're going paddling in the sea.'

'You what?'

'What? You mean somewhere like the Costa Brava?'

'No, you bloody clown. Down on Blackpool Beach.'

Alan Scott looked suddenly downcast.

'Don't look so disappointed, Alan. You'll like it just as much as the Mediterranean.'

'Won't it be a bit cold?'

'Don't be silly. It's a nice little jog down to the Promenade. By the time we get there, you'll be so hot you'll be dying to go in. Anyway, at this time of the year it should be just the right temperature.' It was August. 'You can put your tracksuits on top of your shorts and when we get down on the sands you can take off your tracksuits and leave them till we get back from our little jog.'

'Oh aye! So some bloody holidaymaker can come and help himself?'

'Now Tony, d'ya take me for a complete imbecile. I've already thought about that and I've had a word with Des McClure and he's driving down with Nipper. They can bag a couple of deckchairs and sit on the sands till we get back.'

'Back from where?' Brian Watts asked, suspiciously.

'We're going to run to South Pier and back. Don't worry. It's not far.'

'Run? How can we run in the sea?'

'Well, I didn't mean that literally. I meant a slow jog. Anyway, that's the whole idea. Not only will you benefit from the salt water; you'll also have to work those muscles hard to run through the water. Right! No more questions. Look lively! Chop! Chop! I want you all outside the club in five minutes.'

They were absolutely steaming by the time they reached Nipper and Des. They all stripped off and dashed into the waves.

'Right lads! Further in!'

'What d'you mean? Further in?'

'I mean, in up to yer bloody thighs not yer bloody ankles.'

'I can't swim,' shouted Bob Bentley.

227

'Don't worry about that.' Steve Harris shouted back, amidst gales of laughter. 'I can swim like a fish. I'll save you if you get into difficulties.'

'How do you expect us to jog in three foot of water?'

'By forcing them leg muscles to do some work, that's how.' Danny set off. 'Come on lads. Keep up.'

And that's how it all started. Once or twice a week, Danny, Nipper and Des took the team out on Blackpool sands for their therapeutic water exercises.

The boys mistakenly thought that when the season started, they would be back to jogging round the training ground, especially since there was a nip in the air now it was autumn.

'Oh! No! No! No! We'll carry on going down to that seafront. It's doing you all a power of good. The team's never been so injury-free. I'll tell you what. I'll make a small concession. You can keep your tracksuits on now that it's colder. Nipper can rinse them out when you get back. The team's been doing well lately and I've got the go-ahead to continue with this.'

It was true. Last season hadn't been a good one but this year the boys were doing much better and the Chairman could apparently see the improvement. 'Carry on with the good work, Danny. At least we've stopped losing all the time. It seems those exercises in the sea are paying dividends.'

It was time for Connie and the kids to jet off to Majorca but the peace and quiet Danny was looking forward to had been shattered by Steve Harris. He'd had a terrible accident while playing away. When they got him to hospital they found he'd broken his leg. Danny phoned Nipper. 'I'm staying here till they've set his leg.'

'Don't worry, Boss. I'll hold the fort.'

'Listen! If Connie happens to phone in, tell her what's happened.'

They'd been at Stoke two days. Steve's leg had been set. Then Bob was asked to see the Registrar. He came back looking pleased. 'The news is a bit better. They want to transfer him back to Blackpool.'

'I'm not having that,' said Danny.

'What's wrong with him being transferred to Blackpool? They're just thinking of his family. It's a long way to visit him at Stoke.'

'It's nothing to do with that. They just want rid of him so he's not clogging up the system.'

'So what do you think we should do?'

'I'm going to phone Mr Barnes. If Stevie's got to go anywhere, it'll be Wrightington not Blackpool.'

Within a few minutes of speaking to his friend, all the arrangements had been made and Steve Harris was on his way to Wrightington.

A few days later, Danny got a call from Mr Barnes, asking if he could pop over and have a talk about Steve. When Danny got there the surgeon explained the problem.

'This break is a very bad one. He's broken the tibia about a third of the way down. I thought I'd just have a look and find out how it's been set so I've had the leg X-rayed again. I can tell you, I'm not at all happy with it. The trouble with most hospitals is, they're used to dealing with the man-off-the-street. And normally the way this leg's been set would be

229

perfectly good enough for walking and even running but for a footballer it's all wrong. Every time he goes to kick the ball, the bone will be what we call "riding" and it will cause him a great deal of pain.'

Danny was shocked. 'Oh dear. That's terrible.'

'What sort of player is he?'

'He plays at centre…'

'No! No! No! Not where he plays. What sort of player is he? Is he any good or is he just average?'

'Oh right! Well, I can say, he's one of the most talented players I've ever handled. In fact, it will be a terrible tragedy if he can't play again.'

'Well that's just the answer I was looking for. In that case, what I propose is another operation. I'm sorry to say, it's quite complex. He'll be in plaster for quite a while and he'll need the usual physiotherapy and exercises. Anyway, you did an excellent job for Tony Grey so I know he'll be in capable hands.'

'Well thanks for compliment. As it happens Tony's just been chosen for the England squad so it was time well spent.'

'That's excellent news. Well, keep them boys of yours paddling in the sea, summer and winter. Don't let the cold put you off. After Steve Harris has his plaster off, that will be just the sort of exercise that will help his recovery. There's nothing quite like it, you know. It's particularly beneficial to both man and beast. It's not just because of the salt, though that is good but it's also the constant lapping of the water against the muscles. Tones them up, you know.'

'Aye! I remember you telling me that and you were right. There's been a definite improvement since we started going for a twice-weekly paddle. Mind you, they won't be too keen in the dead of winter.'

'Oh yes! That reminds me. When I knew you were coming over, I put something in the car boot for you. I'll walk down to the car park with you.'

Danny was mystified but when he saw what the surgeon had brought him he knew instantly what a boon it would be. It was a rubber suit.

'It was the wife's but it should fit you. She's a size bigger than you. Her size was the reason for buying it. I told her it was a daft thing to buy. She paid a fortune for it and it didn't make a blind bit of difference. She didn't lose an ounce.' He laughed. 'Not even a sliver. She was just about to sling it out when I thought of you. You slip that on, underneath your tracksuit, this winter. You'll be as warm as toast when you go in that sea. I wouldn't let on about it though, if I were you.'

As soon as Danny got back to Blackpool, he tried the rubber slimming suit on. Mrs Barnes must have been a stone bigger than a middleweight boxer. The suit fitted Danny like a glove. He'd not had it zipped up thirty seconds when he started to sweat. He knew he'd have his work cut out keeping it from his boys. God help him if they ever found out. They'd kill him. They were already starting to complain about the cold and it was only November. Danny decided he'd better wait till the weather got really bad before he wore it. Didn't want to be fainting on the beach.

It was nearly December when Danny decided to try his rubber suit out. He went to great lengths to keep it a secret. 'Right lads. You carry on. I'll catch you up. Just got to change into my tracksuit' Or, 'I won't be long. Just got to make a quick phone call.' He'd nip into his office and lock it as quietly as he could. Then he would unlock the door of his cabinet; get out

231

his tracksuit and the rubber one. Then he'd slip into it, zip up the neck, and pull down the zips on the arms and legs. It was just like a wet suit that you would use to water-ski. Then, when he put his tracksuit on, all he had to do was make sure there wasn't any part of the rubber suit showing. He knew it was a bit dodgy, keeping his locker locked. He heard some of the players talking...

'I don't know why he keeps that old thing locked!'

'What's he keeping in there? The crown jewels?'

'His lunch, most likely!'

By putting on a bit of a sprint, he could catch the team just before they got to Lytham Road. 'Right lads! Let's go! Lift them knees up. Watch that traffic! Straight down Woodfield Road.' From the club to the sands took about ten minutes. 'Come on! Straight in! Don't hang back!' The sea was murderously cold but Danny was glowing like a beacon and the water didn't penetrate the rubber suit at all. But his boys were going mad.

'I don't know how you stand it Danny!'

'Oh Danny! It's too cold! It's killing us!'

'Agh! It's bloody freezing!' Dave Lennox was nearly in tears.

'Come on! What the bloody hell's up wi' you? Ger in! Ger in yer ninnies! It's not that cold. You'll soon get used to it. Don't be soft!'

'Agh! Agh! It's freezing. How can you stand it?'

Danny was already up to his thighs in seawater.

'Danny! Danny! This is ridiculous. We can't go all the way to South Pier in these conditions.' George Wallis was dancing up and down in spite of the fact that he was only in up to his ankles. Of course he, like all the others, still had old trainers on his feet.

'Right lads! Small concession this morning.'

Everyone looked relieved.

'About turn lads! We'll just go up to Central Pier, instead. It's not quite as far.'

There were more screams and objections.

'Central Pier's further than South Pier!' Brian Watts was incensed.

'Oh all right!' Danny could see they were a bit wound up. 'If you like, you can get out of the water at the pier and come back along the sands as far as the Manchester Hotel and then we'll branch off down Lytham Road. It's all for your own good. You've got that important game at Oxford on Wednesday. You all need to be fit for that.'

The game was in progress. Just before half time, the Oxford Manager appeared in the dugout. 'Your Secretary's on the blower. Want's to speak to someone.'

'All right,' said Danny. 'I'll go.' He followed the home team manager to the phone. 'Hello!'

'Hello. Is that you, Danny?'

'Aye!'

'It's me. Des McClure.'

'What's the trouble, Des?'

'Got a terrible weather report for you. They reckon there's going to be a pea-souper tonight on that M6. I don't think you should attempt to get home. I've been making some enquiries and I've fixed you up with a very nice hotel. You'll have to make a slight detour because the only place I could find was at Kidderminster. You got a pen and paper handy?'

'Just a minute.' Danny took out his little fixture diary and a pen. 'Right! Fire away!' He wrote down the name and address.

'When you tell the coach driver, tell him it's on the main road just as you're coming into Kidderminster. Apparently there's a big sign. You can't miss it. Now listen! I've been on the phone to them and they've promised to have a meal ready for you at seven o'clock. That'll be plenty of time for them footballers to have a bath before they get on the coach. But there's just one problem.'

'Oh aye?' Danny was immediately suspicious. 'I hope you're not expecting us to pay for this.'

'No! No! Don't be silly. No! The club will pay. It's just that with there being so many of you: they want to know exactly what you want to eat.' Des sounded harassed. 'They want you to phone them with a list of your requirements.'

'Don't worry Des. I'll sort it out. What's the choices?'

'Well, it's just the main course they're bothered about. They'll do a selection of trimmings and a choice of pudding. But for the main course, it's either steak, chicken or fish. Can you find out what everyone wants and phone 'em back? Here's the phone number.'

Danny wrote it down. 'Don't worry Des. I'll see to it at half-time.'

There were eleven players, five reserves, Danny, the Coach, three Directors, Bob Singleton and the bus driver. As soon as the whistle blew, Danny went and collared them. 'Now listen! I've had a phone call from Des. It's going to be very bad on the M6. It's foggy and getting worse. We can't get home so we're staying overnight in Kidderminster.'

There was a chorus of raised voices.

'Steady on. Don't worry. Des is going to phone your families and let 'em know. Now! Are you listening? The hotel needs to know what you all want for your evening meal and so…'

'Who's paying?' Tony Grey interrupted him.

'Don't worry. The club's footing the bill.'

'Right,' shouted Tony. 'I'll have smoked salmon followed by Lobster Thermidor.'

'There'll be none of that, Tony,' Bob Singleton chipped in, 'not until you win that FA Cup.'

'Settle down you lot! Now listen! I ain't got time for larking around. The hotel needs to know as soon as possible so they can order the stuff and…'

'You mean so they can get it defrosted in time,' shouted Bill Bentley.

Danny ignored him. '…there's a choice of steak, chicken or fish and fish means plain fish not salmon or lobster. You'll be getting cod or plaice,' he continued, ignoring all the catcalls. 'All those that want steak, put up your hands. Right! One two three four five six seven eight. I think I'll have steak as well. Where's those Directors?'

'Gone for a drink in the bar.'

'Oh well, I'll put 'em down for steak an' all. So altogether that's eleven steaks.'

'Twelve!' The whole team shouted.

'Oh aye! Forgot mine. That's twelve then. Right! Hands up those who want chicken. One two three four five six. Anybody not ordered?'

'Me. I'll have fish," shouted George Wallis.

Typical, thought Danny. George Wallis! He had to be different. He looked round. 'Hang on! Where's Alan Scott?'

'Gone to the bog.'

'Oh bloody hell.'

The Coach put his hand up. 'There's me. I'll have chicken as well.'

'Right. That's seven for chicken. I'll see Alan later. I'll go and find the driver. Hang about. What did you say you were having, Bob?'

'Steak. Sorry! I didn't put my hand up.'

'So the final score is; thirteen for steak, seven for chicken and one for fish. I'll go and find Alan and the driver. That's twenty-three. That's it!'

'What about veg?' shouted Tony.

'Don't confuse the situation, Tony. They're doing plenty of trimmings and there'll be an assortment of puddings. You won't go hungry.' He went to find the driver. On the way he decided to put Alan down for chicken. 'Can't wait for him any longer.' Danny muttered to himself.

Danny looked at his watch. Only four minutes to go plus injury time. No one had scored. Bloody hell! Danny knew Blackpool had to win this game. They were getting near the top and needed these points for promotion. In fact, this match was crucial. Suddenly, Blackpool was awarded a penalty. There was only one bloke who took their penalties. Alan Scott! Right! There was an air of expectation amongst the Blackpool fans, the few who'd managed to get to see the midweek match.

'He's got to get this in,' muttered Bob Singleton, 'or we're sunk. We'll be another season in this division.'

The ball was placed on the spot and Alan Scott walked up. The Oxford fans were booing and jeering: trying to put him off. He looked a bit pensive.

'What's up with him?' said Bob.

Then slowly but surely, Alan retreated. He always took exactly eight paces back. One. Two. Three. Four. Five. Six. Seven. Eight. Then he stood looking down at the ground.

'Come on, lad,' shouted the referee. 'Take it quickly now.'

There wasn't the slightest movement. Alan took no notice at all.

The referee shouted at him again.

Scott suddenly looked up, realised where he was; ran up and…

BANG! The ball was in the back of the net and a few moments later while the Blackpool fans were still cheering, the final whistle went.

As soon as they came off the field, Danny grabbed Alan Scott. 'What's up? Are you all right?'

'Aye! Course I am. Scored, didn't I?'

'Well, what was up with you out there, studying that ball, all that time?'

'Oh that,' said Scott. 'I was trying to make my mind up. I don't know whether to have steak or fish.'

'You great teacake! I can't believe you were thinking about your food at a moment like that. Anyway, you're too late. I've already put you down for chicken.'

It was the end of January before Danny pronounced Steve Harris fit to go jogging in the sea. '…and only for ten minutes at a time.'

'Oh Good!' Bob Bentley was ecstatic. 'Ten minutes is all we need in this weather.'

'I never said you lot could go for ten minutes. Oh no! Steve can come down on the sands and jog along the edge of the water, just up to his ankles, as far as the end of Lytham Road and then he can jog gently back to the club, on his own, whilst you lot carry on to Central Pier.'

Steve was so keen to get himself fit that he asked to go in the sea every day.

'Not yet, Steve. You're trying to go too fast. You've got to take it slowly so we don't have a relapse. We'll go twice a week and you can gradually build up the time you spend in the sea.'

On the twentieth of February, Danny was just too busy to take them paddling. 'Listen everyone. We had a very hard game last Saturday and I've got a lot of injuries to see to. We'll have to cancel this morning's run.'

The cheers were heard over at Preston North End!

But Steve Harris wasn't cheering. 'Oh no Danny! That's not fair. You can't say that. Not when I'm doing so well.'

Steve's comments weren't popular at all. 'Pipe down, Stevie. You heard what Danny said. We can't go and that's that.'

'For God's sake, Steve. Shut up.'

'Listen you lot. It's all very well for you. I've not had a game since last September. I can't stand it much longer. Listen Danny. You can't not take us. Can't we go this afternoon?'

'No. It gets too dark after lunch. I don't want you lot crossing those busy roads in the dark. We've got enough injuries without anyone getting knocked down.' The real truth was: Danny knew it was going to take him all day to see to the various injuries.

'Oh Danny. What am I going to do? I'm desperate.'

'If you're that desperate why don't you go on your own?' Dave was pretty cocky; safe in the knowledge that his own pulled muscle meant he wouldn't have to go. The boys that were fit sidled out of the door before they could be picked to accompany Steve.

'Well,' said Danny, thoughtfully, 'you're a clever lad, Steve. You know what to do. You carry on, if it's what you want. The tide will have just started going out. You'll be quite safe.'

'Ok Danny. I'll see you when I get back.'

'Now don't go too far. It should take you about forty minutes, as long as you only go as far as Waterloo Road. I'll have a nice hot bath waiting for you when you get back. I'll get Nipper to throw some of those Epsom Salts in the water.' Danny watched him go. He felt a bit guilty. Maybe he shouldn't be letting him go on his own. Suppose he drowned?

Danny pushed this thought to the back of his mind and started examining his players. He'd been working about an hour when there was a rantantan on the door and such a hullabaloo. 'What the bloody hell? Who's that?' Danny threw open the door and there, to his amazement, stood Steve Harris between two enormous policemen. Tears were streaming down his face and the policemen had a firm grip on him.

'Danny! Danny! Tell 'em who I am. They've arrested me for going in the sea. Go on, Danny. Tell 'em! Tell 'em! Quick!'

'Excuse me sir. Are you Danny McCoy?'

'Aye! That's me.'

'Well this man seems to think you'll vouch for him.'

'Who is he?'

'Danny! Danny!' Steve screamed at him.

'He says he's one of your boys. Says his name's Steve Harris.' The policemen obviously weren't football fans or they would have recognised him.

'Never seen him before in my life,' said Danny and shut the door, firmly.

Everyone could hear Steve screaming and protesting.

'You can't do that,' said George Wallis, looking shocked.

'Oh all right,' said Danny, grinning. He opened the door. 'Only kidding, officer. Bring him in. He's one of ours. He's just recovering from a broken leg and I sent him to do some paddling in the sea. Best cure there is for injuries and sprains. Can I offer you two a cuppa.' The policemen came in and gradually Danny got to know what had happened.

Steve had set off running, at a nice easy pace, towards Lytham Road. There was the usual Blackpool gale blowing. If it had been slightly warmer it would have been snowing! He saw a break in the traffic and hurtled across into Woodfield Road. By the time he reached the Promenade he was almost warm. He jogged on the spot till it was safe to cross and, keeping his eyes open for any stray trams, he dashed across the tracks. Good! Nearly there! Down onto the sands he went. He waded out nearly to his waist. He was slowly trudging along, fighting the rough sea when he heard a siren. He grinned to himself. 'Hello! Who's getting done for speeding?'

After a few minutes he noticed two figures running down to the water's edge. Wonder what they're doing, he thought. Then he saw they were policemen and he could hear them shouting through a loudhailer.

'COME OUT OF THE WATER IMMEDIATELY!'

He looked round. There was no one in the water. Then he suddenly realised they meant him. So he shouted back, 'Who? Me?'

'YES YOU! DON'T BE SILLY NOW!'
'COME OUT AT ONCE!'

He waded back into shallow water and as soon as he got near the policemen, they grabbed him. 'Hey! Hey! What d'you think you're doing?'

They frog-marched him up the beach, through the crowd of interested spectators that had, by this time, gathered. 'You're coming with us.'

'Where?'

'To the police station. Where else?'

Apparently when Steve went in for his therapeutic dip a woman, who was in Blackpool for the International Gifts Fair, was watching him. She was staying in a hotel right opposite where Steve had gone down into the sea. She was sitting in the window having an early morning cup of coffee when she saw this fella, poorly attired, pushing his way across the road in the teeth of a force-ten gale. He disappeared from view, down the steps and onto the sands. Then she saw him again, making for the sea. She knew he couldn't be going swimming in this weather but when he marched fully clothed into the sea, she decided it must be a suicide attempt. In a panic, she phoned the police. It took Steve ages to persuade the police to bring him back to Bloomfield Road.

CHAPTER TWENTY-FOUR

Barring a few incidents, the fifties and sixties had been good to Danny and by 1970 he had his feet well under the table at Blackpool Football Club. It was at least six years since he'd treated Rico Chico. There had been a steady stream of show business folk ever since and the name "Danny McCoy" was always mentioned if someone was in pain and needed help.

Occasionally, someone from the management side of show business would turn up. Today, one of the accountants from the Winter Gardens had come to see if Danny could help him.

'My back's killing me. I can hardly sit down and I can't afford to be off work at this moment in time.'

'Why? What's coming off at this moment in time?' Danny asked as he plugged in his heat lamp.

'Well, you must have heard about our new venture: you know the one? That new bar. The Stardust Gardens.'

Up till now, Danny had only heard a few rumours but here was a chance to get all the details straight from the horse's mouth. 'Well I don't know as I have but you can tell me about it while I get some heat into this back. It'll take your mind off the pain you're in.'

'Well! Honestly! It's going to be the best thing that's ever come to this town. It'll put Blackpool on the map.'

Oh aye! Danny thought to himself. Already been done nearly a hundred years ago, by the fella who built Blackpool Tower. But he didn't say it out loud. He didn't want to stop the flow of information.

'I'm telling you: we'll get them punters thinking properly. It'll be a burster, will this! We'll not be serving all that beer in pint glasses. Oh no! We're going to do what they do in all the posh bars in London.'

'Oh aye? What's that then?'

'Well, for example: we're going to have everyone sitting at little tables spread all over the place and we'll have the drinks coming round on little trolleys.'

'How are you going to measure out the drinks?' Because, thought Danny, if the waiters that he'd seen in there were anything to go by they wouldn't be pouring it into the glasses: they'd be pouring it all over the tables.

'We're not!' The accountant was triumphant, pleased to have caught Danny out. 'We'll be serving all the spirits and the mixes in little miniature bottles just like they do on an aeroplane. We'll make a bomb.'

Some hopes, thought Danny. The sort of people who came to Blackpool on holiday didn't want that. They wanted to get in a bar where they could have a singsong, a knees-up and plenty of mild and bitter in pint pots.

'You wait till you see it. Come over to my office next month. We'll have the plans laid out by then. We're getting a top London designer to do it all. I've seen an artist's impression and…' he rambled on.

Danny's concentration wavered a bit. Oh aye! An artist's impression, ay? Everybody knew what artists and designers were like for exaggerating. He tried to concentrate on what the accountant was saying, again.

243

'…honestly! It looks like something from the South Pacific. You know: that musical all those years ago. How can I explain it? Yes! I've got it. Remember that show a few years ago, at the ABC? Caribbean Cocktail?'

'You mean Caribbean Carnival,' said Danny, wearily.

'Yes! That's the one! Well, it's like that. There's going to be palm trees dotted around under a canopy of stars against a midnight blue sky. The designer's devised a way of doing a false ceiling and he's got all these tiny little lights which look as though they're floating in space: you know: just like stars. It'll look spectacular. Obviously we'll be charging an entrance fee.'

'How much?'

'Oh! Not much. Round about five pounds, I imagine.'

Good God, thought Danny. That's nearly half a week's wages for most factory workers. There wasn't going to be many people coming to Blackpool who could afford to pay those prices. 'Well, I hope it's a success for you.' That's what he said but what he was thinking was, it's going to be a complete and utter failure. Anyway, he hadn't time to dwell on it any further because he was picking up Derrick Horan, his next door neighbour, for a day's racing at Haydock Park. Derrick and his wife Anne owned a hot dog stall on Blackpool Promenade. It was quite handy really. Derrick preferred National Hunt racing and the jumping season coincided with the closed season on the Promenade.

'Oy! Come and look in here,' said Brian Watts.

'What are you doing in Danny's office?' Tony Grey was appalled. 'You can't go rooting round in someone's office, like that. And what the hell are you doing opening his locker? You'll be for the high jump if he catches you.'

244

'Well he won't catch me because he's gone to Haydock. Anyway, I wasn't deliberately rooting. I was told to bring these towels in.'

'Well come out of there before the Manager catches you.'

'Not till you've had a look at this. I'm telling you: you won't be quite so critical when you see this. Come on. Come in, will you?'

Tony went in hesitantly. Brian was standing by the open door of Danny's locker. 'Listen. I didn't open this. The door was ajar when I walked in. See! I'm telling the truth. There are the towels on the desk. But look in here.'

Tony glanced inside the locker. 'His tracksuit. So what?'

'Not just his tracksuit. See what's hanging underneath?'

'What? What is it?'

'It's a wet suit.'

'A what?'

'A wet suit. Come on Dumbo! Think! It's one of those wet suits that they wear for water skiing. You know the sort: made out of rubber: zip up the front and zips at the wrists and ankles.'

'What's he want one of those for? He doesn't go water skiing, does he?' Tony sounded even more confused.

'God! You are thick. Think about it. See! Smell it! He's been in the sea in it. He's been putting it on under his tracksuit.' Brian Watts was furious. 'I'm going to confront him with this.' He grabbed the rubber suit and lifted it out of the locker. 'No wonder he's been so warm in the middle of winter.'

'No! Wait!'

'What d'ya mean? Wait? I'm not waiting.'

'Listen! There's a much better alternative. Put it back and shut the door. I've got a fantastic idea to get him back.

245

Honestly! You'll love it.' He grabbed the rubber suit and shoved it back behind the tracksuit. 'Come on. Let's get out.' He dragged Brian out of the door and off down the corridor.

Danny had a good day at Haydock and next morning he was feeling quite chirpy. 'Right lads. Let's get down to that beach. I'll just get Nipper organised with those Epsom Salts. Won't be a tick. Go on. I'll catch you up.' Danny disappeared down the corridor.

He caught them up just before they reached Lytham Road. 'Blimey! That wind's a bit sharp this morning. Must be a north wind.' They were soon down on the beach. 'Right lads. Get in the water. We'll jog down to South Pier, this morning.'

'Hang on a minute, Danny,' said Tony.

Danny looked round. Some more of his boys were running down the steps. He'd never seen so many of them on the beach at one time. They all surrounded him. 'What's up wi' you lot.' He looked at them. There was a full compliment. Tony Grey. Brian Watts. Alan Scott. Dave Lennox. Steve Harris. George Wallis. Bob Bentley, who still hadn't learnt to swim. These trips in the sea were quite a feat of mental endurance for him. Then there were some of the lads from the Youth Team. Frank Delaney. Wyn Jones. Tony Wright. Stan Woods. David James. And even Keith Graves was there. He was a promising young player from Burnley and he'd only arrived last week. In fact every single player including those who were on suspension or off sick had turned up.

'It's a bit cold, today, don't you think?' Brian Watts sniggered.

'Well it won't be too bad when you've been in a while. Anyway, what the hell are you lot doing here? Hey! What the hell do you think you're doing? Hey! Leave those alone. You kinky or summat?'

Tony and Brian were kneeling on the sands tugging his shoes off. 'The only kinky person here is someone who wears a rubber suit under his clothes,' yelled Tony, above the howling wind. 'Right lads! Let's do it.'

The rest of the footballers piled in. Somehow they'd found out his little secret. Danny quickly realised that one ex-middleweight boxer had no chance against twenty irate footballers His protests went unheeded as they peeled off his tracksuit and then the rubber suit. Danny was soon down to his birthday suit and by God, was he cold? It was absolutely perishing!

'Now you know what WE'VE been going through,' shouted George Wallis. 'Go on! Get in that sea! He grabbed Danny and hauled him up. Some of the others helped him carry the physiotherapist. They dumped him in three feet of water that was as cold as the Antarctic!

'Right, Danny, ' shouted Steve Harris, picking up Danny's clothes and jogging off towards the Promenade. 'We'll see you back at Bloomfield Road.'

'Wait!' Danny gasped, as he crawled out of the water. 'You can't leave me wi' out any clothes.'

'You'll soon get warm if you jog back,' shouted Dave Lennox.

'Come on, lads. For pity's sake. Leave the shoes. I can't run across them tram tracks in bare feet. And if you don't leave me my bottoms, I'll get arrested.'

'Right! What d'ya think, boys. Shall we leave him his shoes?'

'Aye! Go on then. We don't want him cutting his feet to shreds. Everyone agreed? Hands up,' shouted Tony Grey.

'Aye!'

'Aye! All right!

'Aye!'

'Aye! Go on then!'

'Oy Steve!' Tony Grey shouted. 'Chuck us them shoes and that sweatshirt to cover his other bits. Don't want him to frighten any old ladies on the way back, do we?'

Steve duly obliged and the items fell onto the wet sand in front of the naked Danny. Then everyone ran off to arrange a welcoming committee back at the club.

Danny got a merciless barracking from the people he passed on the way back. He reached the grounds just as Nipper came running out with a big bath towel.

'Here you are, Boss. Don't worry. I've filled that bath up with boiling hot water.'

'You'd better check it. Knowing that lot, they'll have pulled the plug and re-filled it with cold. They're as mad as blazes. Can't blame 'em, I suppose.'

CHAPTER TWENTY-FIVE

Danny had been riding on the crest of a wave for so long that he'd forgotten how fate has a nasty habit of dumping on folk without any warning. At the end of March 1970, he got a call from Mr Barnes. 'Listen, Danny. I just thought I'd let you know: I've decided to retire. Been thinking about it for quite a while.'

'Oh no! What on earth am I going to do without you?' Then Danny realised how bad that sounded. 'I'm sorry, Mr Barnes. I really should have said, have a happy retirement. Very bad of me to be thinking only of myself.'

'Well, I'll take it as a compliment but don't worry, I've fixed you up with an old pupil of mine. His name is Arnold Stern. He hangs out at Preston Royal Infirmary but his private rooms are out at Moor Park. This should be good for you. You won't have as far to go. You got a pen and paper?'

'Yeah.'

'Well, write this number down and when you need him, just give him a ring. He knows all about you and the club.'

'Well that's most gracious of you and I'm sorry I reacted so badly but it's awful when you lose a good friend.'

'I agree with you but you're not losing me, I hope. You must bring your wife over in the next few weeks. We'll all go

out to dinner. Give us a chance to have a proper chinwag. Talk
to her and then phone me and we'll make some arrangements.'

But Danny didn't get a chance to talk to Connie about dinner
with Mr Barnes because that bad news was followed by worse
news. The phone rang at two o'clock and it was Connie. She
was in a terrible state. 'Mum's just fallen down stairs. I think
she's broken her ankle. I'm taking her up to Victoria Hospital,
now. I'm not waiting for an ambulance.'

'Right! Now don't panic, love. I'm on my way. I'll meet
you up there.' He put the phone down. 'Nipper! Nipper! Are
you there?' He went down towards the treatment rooms.

'Here I am, Boss. What d'you want?'

'Go and get in the car. We'll have to get up to the hospital.
Sylvia's had an accident.'

'Oh no! No! Is she badly injured?' Nipper looked scared
stiff.

'Don't panic. Connie thinks it's just a broken ankle. Let's
hope she's right. I'm just going to have a word with John
Peters.'

'I'll get your bag and coat,' shouted Nipper, setting off at a
run towards the office.

By the time they got to the hospital, Sylvia was in the
examination room. An hour later, the doctor brought the news
that it was just a very bad sprain, 'but we'll x-ray it anyway.'

Connie was still tearful. 'I'll have to stay here. Will you
pick the kids up?'

'Course I will, love. Don't worry. Everything will be all
right.'

'Listen, you'll have to pick Jack up first. They get out sooner. Then pick up Daniel and Bridget. I've already phoned the schools to let them know you might be late.'

When Jack was ready for school, Danny got his own way and sent him to St Kentigern's. Daniel Dermot had followed the twins to St Joseph's and Bridget Kathleen was at The Convent for girls, which was nearer than both, being only a stone's throw from Victoria Hospital. However, Connie was right. It was logical to leave her till last.

So it would be a quick trip down Newton Drive to get Jack and Daniel and then he'd have to come back up Newton Drive to get Bridget. 'I'd better get going then. D'you want me to bring them back here?'

'Good heavens! No!' Connie was horrified at the suggestion. 'They'll only get upset. Take them straight home. The twins won't be home till six o'clock. They've got football practice.'

The twins had bicycles. Connie had been very much against it because the traffic round St Joseph's was quite heavy. But she'd lost that argument as well. 'You can't wrap 'em in cotton wool. All the fifth formers have got 'em. You'll make 'em a laughing stock at Holy Joe's. They'll be calling 'em mammy's boys.' But even Danny had put his foot down when Bridget, who was only thirteen, wanted one. 'You're too young.'

'I'm only two years younger. It's not fair!'

'Me too. Can I have a bicycle,' shouted Jack.

'No!'

'No!'

For once Danny and Connie were in complete agreement.

251

Danny parked outside St Kentigern's. They were just in time.

'I'll go in and get him,' said Nipper. He was back within five minutes. He bungled the little boy into the back seat.

'I wanna sit in the front. I wanna sit in the front.'

'Stay where you are,' snapped Danny. 'We're in a hurry. We've got to go and collect Daniel and then we've got to get back to that Convent and pick up your sister.'

'Is Gran all right, Dad?'

'Yes. She'll be home tomorrow, probably.'

By the time they'd got Daniel and driven up to The Convent, the girls were filing out of the schoolyard. Bridget Kathleen looked very smart in her uniform, which was bottle green. It complimented her red hair. Danny was always proud when he picked her up. 'Katie! Katie! Over here!' Danny leaned out of the window.

Bridget Kathleen frowned and pretended to check on the traffic. She hated being called Katie.

'Oy! What d'you think you're doing? Get back in at once!' Danny got out and walked round the front of the car and onto the pavement.

Jack was standing on the pavement.

'I'm sitting in the front. She sat in the front this morning. It's my turn tonight.'

Danny grabbed his arm. 'You little monkey. You can't sit in the front because Nipper's sitting in the front.'

'No he's not.'

Nipper had also got out. The only one left in the car was Daniel, who was watching the proceedings with glee, hoping Jack was going to get a thick ear.

'Anyway, if you'd have let me have a bike, I would be cycling home by now.' Jack pulled away from Danny, who was concentrating on making sure that Bridget got across the very busy St Walburga's Road, safely.

'Come on, Katie,' shouted Danny. 'Come on, now!'

Bridget ran across and went round to the front seat.

'No! No! She's not sitting in the front seat,' yelled Jack. 'I'll walk home if she gets in the front seat.'

Bridget pulled her tongue out at him and dived into the front of the car.

'No!' Nipper screamed. He was at the back of the car, half on and half off the pavement.

'No!' Danny screamed. He was on the pavement at the side of the car and he wasn't near enough to prevent Jack leaping off the pavement and running straight across the road.

The driver stood on the brakes as hard as he could. The bus skidded towards Jack, who turned his head in horror as he heard the screech of the tyres on the tarmac.

Danny saw the whole thing almost in slow motion as he launched himself towards the front of the car, knowing he wouldn't make it. Out of the corner of his eye he saw Nipper throw himself into the path of the bus, knocking Jack onto the pavement. The bus hit Nipper and tossed him into the air like a rag doll. 'No! No! No!' Danny screamed.

'Nipper! Nipper!' Daniel screamed, from the back seat.

Bridget in the front seat was screaming. 'Dad! Dad!'

The traffic came to a standstill as Danny ran to the front of the now stationary bus. He dropped down on the road and cradled Nipper's head in his arms. 'Nipper! Nipper!' Danny shouted. 'Speak to me, lad. Come on, lad.'

Bridget jumped out of the car, ran across the road and grabbed Jack.

The Mother Superior had come running over and she grabbed both Bridget and Jack. 'Come here, Bridget Kathleen. Is this your little brother?'

Bridget nodded, unable to speak.

'Sister Theresa!' The Mother Superior looked across at another teacher. 'Go and get the other little boy out of the car.' She could see Daniel's white face staring out of the back window. 'Bring him over here.' She dragged Bridget and Jack to the back of the bus where they couldn't see what was happening on the ground.

A man ran over from the houses opposite the school. 'I've called an ambulance.'

A crowd was gathering and more teachers came running out of the school. They ushered the other pupils away from the scene.

The sound of the siren told them of the approaching ambulance.

Danny left the children with the Mother Superior and went with Nipper, in the ambulance. Then he phoned Derrick and Anne Horan and asked them if they would collect the children from The Convent. Then he phoned the school and told them Derrick and Anne were on their way. 'Are they all right, Reverend Mother?'

She told him they were very shocked but they were being well looked after.

Danny asked how Jack was taking it.

The Mother Superior told him the little lad didn't seem to understand how bad Nipper was.

'He's very bad but don't tell them that. Tell them we're here with Nipper and we'll all be home soon.'

Nipper was in a small private room. He'd just come back from the operating theatre. Danny and Connie were in the waiting room, ready to speak to the surgeon. They'd been waiting over an hour. The door opened. They jumped to their feet. 'How is he? Is he all right?'

The surgeon shook his head. 'There's nothing more we can do. His injuries are too bad. You'd better go in and see him.'

Connie started crying. 'You go in. It will be you he wants to see.'

Danny sat down next to the bed. 'Well, you dozy bugger! Couldn't you have run a bit faster?' He tried to be jovial but it was very hard.

'Listen Boss, how…'

'Can't you, just for once in your life, call me Danny?'

'Ok Danny,' Nipper whispered. 'Listen. Is that kiddie all right?'

'He's safe and sound. Bruised and shocked, that's all. He'll be back home already. I asked Derrick and Anne to collect the kids from The Convent.'

'You won't blame him, will you?'

'No!' But Danny knew he would. He'd always blame him but he'd never tell him.

Nipper breathed a sigh of relief. He could tell just by looking at Danny's face that Jack wouldn't be punished. 'Listen Danny. Do you believe in that stuff they call the fickle finger of fate?'

'Aye.'

'The sort of thing that brings people together for a special reason?'

'Aye!' Danny could only manage one word at a time.

'Well I reckon we were meant to meet up in Newcastle all those years ago, just for this one moment in time. You know?

255

So I could be here today. If we hadn't met, I wouldn't have been here to save Jack. It's thanks to you, Danny that I've had such a wonderful life. It could have been so different for me. I wouldn't have lasted long with Bert Shaw. Would have probably been dead years ago. I owe you my life and today I've been able to repay you. I love you and Connie and all them kids.'

'I love you too. We all do. All the family. All my boxers. All my footballers.' Danny's voice was hoarse with pain.

'We had a great time, didn't we? You and me and George. Oh aye and Mac as well.' Nipper's eyes were clouding over. 'Don't ever forget those times with your boys.'

CHAPTER TWENTY-SIX

The weeks that followed were far worse than anything Danny could have ever imagined. First of all, he had to arrange the funeral and that was a job and a half, in itself. He'd no idea if Nipper was religious. They'd never discussed it and Nipper had never been to Danny's church, except when the children were christened. He had a vague feeling that Nipper's parents had been gypsies from Hungary or maybe Romania. The thing was; Danny had never asked Nipper about his past in case it brought back painful memories.

'What am I going to do?' he asked Connie. 'I can't ask for a service at St Kentigern's when he never showed any interest in our church. And where are we going to bury him?

'What's wrong with Layton Cemetery?'

'Rumour has it, there's no spaces left.'

'Why don't you go along to the funeral parlour and ask their advice?' The phone interrupted her. 'Hello! It's starting,' she muttered, as she went to answer it. 'Danny! Danny! It's John Peters. He wants to come and see you. Is that all right?'

'Aye! I suppose so.'

The Chairman arrived within fifteen minutes. 'Listen Danny. I want you to take as much time off as you want. It's been a terrible shock for you all. It's been a shock for us as

257

well. Everybody down at the ground is devastated. How are the kids taking it?'

'Very, very badly. Nipper's been with me since 1953. They treated him like a surrogate father. In fact, they were probably closer to him than they were to me and he did more for them than I ever did.'

'Have you made the funeral arrangements yet?'

'Well as a matter of fact the only arrangements I've been able to make so far, is to have his body moved to the funeral parlour. But I don't know where to have the funeral or who to ask to conduct the service. Nipper wasn't religious. I think his parents were refugees either from Hungary or Poland or it might have been Romania and they might have been gypsies. They were part of the circus community.'

'I've been trying to remember,' said Connie. They were sitting round the kitchen table. 'I think Nipper said his parents were from Hungary. More coffee, anyone?'

Danny pushed his cup across to her.

'More coffee, John?'

'Mmmm! Oh yes please! Sorry! I was deep in thought. What religion is it in Hungary?'

'Possibly Greek Orthodox although I think the communists have stamped out all religion. Anyway I still reckon they were gypsies, which is probably why they joined the circus.'

'Listen Danny. Will you give me a couple of days? I've got one or two connections that might be able to help.'

'I'll be eternally grateful if you can help me sort summat out. I'm supposed to be going into his flat today, to look for his birth certificate.'

'Do you want me to come in with you?'

Connie butted in, 'No it's all right, John. I'm going in with Danny. We're doing it together. We'll be all right. You'll be helping a lot if you can sort out our funeral problems.'

'Yes, ok. I'll try my best. Oh by the way. There's something else I need to talk to you about. I've had them newspaper men on the phone. They want to do a report on him. He's a hero as far as the media is concerned and that always makes newspapers sell. Will you give them an interview? You don't need to if you don't feel up to it. I can cobble something together for them.'

'Bloody newspapers! Who is it?'

'Only someone from the Evening Gazette.'

'Well, I don't mind speaking to them. At least I can make sure they only print the facts. Better than leaving them to make summat up.'

After John Peters had gone, Connie looked at Danny. 'Don't you think we'd better get it over with, while the kids aren't here?'

Derrick and Anne had taken the children to Stanley Park, to feed the ducks. There had been a bit of an argument from Michael and Patrick since they felt it was beneath them to go feeding ducks. They'd soon changed their minds when they realised that Danny and Connie were going into Nipper's flat.

'Yes. All right.' Danny heaved himself to his feet. Everything was such an effort. He wished he could go and lie on the bed and fall asleep and not wake up till it was all over. He knew Connie felt exactly the same. The trouble was, neither of them were sleeping. Connie's eyes were puffed up: a combination of too much crying and not enough sleep. And he was completely wrecked and numb with misery.

The flat was cold and silent. 'I hate this,' said Connie. 'It's like an invasion of his privacy.'

'Well, someone's got to do it and we're the only family that poor little bugger had. Listen, you just go and take the bedclothes off and take them down to the laundry room. I'll have a look in the cupboards in here. And let's get that bloody heating switched on.'

There was silence for a while then Connie came out of the bedroom with the laundry. 'What's that?'

Danny was pouring over a book on the coffee table. 'It's a scrapbook. Have a look for yourself. He's kept every newspaper cutting that's been written about me, from every newspaper that's ever given me an interview. Look. All about my boxers. And here's some stuff about our wedding. And there's loads about Blackpool Football Club. I can't stand it.'

Connie could see Danny was broken-hearted. She sat down on the sofa and put her arm round him. 'Let's leave it till after the funeral. Did you find a birth certificate?'

'No and I don't reckon I ever will. I don't think he had one. If you think back, when he came to Chesterfield, he came in just the clothes he stood up in. He'd got no baggage at all, absolutely nowt. Don't you remember? I took him into town and bought him some clothes.'

'I remember Danny. His life started when you gave him a job and this scrapbook proves it. You'd better take it back to the house. It was probably his most prized possession. We should keep it in the family.'

A few days later, John Peters was back. 'Brought you last night's Gazette. There's nearly a full page. It goes into great detail about the accident. They've even managed to interview some of the passers-by as well as the bus driver. Oh yes! By the way. They've interviewed some of your boys down at the ground. It's a lovely piece. Anyway, listen. I think I've sorted something out about the funeral.'

'Thank God!'

'I've got a pal who's Minister down at Rawcliffe Street Methodist. You know the one? The one down by the side of The Lido? The one with that lovely slender steeple?'

'Oh Aye.'

'Well if you go and see him at his house in Hampton Road, he says he'll talk to you about it. Here's all the details; the address and phone number. He's called Peter Seddon. My friend says he's a nice man: true Christian and all that. Well he would be, wouldn't he? Goes without saying. Anyway, he'll do a nice job for us.'

'We want a proper burial not a cremation. Still got to sort out where. No places left at Layton. But I definitely feel he would like a Christian burial even though he didn't go to church. So do you think you could conduct the service for us, Mr Seddon?'

'After all you've told me about the way he saved your little boy, I'd consider it an honour to do that for you. Where would you like to hold the service? You've got two options. There's usually a little church at every cemetery. Or you could hold a service at my own church.'

'Well he's got no family so a small place…' Danny stopped in mid-sentence. 'Oh dear! I've just thought. All my boys from Bloomfield Road will want to come. We need somewhere fairly large.'

'Right. That's decided then. Rawcliffe Street it is. When do you want it? And we need to discuss the hymns you want.'

'Well I know this might sound strange but it can't be a Saturday or a Wednesday because those are match days and we're bound by the Football Association rules. Perhaps next Monday would be the best day. That gives me a week to make the arrangements. And I think we should have a fairly simple service, nothing too elaborate. I'll leave that to you.'

'Just one more thing. Do you have his details? You know? Where he was born and how old he was. Just things I can talk about.'

'Well, the trouble is, I don't know anything about him. I came across him on a fairground. He was being kicked around by a big brute of a man, if you could call him a man. Poor example of the human race if you ask me. He'd nicknamed him Frankenstein. I renamed him Nipper. My wife says his life began when he came to live with us.

'Oh dear. That is a problem.'

'Why? Does it make any difference to the service if you don't know his real name?'

'No! Good gracious me! It doesn't make a scrap of difference to me. It's the funeral directors you'll have to worry about. They'll need a name for the gravestone.'

The Minister had set Danny a serious problem but he had even more to think about than just a name. Finding an available plot in a local cemetery was now a priority. Looked like it would have to be Carleton. He decided to call in and see John Peters on his way home.

'Listen. I'm glad you've popped in. I've found someone who owns a plot in the non-conformist section of Layton Cemetery. Friend of mine. We were just chatting casually about it all, in the pub last night. She says she's got a family plot and there's room for one more but it won't be her. Says she wants to be cremated. Anyway, the thing is; there's no stone on this plot and she can't afford one. She says you're welcome to put Nipper in but she would appreciate if you could arrange for a small discreet stone to be put there. What d'you think? It'll kill two birds with one…' He stopped speaking in mid-sentence. 'Oh hell. I didn't mean to put it like that.'

'It's ok, John. Don't worry. I'm grateful for what you've done. Tell her I would be pleased to sort out a stone. It's most kind of her to let me do this. We'll get together after the funeral. She can choose everything. No expense spared. Tell her it can be as fancy as she wants. As long as Nipper gets his name on it as well. I'll pay for the lot.'

'No! You can't do that.'

'What? I can't put Nipper's name on? I thought that had been settled.'

'No! I mean you can't pay. The club will be paying. We've already had a collection. The directors have been extremely generous and the boys have all contributed. There will be more than enough.'

'I can't believe it. That is so kind of everyone.'

'They all loved Nipper, probably more than you know.'

Danny was glad to get home. Connie was waiting anxiously. 'How did you get on?'

'Good. I've got a Minister, a church and a grave plot. And the club's paying.' He gave her all the details.

But Connie could see he was still worried about something. 'What's bothering you, Danny?'

'I need his surname for the gravestone or I will do, eventually. I haven't got a clue how to find it.'

There was a moment's silence and then Connie said, 'Nipper McCoy!'

Danny looked at her in shocked surprise. He was immediately transported back to a ferryboat ploughing its way across the Irish Sea.

"What about training boxers?" Those few words that Connie had spoken in 1952 had put him on the road to success when he hadn't a clue where he was going. And now here she was, eighteen years later, solving another of his dilemmas with just two words. She'd turned out all right. In spite of their altercations, they still made a good team.

'What? What?' Connie looked bemused. 'You haven't looked at me like that for donkey's years. Don't tell me you're beginning to appreciate me?'

'Aye. Well. I've always known you had a good brain. Just never said so. Don't want you to get bigheaded.'

'Thank you. I take it that name is ok then?'

'Aye. Reckon Nipper would like that.'

'I reckon that Nipper would love it. He was always one of your boys.'

The following day, even before Danny'd had a shave, John Peters was on. 'Just thought I'd warn you. Fleet Street's got hold of it. There's a write-up in every newspaper this morning, all about Nipper, Jack and you. Unfortunately they've had Sherlock Holmes on the job, down at the Daily Mail. They've raked up all that stuff about that barefoot boxing match. Got pictures an' all. I must admit, up until today, I always thought you were making up some of your tales.'

264

'Well thank you for letting me know.' Danny spoke quietly, replaced the receiver and then... The explosion reverberated through the house. 'Shit! Shit! Shit!' Danny roared. He was incandescent with rage.

Connie came running. 'What's the matter now? What's happened?'

'The papers have got hold of the stuff about that boxing tournament that Abe Rosen put on.'

'How did the Evening Gazette find out about that?'

'Not the Gazette. The Daily Mail. That was John Peters on the phone. He says the story about Nipper saving Jack is in every national this morning but the Daily Mail have dug a bit deeper and done a piece about me. Bastards!'

'Well so what? You're not in the game any more so what harm can it do? Forget it. Calm down. You're on a knife-edge. Anyway, you never did anything illegal, did you?'

'No! No! I didn't. You know that.' Danny didn't want Connie delving any deeper. He'd managed to pull the wool over her eyes all these years. 'It's just a shock that's all. Might mean there's a few more at the funeral, that's all.'

There were certainly going to be more than a few at the funeral. Ron Charleton had phoned. 'Listen Danny. Me and some of the boys want to carry the coffin.'

There was consternation at the club when his footballers found out that his boxers were carrying the coffin. 'But we thought we'd be the ones carrying the coffin.' In the end, Danny worked out a solution to the conundrum. It was decided that Ron Charleton, Bert Longthorn, Steve Riley, Jackie Hudson, Joe Clark and his brother Ray would carry the coffin into and out of church. Then when they arrived at the cemetery, Tony

265

Grey, Brian Watts, Dave Lennox, Steve Harris, George Wallis and Alan Scott would carry it from the hearse to the graveside. And even that was fraught with problems because there were far too many footballers for the job.

The funeral director was clearly anxious. 'I've made special arrangements to leave the hearse just inside the gates so your footballers can carry the coffin from the car to the graveside but one of them suggested they could change over halfway. It just wouldn't look dignified, Mr McCoy.'

'Nipper wouldn't mind.' Bob Bentley was horrified he'd been left out.

'There will be a lot of wreaths, Bob. We've already had fifty and there's another two days to go. Perhaps you could organise the boys to carry those.'

'We're going to need extra cars to get all those wreaths down to the church and the cemetery, Mr McCoy. It's going to mean extra expense for you. You could always take them down yourself, after the funeral,' the funeral director said, obviously trying to save him some expense.

'No!' Danny said, firmly. 'I want all the wreaths to go down with Nipper. And I want them all on view even if it means ten extra cars.'

It was the biggest funeral procession that Blackpool had ever seen. Danny, Connie and the children were in the seventh car because five extra cars had been needed for the flowers. The police had been to see the Chairman about stopping the traffic. On the day, they found they didn't have to do anything. The traffic along Lytham Road and Bloomfield Road pulled to a halt along each kerb, to leave room for the funeral cars. The flag at the club was at half-mast and the groundsmen were lined up and standing to attention. There were hundreds of football fans lining the pavements because everyone had read all about Nipper and his bravery. Everything went off perfectly and the coffin was carried all the way, from the gate of the cemetery, to Plot 306 in the non-conformist section.

Most of Danny's boxers stayed for a week, camping out in Nipper's flat. They packed up all his belongings except for the most personal items like the scrapbook, which they pored over and his cufflinks, which they gave to Danny. Then they built a big bonfire in the grounds and burnt everything. 'Be just like a gypsy funeral. Honestly Danny. It's exactly the right thing to do. Nipper will love it. He'll be watching us from up there.'

'At least the children seem to be getting over it,' said Sylvia, from her wheelchair. The ankle was still very painful. 'It's all thanks to your boys, Danny. They've helped enormously.' The tears sprung to her eyes again. 'If only…'

'Don't start again Mam. You can't keep blaming yourself. It's just what Nipper said to Danny, in the hospital. It's the fickle finger of fate.'

But when it was all over and Danny was back at Bloomfield Road he knew that it was going to be impossible to forget his little helper and close friend of seventeen years.

After John Peters found him in tears whilst shovelling Epsom Salts into the bath, he put his foot down. 'Listen Danny. I want you to take some time off. In fact, I'm ordering you to take some time off. From today, you're suspended on full pay for a month. There's no argument. I'll get someone to stand in from somewhere. So pack that bag and get out.'

Connie was in full agreement. 'He's right, Danny. We all need to get away. Don't worry. I'm not suggesting Majorca though goodness knows we could all do with a bit of sun. But I know you'd hate it so why don't we all go to Ireland?'

'Thought you didn't like them kids missing school?'

'Only in an emergency and this is an emergency. Anyway, I've had a word with Father Jackson and he thinks it would be a good thing. The boys aren't doing as well as normal. He thinks a short holiday away from Blackpool and all its reminders will settle them down again. He says they can have some extra tuition when we get back.

CHAPTER TWENTY-SEVEN

Maybe it was for the best, thought Danny, as he stared out across the sea. The promise of a holiday had certainly cheered the kids up. Luckily, the sea was as calm as a millpond and no one was being sick. The sun was shining and the sky was an azure blue.

Paddy McCoy met them in Dublin so he could drive them to his father's place in Leitrim.

'Well! I can't believe it. Young Paddy McCoy, a boxing manager! Good God!'

'Don't be so surprised, Danny. I always said I would give up the boxing as soon as I reached thirty.'

'Never! You're never thirty already!'

There was a wonderful welcome waiting for them at the house that Maggie and Peter McCoy had bought with the proceeds from selling their shop. 'Come in! Come in! And a t'ousands welcomes to you all. We'll be having a party, will we?' His Uncle Peter was still as jolly as ever even at seventy years of age. He got out a new bottle of Irish Whiskey, opened it and threw the screw top in the fire.

Danny could see his two eldest lads were quite intrigued. 'D'ya know why he's done that, boys?'

'No! Why?' Patrick answered for them both, as he always did.

'Well, t'is the biggest honour you can receive in Ireland. It means no one can leave or in our case, no one can go to bed, till the bottle's empty.'

'So will we have a drink of it, Dad?'

'No you will not,' said Connie. 'You will have some orange juice like Jack and Daniel and Bridget Kathleen.'

By the time the two youngest children were packed off to bed, there were about twenty in the small lounge and it was like that every single night they were there.

'And where are you taking the family tomorrow?' Peter asked.

Danny had hired a car so he could show the children some of the local beauty spots. 'I thought we'd go and have a look at Carrick-on-Shannon.'

'It's the longest river in the British Isles. It flows for a hundred and fifty-nine miles,' said Michael, showing off a bit.

'Now will you look at that, Danny? Young Micky knows more about Ireland than me. What are you going to be when you grow up, Micky?'

'I'm going to be a solicitor or an accountant. I want to make plenty of money.'

'And what about you, Paddy?'

'I might be a teacher. They get good long holidays.'

'Mmmm! You've both got your heads screwed on. What about our Katie?'

'I'm going to be a model,' she paused. 'Actually, I'm called Bridget Kathleen.'

Connie frowned. It was obvious she was thinking there was no way that her daughter was going to be a model. 'I think both Bridget and Jack will have to do better at school before they make any decisions about a career.'

Danny could smell a confrontation from a hundred yards and he quickly changed the subject. 'Thought we'd stay at that old coaching inn. You know? The one right on the riverside. Might take everyone out on the river.'

'Will you be going to Cavan?'

'Aye and then I thought we might pop over to Fenagh and see Patsy. I wanted to see that nice little dance hall that he opened in the fifties.'

'Is he still alive?' Connie asked.

'Give over. He's only about twenty-five years older than me.'

'Well that makes him seventy-five at least.'

'Jesus, Mary an' Joseph!' Peter started laughing. 'Where have all the years gone?'

They were well on their way to see Patsy McCoy when Connie suddenly said; 'Did you ask your Uncle Peter how to get to your Patsy's house?'

'No! I forgot. Anyway, I know Fenagh and t'is only a small place, so it is. Will you stop worrying?'

'Have you ever been there?'

'Er! Well! Actually, no!'

'So how do you know where it is?'

'Well. I thought as I'd ask someone when we get near.'

'Ask someone? Ask who? As usual, there isn't anyone around. Sometimes I wonder about your lot, Danny McCoy! They never seem to be out in the fields doing any work. They're always inside with a drop of the Irish!'

'Or Guinness, Mum.' Michael was well aware of his father's habits by now.

271

'He's growing up fast, our lad.'

'Yes! Well! Don't you think he's going to be joining you in the pub, just yet,' snapped Connie.

Danny changed the subject. 'Look! There's a little shop.' It was a small dark green corrugated shed with the name Carroll above the door. The windows were all steamed up. 'I'll nip inside and ask if we're on the right road.'

'Don't you be having anything to drink in there,' she shouted through the open car window.

There was a little old lady behind the counter, such as it was. Danny smiled at her. 'Good morning to you.'

'Good morning to you and the blessings of God be upon you.'

'Thank you. That's most kind of you.'

'And what will you be having to drink?'

Connie's instructions were still ringing in his ears. 'Oh, I won't bother today, thank you. I only popped in to ask the way. Am I on the right road to Fenagh?'

But the old lady answered his question with one of her own. 'Fenagh? And who would you be looking for? There's only a few houses there. Who would you be wanting then?'

It was obvious she was keen to get into conversation with an interesting-looking stranger. Danny could see he was going to have trouble escaping. 'I'm looking for a cousin of the mammy's. Patsy McCoy.' It was like he'd waved a magic wand.

'Oh! Oh! Patsy McCoy! The man himself!' she exclaimed and all the while filling a glass. She placed the glass on the counter.

'What's this? This isn't for me, is it?'

'Sure an' it is. You don't think I'd be letting a cousin of Patsy's go without a drink of friendship, do you?'

272

This is a bit tricky, thought Danny. 'Well, I've got my family waiting outside for me, in the car. I can't stay in here drinking. I only came in to ask the way.'

'Well! Bring them in. Don't leave them out there, on no account.'

Some more glasses appeared on the counter and Danny started to panic. Connie would never believe this wasn't a set up. He went outside before she came beetling in. 'Listen you lot. You'll have to get out and come inside. The owner of the shop is in there pouring drinks.'

'What? Are you an alcoholic? For goodness sake, Danny! You surely don't need a drink at ten o'clock in the morning.'

The children were listening with interest and giggling.

'It wasn't my idea. She won't tell us if we're on the right road until we've had a drink with her. Anyway, she knows Patsy.'

'I just do not believe this. How many people are there over here who know your family? For God's sake how many relations have you got over here?'

'You should know. You saw about half of them at our wedding. They're all over Leitrim and Cavan for a start off. Anyway, come on. You'll have to come in. We can't be rude to the poor old lady.'

'What about the children?'

'They can come too. Don't worry. There's no one else in.'

They all trooped into the shop.

'Here's a little seat for your wife.'

'Could the children just have a glass of water?' Connie asked.

'Surely they'll be wanting a glass of milk, at the very least?'

'Are we on the right road, Dad?' Patrick asked him.

273

'I don't know Paddy. She hasn't got round to that yet.' Just as he spoke, the door opened and three farm labourers came in.

'Ah! There you are then! See! He's a cousin of Patsy McCoy. Remember Patsy? The fella that's just come over from America?'

Danny had to laugh at that. His cousin Patsy had come back to live in Ireland about thirty years ago. He'd been a bootlegger in America. When he finally came back, he'd had enough money to open one of the first dance halls in Ireland.

'Patsy McCoy! To be sure an' didn't he open "Fenaghville" an' on the opening night, he flew the "All Ireland Champion Ceili Band" all the way from New York specially for that opening night?'

'That's him. An' didn't our own Val Doonican sing there an' all?'

Danny could see the children were captivated and then he looked round. There were at least thirty people crammed into the tiny shop. News travels fast, he thought to himself. The drink was flowing even faster but every time Danny tried to pay, the old lady pushed his money back over the counter. Connie looked resigned to her fate and had struck up a conversation with her.

'Daddy!' Jack tugged at his arm. 'That man over there has got a fiddle.'

'So he has,' said Danny and just as he spoke the man struck up a tune. Not much had changed and eventually Danny couldn't help himself. He asked the fella to play his daddy's favourite tune. Danny could just about remember all fifty-two verses and when he stumbled slightly, the fiddle player helped him out. Together they sung all the verses of "Leitrim, Lovely Leitrim" and Danny wondered why he'd stayed away so long.

Round about four o'clock, Patsy McCoy arrived with his son. Someone had sent for him. 'An' t'is just as well that they did, for you're not in any shape to be driving. So my son, Liam will drive your wife and children and you can come back with me.'

'That was some party, wasn't it, my love?' They were sailing back to Liverpool. The children were playing cards in the cafeteria. Danny and Connie were up on the deck, leaning on the rail. 'Sure an' I wish we'd made the effort to go to Ireland more often.'

'Yes! Well! That's all down to you,' Connie retorted. 'Maybe you'll listen to me the next time I want to go away. We won't have the children much longer. Soon they'll be grown up and wanting to go away on their own.'

'Don't go on. I feel depressed enough as it is.'

'You? Depressed? What have you got to be depressed about? You've just spent three weeks in your beloved Ireland and now you're going back to your boys. How can you be depressed?'

'I don't know. I'm not right sure but I've got this feeling.'

'What feeling? What about?'

'I'm not sure but I feel queasy when…'

'Queasy! That'll be seasickness.'

'Don't be daft. The sea's as smooth as a baby's bottom. It's got nothing to do with being on this boat. It's a premonition. Something's wrong back at the club. I know it is.'

'Don't be silly. It'll be all the upset about Nipper. You've got to put it behind you.'

Danny went into Bloomfield Road as soon as he arrived back in Blackpool, which was Friday afternoon. He took the same taxi that dropped Connie and the children at home.

'Don't think you're leaving me to do all the unpacking. It'll be waiting for you.'

'Leave it for me. I don't care. I know there's something wrong and I've got to go and see what it is.'

CHAPTER TWENTY-EIGHT

'Thank God you're back.' Des McClure met him at the door of the gym. He looked white and gaunt, quite unlike his natural cheery self.

'Why? Whatever's up, Des?'

'John Peters had a heart attack while you were away.'

'Oh! No! No!'

'Don't worry. He's recovering all right but he's had to resign. There's a Board Meeting to discuss his replacement, today.'

'I knew there was something wrong. I had a premonition, on the boat, coming back. Are you sure he's all right?'

'Yes! The doctor says it was just a warning but he's got to rest. It's put the wind up a few of them directors, all right. Richard Redman's resigned and so has Philip Burton.'

'Why didn't someone let me know?'

'Well! No one knew where you'd gone except John and when he was well enough to have visitors he told us we hadn't to bother you.'

'Can I go and see him?'

'Aye! But phone his wife first.'

'Do any of my boys need any treatment today?'

'No! Funnily enough, while you've been away, they seem to have been keeping out of trouble. D'you know something,

Danny? It's always been my belief that half their injuries are made up.'

'Give over. Why on earth would they want to make them up? They're too keen on getting a game every Saturday to pretend to be injured.'

'Yes and I've seen 'em recover in time for every game. It's just like you've waved a magic wand over 'em.'

'Well that's my expertise.'

'No! I reckon it's your tales.'

'Well, I know that does help as well.'

'No! You're missing the point. I reckon they pretend to have a minor injury so they can spend an hour or two listening to your Irish blarney, that's what.'

Danny laughed. 'Well maybe you're right at that.'

Having phoned Freda Peters and got her permission, Danny beetled down to see his friend. 'Thank God you're all right. You'd better take things easy from now on.'

'Yes. And I shall make sure he does just that,' said Freda, 'which is exactly why I'm limiting this visit to ten minutes and no more. And no talking about the club either. You can tell him about your trip, Danny.'

'Aye! It would do you a power of good, would Ireland. You know, there's one thing I'd forgotten about Ireland.'

'What?'

'Well it's got that air of relaxation. As soon as you get over there, you find that life goes on at a much slower pace. You do feel far better than what you do, here in England, rushing about all over the place. Nothing changes. There was a fella with a fiddle. He was singing my daddy's favourite song. There were tears in my eyes like October cabbages.'

'So would you go and live over there?'

'Like a shot but Connie wouldn't. She's got that bloody boarding house to look after and now Sylvia and George are talking about retiring and putting it in her name. She'll be taking over the reins and she'll be wanting me to help.'

'Good job you've got your boys down at Bloomfield Road then.'

Freda came bustling in. 'Right! That's it! I was just passing the door and I heard those words, Bloomfield Road. Off you go Danny.'

'But I haven't told Danny about that new Director.'

'Too bad. It can wait till you're better. Someone else can tell him.'

It was a real pity that Freda put the block on John telling Danny about the new Director because he popped in to see Danny the following day.

'Well! Well! Well! So this is where you've been hiding for the last ten years.' Billy Battle was jubilant.

'What the bloody hell? What the hell are you doing here?'

'I'm one of the new Directors now, so watch your language.'

Danny ignored the jibe. 'How the bloody hell can you be a Director?'

'Because I bought a pile of shares and wormed my way in while you were cavorting round that precious emerald isle of yours. I've been looking for you all these years and now I've found you.'

'How the bloody hell did you find me?'

'By reading all those very interesting newspaper articles about you: the ones about that midget friend of yours. The ones in the Daily Mail were particularly informative.'

'How long have you been here?'

'Long enough! I've bought some shares in the club and I've informed the new chairman about your dirty tricks and all those illegal scams of yours. They were particularly interested to hear about them Steel Drops which, by the way, I managed to get analysed.'

'What d'ya mean? Analysed? You dropped that bottle. I saw it smash.'

'Well, now! Guess what? I managed to soak up some, off the platform, with my hanky. I asked the woman in the cafeteria for a plastic cup. Then I squeezed the hanky into the cup. D'you know something, McCoy? They only need the tiniest of drops at those fancy labs. Minuscule in fact! My God! You should have seen the lab report. It was horrendous. It was like a shopping list for ICI. And of course I made photostats. Twenty in fact. More than enough for the Board Meeting, this afternoon. This time you're finished, McCoy. I've waited for this for so long. It's been my life's ambition to bring you down.'

Danny was too tired to argue. Nipper's death had left him drained. He knew his time at Blackpool Football Club had come to an end. 'You're a bastard! They'll regret letting you on the Board. This will be the start of Blackpool's decline. In five years time you'll be down in the Fourth Division.'

'Well, don't bother about what happens to the club. Worry about yourself because your days here are numbered. In fact, when all this gets into the papers, nobody in sport, any sport, in fact, will want your services. This is it, McCoy. Your future is very bleak from now on. You're gazing down into the abyss, all right.'

Left on his own, Danny packed up his personal gear and wrote out a letter of resignation. By the time he was ready to leave

Bloomfield Road for the last time, the Board was already meeting. He opened the door and marched in. He flung the envelope down on the table. 'Here you are! My resignation! Find another resident physiotherapist. There's no way I'm working for a club with a loser like him on the Board of Directors. He'll bring this club nothing but bad luck. When you get demoted you just remember I told you what would happen.' He stomped back out with his head held high. But as he drove out of the car park, Danny knew he'd lost everything. He could still see the look of triumph on Billy Battle's face. He knew that look would haunt him forever.

'You what? What d'you mean? You've quit the job?' Connie was bewildered. 'Listen to me Danny. You will get over Nipper's death. He wouldn't have wanted you to do this.'

'It's got nowt to do with Nipper. That bastard Billy Battle's turned up again.'

'Billy Battle! Billy Battle! What the hell d'you mean? Billy Battle's turned up? Turned up where?'

'At Blackpool Football Club. He's one of the new Directors.'

'What on earth are you talking about? How can he be a Director?'

'He's bought a pile of shares, pulled some strings and got himself invited onto the Board. That's how.'

'But why would he want shares in Blackpool Football Club? He lives in Derby!'

'So he can get at me. Anyway, he's living here now.'

'But how on earth did he find you?'

'He saw that newspaper report in the Daily Mail about…'

'What report?'

Danny was weary of getting the third degree. 'The one about Nipper's death. I told you about it at the time,' he replied, tersely. 'The one about that boxing tournament.'

'I can't believe it. Are you seriously suggesting that an inspector of the British Boxing Board of Control has come all the way to Blackpool, bought a house, bought some shares and got himself on the Board just so he can have some sort of influence over you?'

'That's about the size of it. Yeah!'

'But what about his job?'

'He must have left or retired. I didn't stop long enough to find out. I just wrote out my resignation letter, packed my bags and left.'

'Are you sure it isn't just a coincidence?'

'Nope! He actually told me that he'd come to Blackpool so he could let them Directors know all about the scams I've been involved in.'

'What scams?'

'Just scams. You don't want to know.'

'Well! That's just it, Danny McCoy! I do want to know and I'm no longer that innocent twenty-three-year-old that you was courting. So you can stop telling me lies and you can forget all that "you don't want to know" stuff and you can tell me the truth for once. I want to know what he's got on you and how it's going to affect me and the kids.'

'It ain't goin' to affect you an' the kids because I've left.'

'I see! So who's going to be putting food on the table and paying for the kids…'

'For goodness sake stop moaning. I'm going to get another job.'

'What? Where? At your age? I'll tell you what! You can forget going back into boxing. And you can also forget about leaving Blackpool.'

'You've never liked Blackpool. You didn't want to come in the first place.'

'That was before my mam and dad came to live here. We're all nicely settled now. I'm not moving the children: not so close to their exams. So if you want a job you can get yourself down to the Briardene and help me run it.'

'Not bloody likely!'

'Well you can't sit at home doing nothing all day.'

'I'm not going to be sitting at home. I'm going to set up on my own.'

'What? How? How the hell can you set up as a football physiotherapist? You thinking of buying a football club?'

Connie could be extremely sarcastic when she was riled and Danny wished he'd not said anything about setting up. The idea had just popped into his head and he hadn't the foggiest idea how he was going to set up on his own. But the more he thought about it, the more he liked the idea.

'Come on! How?'

'I'm not just a football physiotherapist. I've been treating all them famous people. They've been coming to me from all the stage shows.'

'From all the stage shows? What d'you mean? Have you been using the facilities down at Blackpool Football Club to line your pockets?'

'No! I haven't! I've never charged anyone a penny.'

'You've not resigned at all!' Connie's voice was getting louder. 'I know exactly what's happened. Billy Battle's found out you've been using the club to treat your own private patients and he's sacked you.'

'That's absolute rubbish. You can ask John Peters. I've had his blessing to treat all them stars. In fact, it was his idea. It's supposed to be a bit of goodwill to all the stars from the summer shows. It all started with Rico Chico. Anyway, I'm not arguing with you. I'm going out.'

'Where are you going?' Connie screamed after him.

He turned round in the doorway. 'I'm going to find myself some rooms in town.'

'Well when you find them, you can take your bed down there, an' all!'

'Listen Danny. I'm dead sure I can help you out.' The two men were sitting in a little coffee bar in Church Street. 'There's some first-floor offices in King Street. They've got a notice up in the windows.

OFFICE SPACE TO LEASE.

'I know the landlord. I'll have a word with him and see what he wants to charge you.' The accountant rattled on.

Danny was thinking about his proposal.

'By the way, I told you that the "Stardust Gardens" would be a blinding success, didn't I? We had a fantastic opening night. You should have come along. I sent you and the wife a couple of invitations. I think you must have been away.'

It's all very well, thought Danny, to himself, saying something is a blinding success when all the seats are free. It still remained to be seen if holidaymakers would pay to get in. However, in view of the fact that he was quite interested in Brian Thompson's proposal, he refrained from voicing his opinion on The Stardust Gardens.

So here he was: sitting in his new office with the afternoon sun streaming through the window, catching the small crystal pyramid on his desk: a little present from one of his footballers. "Here, you can use this as a paper weight for all those notes you'll be making about your private patients," George had joked. At least he was out of Connie's clutches. She'd hinted that there were a lot of odd jobs that needed doing down at the Briardene but he'd ignored all her pointed remarks. He had a quick peep in his diary. He'd got a bloke called Billy Dainty coming at four o'clock. He was quite a well-known comedian and the stage manager of the ABC had phoned Danny, that morning.

'Can you fit him in about four o'clock? Then, after you've treated him, all he has to do is nip across the road into that stage door. He'll be in plenty of time for the First House.'

'What's wrong with him?'

'His feet are playing him up.'

That figures, thought Danny. Billy Dainty had an act that involved walking about like a penguin. It was likely he was suffering from flat feet.

Billy was right on time. 'My feet are giving me hell. I just hope you can help me.'

'Well, I'll see what I can do. I'll give them some ultrasound but really you'd be better with some special exercises. I want you to practise walking on the outer edge of your feet. You'll have to hold onto a table until you get the hang of it. You need to strengthen the ligaments in those feet. If I were you, I'd lock the dressing room door while you do it because if anyone sees you, they'll think you've gone barmy.' He waited for Billy to stop laughing and then he said to him, 'I want you here, every afternoon for treatment. And between houses you can sit with your feet in a bowl of hot water and Epsom Salts.'

The summer passed so quickly, Danny didn't seem to have a moment to spare. Word spread like wildfire. Blackpool Football Club's physiotherapist was in King Street. There were hundreds of people coming to see him. People from the summer season shows. Dancers, ice skaters, trapeze artistes, clowns, jugglers, even a double-base player with a stomach strain. Then there were the men and women from the world of sport. Swimmers, runners, cricketers, snooker players but no footballers. There was a big surprise in the shape of an American baseball player, whose team was giving an exhibition in Blackpool. But the most important people as far as Danny was concerned were the folk who were the backbone of Blackpool. People who worked behind the scenes: keeping the razzle dazzle wheels of fortune turning, like the joiner from the South Pier.

'I've just had to put a notice up. Did you see the Evening Gazette, last night?'

'No! Why?'

'Someone's stolen Gypsy Petulengro's crystal ball.'

'Never!'

'Yes! It's right! I'm telling you. That's why I've had to knock up a notice for her and I've nailed it to her door. Closed due to unforeseen circumstances. What's funny about that? What you laughing for?'

'Well! You bloody fool! You'll have to do another one. How can you put that on the door of a gypsy when she's supposed to be able to see into the future?'

Soon it was winter: the first winter without his boys. Some of them had been to see him. 'We can't come to you for treatment. That bastard Billy Battle has put you off-limits.

Honestly Danny! It's like a concentration camp down there. Can't you come back?'

'No lads. I'm sorry. I'm far too busy with my new clients. You'll be all right. You've got a new physio, haven't you?'

'Yes. But he's not like you, Danny. He's awful.'

'What's wrong with him? He's got plenty of qualifications, hasn't he?'

'Yes but he doesn't tell us any funny stories. It's awful. We're so depressed.'

'Well I'm very sorry, boys. I can't give you any treatment. Even if I had time, it wouldn't be allowed. You must know that. But if you are getting depressed like you say you are, you can always pop up here for a chat. He can't stop you coming to see me.'

What he'd told them was true. Even though it was winter and the theatres were closed, there were still plenty of people coming to him and they were coming from all walks of life. Connie had had to resign herself to the fact that she was going to have to run the Briardene on her own. So just before Easter, she started taking on staff.

Shortly after Easter, Danny got a long-distance phone call. 'Hello! Hello! Who is it?'

'It's me, Danny. It's Paddy. I'm calling all the way from Leitrim.'

Paddy McCoy! Calling all the way from Leitrim! 'What's wrong, Paddy? Is someone ill?'

'No. Don't be worrying yourself, Danny. Everybody's all right. It's not the family I'm phoning about. It's about one of my boxers: the one who won that Gold at the Commonwealth Games. By the way, thanks for the telegram.'

287

'Mick Maguire! What's wrong wi' him?'

'He's damaged his left hand. He's been resting and I've done everything I can think of but it's getting worse. We were hoping for Gold at next year's Olympics but it's looking like the end of the road for him.'

'Right. Don't worry. Just put him on the next plane to Squire's Gate. Let me know what flight he's on. I'll check the landing time and I'll be there to pick him up. Now I don't want you to worry about a thing. I'll look after him while he's here and I've got that friend at Preston Royal Infirmary who'll take a look at his hand and then he'll advise me what to do. We'll have him better for those Olympics, don't you worry.'

As soon as he found out what flight Mick Maguire would be on, Danny rang Mr Stern. His secretary answered. Danny explained the problem and told her he was picking Mick up at Blackpool Airport in four day's time.

'We have a two-thirty appointment free, a week on Wednesday at Moor Park. If you bring him over, Mr Stern will see him then.'

Good, thought Danny, after he'd replaced the receiver. Now that's sorted, there's time for a cup of coffee before my next patient. He was just putting the cup on his desk when the phone rang.

It was Connie. 'Hello! Danny? Is that you?'

'Who else would it be answering my phone?'

She ignored the sarcasm. 'I just want to know if you're planning on coming home for tea at a respectable hour?'

'Why?'

'Because I want to talk to you about something and if you're not coming home for tea, I'll come down to King Street.'

Danny could hear a determined note in his wife's voice, which meant she had a bee in her bonnet about something. At least it wouldn't be about a holiday, not between Easter and Whitsuntide, so he knew he was safe. 'Ok. Don't worry. I'll be home at six.'

She was waiting for him.

Danny hung up his jacket in the hall. 'So what's the matter now?'

'Nothing's the matter. I just need to speak to you, that's all. Go and sit down. I've laid the table already. I'll pass the food through the hatch.'

'I'll just go and swill my hands.' Danny trundled off into the downstairs cloakroom. Her and her bloody serving hatch, he thought. Connie'd had a serving hatch built. Danny had argued that it was a waste of money.

'It is not a waste of money. We've got one down at the Briardene and it's a boon.'

'This isn't the Briardene. It's a bloody house not an hotel.' But he might as well have saved his breath because he came home a few days later, to a dining room filled with dust and a big hole in the wall.

'Where are the kids?' Danny asked.

She passed some dishes through the hatch. 'Michael and Patrick are upstairs doing their homework. Bridget has a rehearsal for the school play and then she's going to tea at Mary's'

Mary McAvoy was Bridget's best friend.

'Daniel and Jack are playing in the garden. I gave them tea early.'

Can't be anything riveting, thought Danny, because if it was, the kids would be here hanging on every word. 'So what d'ya want to talk about?'

'Hang on till I'm sitting down.' Connie came through into the dining room and sat down. 'I want us to sell this house.'

'Bloody hell!' Danny blurted out. This was a bombshell, all right. 'What the hell d'ya want to sell the house for? Don't tell me! That bloody boarding house has finally gone bust. I can't believe it!'

'Don't be ridiculous. The Briardene is making us a fortune. In fact, I could go as far as to say, we could even do without your money coming in but don't get any ideas.'

'So what's your problem?'

'Time! That's my problem. Time and the lack of it. I'm fed up of dashing back and forth to South Shore. It's wearing me out.'

'Oh no! We're not living in a boarding house.'

'I wasn't going to suggest living down at the Briardene, you stupid idiot. There isn't room for us. There was barely room for Mam and Dad at the height of the season, when they were fully booked.'

'Good. Then in that case you can live there on your own and me and the kids'll stay here. We like it here.'

'You never change, do you? If I had my time over again, I wouldn't marry you in a month of Sundays. You are such a bastard, Danny McCoy.'

'Oh aye! Well if I remember correctly, it were you that chased me.'

'You didn't run very fast.'

'Only because you blackmailed me into marrying you.'

'Blackmailed? What the hell d'you mean? Blackmailed?'

'You said your father would let me use the ballroom if we...'

'Oh! For Goodness sake! Don't keep pulling that old chestnut out of the fire. I know very well and so do you; Father Murphy had some rooms at the church you could have used. You could have got out of marrying me if you'd wanted to. Anyway, forget all that. Just shut up and listen to what I've decided. I don't want any arguments. We're selling this house and the land, which will make us more than enough to buy a nice house down South Shore, as near as possible to the Briardene.'

'What about the kids' schools? It's not that long since you said you didn't want them to change schools so near to the exams.'

'That won't be a problem. They can stay at the same schools. If we're both tied up and there's no one to take them to school, we'll use a taxi firm. At least all their schools are close together. Anyway, it won't be long before the boys are at university and by then Bridget might be at a teacher's training college and...'

'Give over. You'll never persuade our Katie to be a teacher. You're wasting your time trying. She'll only do what she wants to do.'

'We'll see! Like I was saying, Jack will soon be at St Joseph's with Daniel. It will work out very nicely.'

'You've got it all planned, I see. Never mind what I want.'

'Well, there is something else. Me and the kids need a fresh start. We need a new house. This place is full of memories. We all miss Nipper, the kids especially. Seeing that flat all closed up is bad for them. It's all right for you. You've got a new job and new surroundings. But it's different for me and the kids. It'll do us all good to move to a new house and we can be

291

nearer my Mam and Dad.' George and Sylvia had bought a little bungalow out on Marton Moss.

'We won't be any nearer to them at all. Going from here, you've only got to drive through Staining and up that hill and you're virtually there. If we live down South Shore, you'll have a load of traffic to contend with all the way along Lytham Road or St Anne's Road; whichever way you go.'

'For goodness sake, stop throwing a spanner in the works. You know I'm right so either you get involved with the choosing of a new house or you can resign yourself to moving into the one I choose.'

Danny could see she was determined. Maybe she was right about the memories. That's just what it had been like at Bloomfield Road. He had to admit, he felt much better now he was working from his new rooms in the town centre. Maybe he wasn't being fair to her and the kids.

'So what do you say, Danny?'

'Ok. Do what you want. I'll go along with anything you choose as long as there's plenty of room for all of us. I want a room for each of the kids.'

'The boys won't like that.'

'Well, they can still bunk together, if that's what they want. And so can Daniel and Jack but I want the rooms readily available in case they do want them. Once they get to university, they might need peace and quiet to study during the holidays. By the way, our Paddy's sending a boxer over for...'

'Oh no! No! No! You're not getting involved in that boxing...'

'For God's sake. If only you'd listen to a full sentence instead of going off half-cocked. I've got no intention of going back into boxing. Paddy's sending him over for some treatment. I've got to pick him up at Squire's Gate Airport on

Friday. I've found a nice little billet for him, close to my rooms. I'll be taking him over to see Mr Stern the following Wednesday.'

The next day he got home from work just in time to see the estate agent driving a "FOR SALE" board into the lawn. Bloody hell! She ain't wasted any time, he thought.

'Good! You're home. I've got to go back to the Briardene. I had to ask Doreen to hold the fort because you weren't here to see to the estate agent.'

'You never asked me.'

'And would you have been here for me?'

'Humph!' Danny grunted as he went upstairs.

When Mr Stern examined Mick Maguire's X-rays he shook his head in amazement. 'How long has it been like this?'

'About six months.'

'And you've boxed with it like this?'

'That I have and won, so I have.'

'Well, I can't believe it. What you have here,' he pointed to the X-ray, 'is a sliver of bone floating around.'

'You what? Where from?'

'Well, at some time or other, you must have split a metacarpal bone in this hand. Which hand do you punch with?'

'The right hand.'

'Well, if you'd been a southpaw you wouldn't have been able to fight at all. As it is, I'm very surprised you could fight with this left hand damaged so badly but we know what you boys are like for hiding your pain, don't we, Danny?'

'Dear me!' Danny looked worried. 'Are we going to need an operation?'

'Oh No!' Mick Maguire gasped. 'It'll ruin my career.'

293

Here we go again, thought Danny.

'No! Certainly not. Calm down. I think I can cure this with an injection that will encourage the sliver to knit together with the bone. I can do that now but you're going to need a lot of follow-up physiotherapy.'

'You can leave all that to me, Mr Stern,' said Danny.

So back they went to Blackpool and commenced with the treatment: three times a day. As each day went by, Mick said he could feel his left hand getting stronger and stronger. Soon there wasn't any pain there at all. Three weeks after the injection, Danny decided to let him try it out. He had a speedball in the office that had been presented to him by a boxer called Kid Gavilan. He held it up and told Mick to throw a few punches at it. Being mindful of what had happened with Paddy McCoy and the punchbag, he told Mick to take it easy.

RAT-A-TAT-TAT! RAT-A-TAT-TAT!
RAT-A-TAT-TAT!

'That'll do nicely Mick.'

'God love us. This left hand feels stronger than me right hand now,' gasped Mick. 'You've done wonders. Paddy told us how good you were but he never told us what a good storyteller you were. D'you know Danny? I don't want to go back home. I've loved every minute of being in your company. Sure an' you must have kissed the Blarney Stone itself.'

'Sure an' I never needed help from that old stone. All my stories are true. All I have to do is remember how it was.'

'An' do you remember everything: even about Ireland?'

'Everything,' said Danny, firmly, 'and especially about my childhood in Ireland. It was like Paradise. It was idyllic. I used to run about like a wild pony. I told all my boys about it: my boxers and my footballers. I had a lovely time. People were

294

always so warm and friendly. Oh aye, Mick. I might have been born in Sheffield and spent most of my time over here but it's Ireland that fills my thoughts. Ireland was all my childhood dreams come true. I remember it as if it were yesterday.'

CHAPTER TWENTY-NINE

It took Connie till 1972 to find a large rambling house on Windermere Road.

It had six bedrooms, two bathrooms and it took her five minutes to get to the Briardene. Danny was very surprised when she said she'd decided to employ a married couple to act as managers.

'How the hell do you expect to make a profit?'

'I'm taking over the property next door. It's up for sale and I've put an offer in. Mam thinks it's a brilliant idea. We'll be knocking the two boarding houses into one.'

'You never mentioned it to me.'

'I didn't have time and I didn't think you'd be interested. I only found out it was going up for sale yesterday and I thought I'd make an offer before it was advertised. The owner, Jean Piper, was delighted. It will save her a lot in estate agent's fees. But I'll tell you this much; I'm not going to be slaving away till my dying day down there. Another ten years and I'm selling up and retiring. I'll be fifty-two by then and I'll have had enough.'

Danny had a bit further to drive to King Street each day. It was a bit of a drag having to negotiate the maze of streets from South Shore to his office but if it kept Connie happy, he'd put up with it. He usually took the kids to school first and then he'd drive into town and try and find a parking space. It was always harder in summer but summer had its compensations. For one thing the summer season shows brought more interesting patients to King Street.

The summer of 1972 brought Danny one of his most celebrated clients when Frankie Vaughan climbed wearily up the stairs to Danny's office. 'Come in and welcome. What can I do for you? How can I help you? Do sit down and rest your weary feet.'

'It's not my feet that hurt. It's my hand.'

'Well that's a bad do when you've got to throw that cane around every night. So tell me what's wrong. By the way, how did you get to know about me?'

'It was one of the stagehands that told me about you. I must have looked in pain when I came off stage, because he asked me if I was all right. I told him I wasn't. I'm in agony. It's when I throw that cane from hand to hand that it hurts.'

'Is it only the one hand that's bothering you?'

'Yes.'

'That's a bit strange. It can't be the cane that's causing it, then.'

'Do you think it could be my fishing that's causing it? I'm absolutely mad about fly fishing and I cast with this hand.'

'That sounds about right.' Danny examined both hands. 'I'll give you some ultrasound but I'd also like you to go and see a friend of mine out at Preston.' While Frankie had his wrist under the heat lamp, Danny phoned Mr Stern and made an appointment. 'I told Mr Stern you've got a show every night so he said he'd see you at Preston Royal Infirmary tomorrow morning.'

A couple of days later, Frankie Vaughan came bounding up the stairs and burst into the office. 'Danny! I can't believe it! This hand is much better. Your friend gave me an injection and he said you've to follow up with some heat and ultrasound. Says I should have no more trouble with it.'

'Good. I'm very pleased. You found the hospital all right?'

'Yes, it was easy with that map you drew and my wife drove me. By the way, I caused a bit of a commotion.'

'Why was that?'

'Well, we were sitting in the waiting room and it was packed. One of the doors opened and a hospital porter came out. As soon as he spotted me, he called out to me and then he went straight into my dance routine. He was singing my song: you know the one. Gimme the moonlight and all that jazz. Well! Laugh! The place was in chaos. Mind you, he was good. He did the whole song, word for word. The only thing missing was the stick. I told my wife to get his name and address. I can get him to stand in for me if ever I'm sick. Anyway, when he finished, everyone gave him a standing ovation. And then your friend suddenly popped his head out of the door to see what was going on. Luckily he saw me and started laughing, thank God.'

'I'm not surprised. He's got a wonderful sense of humour. Now I'll get going with your treatment and while I'm treating you I'll tell you about my time as a physiotherapist to Blackpool Football Club. There was one time when I had another song and dance man like you to treat and he came to the club...'

Frankie had just gone when there were more footsteps on the stairs. 'Good God! What a surprise to see you after all this time. Should you have walked up all those stairs? You'd better sit down straight away.'

It was John Peters. 'Yes. Well! I've been meaning to come and see you for ages but I was waiting for the doctors to give me the all clear for climbing stairs.'

'Oh aye! I heard you'd bought a bungalow out at Wrea Green.'

'Aye and that's the other problem. I've been waiting to cadge a lift off the wife but she's been too busy. She's in this amateur operatic company and they're always practising for something or other. Anyway, I had to come and see you urgently so I've come in a taxi. Got some news. Didn't want to tell you on the phone.'

'Bad news is it?'

'Depends on how you look at it. Remember that Director that had it in for you: the one from your neck of the woods? Billy Battle?'

'Aye. What's he been up to now?'

'Well, nothing, actually. He's gone and resigned, right out of the blue. There's an ugly rumour going round that he's in hospital with something serious.'

'Oh dear! Is the rumour true?'

'Well I don't know. I thought I might nip up to Victoria Hospital and see what I can find out. I've been round to his house but there's no one there. I know he lived on his own.'

'Don't you go bothering yourself. You'll make yourself ill again if you go worrying about someone else's problem. I'll go up to the hospital and find out what's happened. Leave it with me. I'll let you know what I find out. In the meantime, can I offer you a cup of tea?'

Danny hated hospitals. He followed the nurse down the corridor. There were only six patients and every one except Billy had a visitor or two. 'Now then Billy, you've got a visitor.' The nurse pulled some screens around them. 'It'll give you a bit of privacy.'

Sounded like Billy was bad. Danny sat down.

'You come to gloat, have you, McCoy?'

'Nope! Just come to give you these.' He chucked the brown paper bag, containing the obligatory grapes, onto the bedcovers.

'Well you can creep back into that job now. The one they've got is useless. He doesn't have a clue. You must have heard.'

'I don't want my old job back, Billy. I've got enough to do, down at King Street. In fact, you did me a favour.'

'Aye! I'll bet. You could always fall in a pile of horse shit and come up smelling of roses, McCoy. I'll tell you summat: I've always envied you. You've got it all and I don't mean money. You've got a beautiful wife, five lovely kids, a good job and every bugger you talk to has nothing but good to say about you an' what a miracle worker you are. You don't know how lucky you are.'

Danny was flabbergasted. Coming from Billy, well, it made him think. Me! Lucky! Well maybe he's right. But there was something else puzzling him. 'Why didn't you tell the newspapers about them Steel Drops Billy?'

'Dunno! When it came down to it I realised all the fun had gone out of it. You know. What they call the thrill of the chase. And those snotty-nosed Directors were a bit too po-faced for my liking. They always thought they were better than a bloke like me from Derbyshire. So in the end, I decided not to give them any more ammunition by involving the media. Anyway, it's all water under the bridge, ain't it? So you can go now: now that you've seen I'm at death's door.'

'I didn't come to gloat. I came to see if you want me to do anything for you.'

'Why the hell would you want to do owt for me after what I did to you?'

'You never did me any real harm, like you said, Billy, I've come through all right. In fact, I dare say you kept me on my toes. Anyway, like you've just said, it's all water under the bridge. There ain't many of us left now. Nipper's gone and so have my parents. Even my sisters have gone, bless 'em. Father Murphy's dead. My Uncle Frankie's dead and so are all my uncles in Ireland. I guess I'm feeling morose. Blimey! I came to cheer you up and listen to me. What I'm trying to say is, life's too short for bearing grudges so let's bury the hatchet. Come on Billy. There must be summat I can do.'

'Well, if you put it like that: there is summat needs doing. I've got a niece living in Clay Cross. She'll need to be told so she can arrange the funeral.'

'Now then, Billy. Let's not talk about funerals. You're in here to get better.'

Billy Battle stared at him in disgust. 'Oh come off it, McCoy! Let's not pussyfoot around. I've been told I've got cancer and I've only got a few months to live. If you really want to help me you'll help me sort out my affairs so I can die in peace. I've been lying here, worried sick, in case our Muriel finds out I'm ill. I don't want her sitting by my bedside. She's a nice young woman but she's had too much illness in her own life. She insisted on nursing her mother and father. I told her at the time to put 'em in a home. My brother went senile and then to cap it all, just before he died, my sister-in-law had a stroke.

301

Muriel gave up work and looked after both of them. My sister lingered on for ten years. It was a terrible burden for Muriel.

'Ok! Ok! Stop worrying. I'll do whatever you want.'

'Here. Take my keys. They're in the locker. Let yourself in the house. Give us a bit of paper.' He wrote his address on and his niece's address. 'Listen. Make sure she doesn't come to the funeral. Get it done as cheap as possible. Right?'

'No Billy. It's not right.'

'What d'ya mean? It's not right? What's not right about it? I've never been religious. I don't need a fancy church service.'

'You can't have a cheap little funeral: not when you're a Director of Blackpool Football Club.'

'Ex-director. Anyway, I can't afford a big do and there won't be anybody there.'

'What d'ya mean? You can't afford it? What about your shares in the club?'

'Not worth the paper they're written on. You must know that.'

'What about your house?'

'Mortgaged up to the hilt. Had to get a second mortgage.'

'What the bloody hell did you do that for?'

'To pay the bills and put food in my mouth. See what revenge does for you, McCoy? Serves me right. Reaping my just deserts now, ain't I? So you can forget a flashy funeral. I've got a little put by, in a suitcase under the bed. But it's only just enough for the funeral. They'll be nowt left for Muriel.'

'You leave everything to me Billy. I'll arrange a decent funeral and I'll get all them Directors there and my boys as well. I'll see to it that everyone from Bloomfield Road turns out, don't you worry. We'll give you a good send off. Your Muriel will be proud of you.'

'Haven't you listened to a bloody word I've said. I can't afford it.'

'Forget it Billy. I'm paying the lot. I'll do it whether you like it or not and when you're dead and gone you won't be able to stop me so you might as well accept the offer and then you can choose one or two hymns and stuff.'

'Ok, I give in,' Billy sighed. And then he brightened up a bit and said, 'Go on, McCoy, tell me about them boxers from the South Pacific.'

'What d'ya want to know, Billy?'

'Rumour has it that you paid for them to come over from Tonga.'

'Aye! And I paid for them to go back, an' all.'

'Why did you do that? They got plenty of purse money and all that?'

'You're quite right and I made sure they stashed it all away in bank accounts an' all. But I knew when them young boys were thirty, they'd be past it and then they'd need that money more than I would'

'Them Steel Drops: you get 'em from your Uncle Frankie, did you?'

'Aye. That stuff wasn't banned in the States, y'know. And it wasn't the worst thing I could have used. It wasn't like taking drugs, y'know. In fact, I'd have got the same result if I'd used a bloody big lump of ice.'

After he left Billy, Danny organised a transfer to a private nursing home where he knew Billy would be more comfortable then he re-scheduled all his appointments so he could close up at three o'clock everyday.

303

When he got back home he told Connie his new working hours '…and don't ask me to pick the kids up just because I'm packing up early. I've got to visit someone in hospital. He's not going to be coming back out.'

Connie didn't argue because she could see by his face that it wasn't just one of his excuses. 'Who's ill?'

'One of my patients. He's got cancer. He's got no one to visit him so I thought I'd nip up there every afternoon. Got special permission from the Matron to pop in any time I want. Anyway, don't worry. He's only got a few months so I won't be doing it for long.'

'Don't be so crass, Danny. I thought you knew me better than that. I would never grumble about you visiting someone in those circumstances.'

'Aye! Right! Sorry!' Danny mumbled.

One day, a few months later, the matron met him at the door of the nursing home. Danny could see she had bad news.

'…and he asked me to write this letter to you.' She gave him the envelope. 'Would you like to see him?'

'Aye. All right.'

'Well, come with me. We've got a little sitting room where you can have a quiet few minutes. I'll come and collect you when he's ready.'

Danny sat down. It was a pretty little room with a gentle melody playing in the background. He opened the letter. 'Thanks for everything, Danny. Sorry I gave you such a hard time. You're a good man. You have a heart of gold. You won't ever be forgotten. You'll go down in history.'

Danny organised the funeral for the following Friday. Then he spent Sunday phoning all the Directors, past and present, making sure they would be at the funeral. His footballers were eager to help him out and so were men like John Peters, Bob Singleton, Des and Paddy. But he had to threaten a few of the Directors. 'It won't look good in the Daily Mail, all that stuff about how you…'

'Can you take a day off, next Friday?'

'Where are we going?'

'To a funeral.'

'Who's died?' Then Connie remembered. 'Is this the patient you've been visiting?'

'Aye but he ain't a patient. It was Billy Battle I was visiting.'

Connie looked worried as she asked, hesitantly, 'Is this some sort of celebration?'

'Like you said to me a few weeks back, I thought you knew me better. We're just going to pay our respects to an old adversary.'

There were thirty-five, give or take, at the funeral. 'I didn't know Uncle Bill had so many friends. And some of them are footballers, aren't they?'

'Oh yes, Miss Battle. He was very well liked.'

Connie stared at him in astonished silence but for once she had the good sense to keep her mouth shut, until they got in the car. 'You got all them Directors and footballers to come today, didn't you?'

'Aye. Most of 'em were ok about it but I had to twist a few arms.' He told her what some of them had been up to in the past. Laughing about it cheered them up on the drive home from Layton Crematorium. But what he didn't tell her was who had paid for Billy's nursing home fees and his funeral.

He felt very depressed the following Monday but he still had to go in and open up. He'd got no one booked in and he was sitting with his back to the door, staring out of the window, watching the traffic buzzing up and down. Footsteps echoed on the stairs. Good! Thank God someone was here to relieve the monotony. He spun round in his leather swivel chair. It was the accountant from the Blackpool Tower Company. He looked very glum. 'Hello Brian.'

'Morning Danny. Is it all right if I have a little sit down?'

'Course it is. You in pain again? That back playing up, is it?'

'No. It's behaving itself at this point in time, thanks to your ministrations. No! I'm just feeling fed-up at the moment.'

'Why is that then?'

'We're going to have to close The Stardust Gardens.'

'Oh dear. Why's that?'

'Because it's making a loss. I can't understand it. It was such a fantastic idea but it's half-empty every night. Anyway, how about a coffee? I'll make it, if you like. Personally I could do with a slug of brandy but them pubs aren't open yet so I'll have to make do with one of your cups of coffee.'

Danny was glad when the accountant left because he was finding it very difficult to be sympathetic. He felt like bursting into laughter but it wouldn't have been a nice thing to do, to the man who'd found him rooms to rent in Blackpool town centre. He was quite pleased when Frankie Vaughan popped his head round the door.

'Hello Danny. How are you feeling this morning?'

'Not too bad. How's yourself?'

'I'm feeling much better in myself, mainly due to the fact that I'm getting very little pain in this wrist.'

'Excellent. You probably need another couple of weeks of treatment and then you can stop coming.'

'Oh dear. I don't really want to stop coming. I love our little chats about your life in Ireland and your boxers.'

'Well, just because you're better, it doesn't mean you're banned,' said Danny, laughing at him. 'You can pop up for a chat anytime. You know that.' He got him settled under the heat lamp. 'Now did I tell you about them Steel Drops that got me into so much trouble?'

Once Frankie was better he was full of energy. He came flying into the office, one morning. 'Danny! Danny! I thought I'd just come in and tell you about a wonderful place we went to last night. My songwriter and his wife came down to see the show and I took them for fish and chips at a place called The Cottage. Honestly, I've never had a nicer meal. I'm taking the cast there at the end of the season. I always treat them to a meal. Have you heard of it?'

'Well yes as a matter of fact I know it quite well.'

'Well I'd like to take you all out for a meal there as a little thank you for all that you've done for me.'

'You don't need to that, Frankie. You're paying me for my services.'

'Yes I know and I could have paid any old physiotherapist but they wouldn't have done as much for me as you have with all your anecdotes. Anyway, I'd like to meet your wife and kids. Shall we say next Sunday night?

'Well, that's most kind of you. The wife and kids'll be thrilled.' This'll be interesting, he thought to himself.

307

As soon as Connie got home from the Briardene, he told her, '...so he wants to take us all out to dinner. He suggested next Sunday night. Best bib and tucker, love.'

'Oh how nice. Where are we going'

'He didn't tell me, love. Probably wants it to be a surprise.'

The following Sunday night Connie was done up like the dog's dinner and the kids were so spruced up, Danny hardly recognised them.

'You can't go like that, Danny.' Connie was horrified.

'What's wrong wi' me?' He had on a pair of casual slacks with a knitted cardigan over his white shirt.

'Can't you put a suit on?'

'Don't be silly, love. I might spill summat down it.'

'Well can't you at least put a tie on?'

'What? And choke mesel' to death over the table.'

They had a wonderful time but Connie let him have a real mouthful as soon as they got in the car. 'You knew we were going to that fish and chip shop, didn't you. You pig!'

When Danny eventually gave Frankie his bill for all the treatment he'd had, Frankie nearly hit the roof. 'This can't possibly be right.'

'Oh dear. I'm sorry. I must have added it up wrong.'

'No! No! It's not the additions: it's the hourly rate that's wrong.'

'Oh dear. A bit high, is it?'

'Don't be ridiculous. It's far too low. You can't possibly be making enough.'

'I'm doing quite nicely, Frankie. Anyway, I'm not here to make a packet out of people's misfortune.'

'Well, I'm going to triple this hourly rate and there's no arguing. Put this in the bank for a rainy day.' He pressed a wad of notes into Danny's hand.

Danny felt a bit embarrassed at accepting so much money but he could see by the look on Frankie's face that he had no choice. 'Well, thank you very much. Now don't forget, you can pop in for a chat any time you're passing. You don't need an excuse.'

It wasn't long after Frankie's visit that Danny was further rewarded for all his hard work when Mick Maguire got a gold medal at the Olympic Games.

CHAPTER THIRTY

'D'ya know summat, Ashley, it's a well-researched fact, the older you get, the quicker the years pass.'

Ashley Mitchell laughed at Danny's revelation. 'You're a comic, Danny. Anyway, how can you say that when you're in the prime of life.'

'Not me. I'm well over the hill.'

'Give over! How old are you?

'How old do you think?'

'Fifty-eight. Give or take a couple of years?'

'Add another ten years onto that. I've been getting my pension for the last three years.'

'You certainly don't look sixty-eight.'

'Well, I'm starting to feel it.'

'How many years have you been here in King Street?'

'Eighteen.'

'Good God! That's unbelievable!' Ashley tried to distract Danny. 'You must have had a good many famous people through your hands.'

'Aye!'

'Anyone stick out?'

'Well, there was Rico Chico and Billy Dainty and Frankie Vaughan. Oh aye. Then there was Rudolf Nureyev. I remember him coming to Blackpool in 1977.'

'You've got a good memory.'

'Only because I came across my old desk diaries the other day. He was over at the Illawalla Country Club, making that film about Rudolph Valentino.'

'That's right. I remember now. They used the Tower Ballroom as well. So how come you got to treat him?'

'He had a slight accident whilst he was filming and one of the stagehands had already been for treatment here so he recommended me. Same as you do with your circus performers. It's all word of mouth. You've sent me a great deal of business yourself over the years.' The phone rang. 'Hang on a minute till I've dealt with this and then we'll have a cuppa.' He picked up the phone. 'Hello! Hello! Danny McCoy. Yes, I see. Well that can be very painful.' He flicked the pages of his diary. 'Now I can see you tomorrow at two o'clock.' He paused. 'Now you mustn't worry about money. I've got special rates for pensioners. The important thing is to get you feeling better.' He put the phone down and saw Ashley's raised eyebrows. 'Poor old lady with a bad back. Can't charge 'em much. They can barely manage on that pittance the government likes to call a pension.'

'How's the family, Danny?'

'All very well. No problems at all.'

Unknown to Danny, his son Michael, who was now an accountant, was sitting a stone's throw away from King Street. He was in the offices of Frost, Briggs & Summerland, in Church Street. After getting an urgent phone call from Ted Briggs, he'd managed to re-schedule his workload and he'd come all the way from his offices, which were in Lytham-St-Annes. And he wasn't best pleased. The traffic had been abysmal due to the crowds attending the Open.

311

'Now I know what I'm about to do is highly irregular. I could probably be voted out of the company so it must remain between you and me. The thing is, I've been worried about your father for the last two years. I've talked to him, every time he's been in here but it seems to have made no difference at all. The fact is, he's about to go bankrupt. He's been in the red at the bank for at least five years and each year he goes a bit further into the red. This year's rates for the half-year haven't been paid and neither have the water rates. I was hoping you could persuade him to retire before people start screaming for a pound of flesh.'

Michael looked up from his father's accounts. 'These are terrible. What's he been doing? Where's all the money going?'

'Well, I suspect he hasn't been charging enough. I've heard on the grapevine that he only charges five pounds an hour. I've also heard that he doesn't charge pensioners if he knows they can't afford to pay.'

'What d'you mean? He doesn't charge them?'

'Just what I say. He doesn't charge them.'

'Nothing?'

'Nothing! Zilch! Not a penny. It's free.'

'He can't do that. It's ridiculous. He's not running a charity shop.'

'Well actually, even charity shops charge.' Ted Briggs grinned, trying to ease the tension a bit. He didn't want to get the old fella into any trouble.

'Yes! Yes! It was just a figure of speech. God! I don't believe this. My mother's been trying to get him to retire for ages. We've got a lovely house down South Shore. He could have his own sitting room with his own TV. He could lounge about watching the television all day.'

312

'Well, that's what he's doing now, basically.'

'What? He's just lounging around?'

'Yes. And he's watching the television.'

'What d'you mean? Watching television? What television?'

'How many times have you been to see him at King Street?'

Michael looked slightly ashamed. 'Well, actually, never.'

'Right, well. Let me put you in the picture. He's surrounded by loads of knick-knacks. He's got a coffee percolator as well as a kettle and a toaster. All presents from grateful clients. And the television he's watching, well, I believe some people from a local insurance company clubbed together to buy him that.'

'So what you're saying is, basically, he's just sitting there all day, watching telly, on his own with no one to see.'

'Oh no! Well, not if his desk diaries are anything to go by. And that's another thing. If the tax man gets his hands on those diaries, he'll never believe the figures.'

'So where's all the money going?'

'Well, there are all the overheads. You know? Things like the rent, rates, water, electricity, phone, cleaner…'

'What! What? He's got a cleaner?' Michael exploded. 'Sorry! Sorry! Didn't mean to shout but what the hell is he doing with a cleaner when he can't afford to pay the rates?'

'Yes well maybe you'd better go and see her. She's called Mrs Fish.' Edward Briggs showed him the address. 'Know where that is?'

'Yes thanks, Ted. I'll go and see her. And thanks for all your concern. I won't breathe a word to anyone how I got all this. I take it I can borrow these accounts?'

'Well it's most irregular but I can't see another way out. As long as you give them back to me personally and in private, please.'

Michael knocked on the door. A neat, elderly lady opened it. He gave her his card but she didn't look at it. 'Mrs Fish?'

'Yes and you would be either Michael or Patrick.'

'How on earth do you know that?'

'I've dusted your photos for the last fifteen years.' A look of alarm crossed her face. 'Nothing's happened to your father, has it?'

'No! No!' Michael hastened to assure her. 'He's fine. I just want to talk to you about something. May I come in?'

She looked down at his card at last. 'Ah! It's Michael. Well, do come in.' She ushered him into the lounge. 'Please sit down.'

He sank into a pale green velvet armchair. He noticed the house was spotless. It was a good advert for a cleaner. 'I think my father will be retiring shortly. I wanted to tell you.'

'So he's decided to go at last.'

'Not quite. I think we may have to force him.'

'Oh dear. Why would you want to do that? He's so happy at King Street.'

'I shouldn't really be telling you this so I would ask you not to repeat it to anyone, including Dad. It appears he's not able to make ends meet. And I think he's rather outlived his usefulness in the field of physiotherapy.'

'Oh no! You mustn't say that. He's got hundreds of clients and he's such a wonderful storyteller. It does everyone a power of good just listening to him. Some of them come to him because they've had no joy at those expensive clinics. You can't cure someone just by putting a new paper towel on the pillow and leaving them on their own, under a heat lamp and I should know. I've had the odd problem with my own back. Anyway, he makes plenty of money out of them stage folk who come to him every summer. Surely he must have something in reserve for when business is slack. Listen, Michael. Please don't make him retire. He would just fade away, sitting at home with no one to talk to. I'm already retired myself. I know what it's like.'

'Then how come…'

'How come I'm still cleaning for your dad? Well, when my back was bad, we came to a little agreement. I clean. He treats my back. The thing is, I really only go to clean so I can sit for a while and listen to his stories and I always feel much better for it.'

It was whilst he was on the way back to the office and stuck in another traffic jam that Michael realised, this was just the chance the family had been waiting for. He'd got the ammunition but how to use it: that was the problem.

His mother would be delighted. She'd been nagging Danny for ages to give up work. Funnily enough, Michael couldn't think why because if his father did give up work, he'd only be at home all day, getting in her hair. Michael had his own suspicions about it. He reckoned his mother had ideas about getting her own back for all the years of neglect: all those anniversaries he'd missed: the births of his children: all the times he hadn't been there for her.

His secretary looked very suspicious when he said he was taking a few days off. 'Listen Susan. I've got some urgent family business to attend to. I'll have a word with Philip and see if he can take over some of my more urgent work. And don't look like that. I am not going to the Open!' Philip

315

Cunningham was one of the partners and he was quite happy to help out.

Michael was back at their old restored farmhouse, on the outskirts of Wrea Green, by lunchtime. His wife, Anne, was amazed to see him. 'I didn't know you were coming home for lunch. You never come home for lunch. This must be the first time ever!'

'I've got some boxes to go through. Family stuff.'

'Family stuff? Whose?'

'Dad's. It's a pile of old accounts he wants me to look at.'

'I thought you didn't do family stuff?'

'I don't. It's bad practice to get involved with one's own family in matters like this but I've got no choice. Listen Anne. If I tell you what it's about I want you to keep quiet about it.'

He told her everything. He wasn't sure he liked her sympathetic looks. Why did everyone want to stick up for his dad? No one had any idea how he'd treated his family. He'd never been there for any of them. It had always been Mum or Nipper who sorted everything out. She always said he thought more about his boys at Bloomfield Road than he did about his own family. 'Keep the kids out of the way, when they come home from school. This lot looks like it will take me till Christmas to sort out.' There were four large boxes, which still had a faint aroma of French Golden Delicious hanging over them and Christmas was months away! Luckily Michael was a fast worker.

But two days later, he was no nearer making a decision but one thing was clear. He now knew who'd paid for Billy Battle's funeral and his nursing home fees and it had taken a huge chunk out of his dad's bank account.

Early the following morning, he went back to Blackpool and parked his car in the car park on the corner of Topping Street and Talbot Road. Then he walked up King Street and found himself a table in the café right opposite Danny's rooms. It was just coming up to nine forty-five. Jack, who had his own sports emporium up Church Street, always gave his father a lift and usually dropped him off at ten o'clock.

By twelve-thirty, the woman behind the counter was looking decidedly suspicious and Michael was feeling quite bloated. He'd had three crumpets, a buttered teacake and six cups of tea. He'd put his Financial Times up to his face on several occasions whenever he saw his dad looking out of his upstairs window. He'd seen a variety of people coming and going. Most were walking normally. One old man went in stumbling a bit. 'I'm just waiting for my wife,' he mumbled as he asked for another cup of tea. By the filthy look the café owner gave him, it was clear she thought he was waiting for someone else's wife!

Good God! He recognised that bloke, easing himself out of a taxi, with help from the driver. In spite of the rain streaming down the windows of the café, he could quite clearly see it was Seve Ballesteros. He knew he was playing at Royal Lytham but it had been rained off today. Well, thank God for the rain because now his secretary would know he wasn't off enjoying himself at the Open. She was a bit of an old dragon. Anyway, it was time to take some action and by the look of Seve

317

Ballesteros, he had plenty of time. He wanted to find out what was going on over there. Was his dad working for free?

He stepped quietly into the downstairs hall. A pungent smell of olive oil hit him and he was back in the gym at the Wellington. He'd only been a little kid but the memories of the smell and the noise were amazingly clear: crystal-clear in fact. It was a weird feeling for the hard-bitten accountant. He leaned against the wall. It was such a shock being transported back in time like that. Those boxers had loved him and his brother. He took a deep breath and sneaked up the stairs. One of the runners creaked and he stopped and held his breath. No one had heard because Danny's latest client was laughing quite loudly.

'…and that's why they called me the eye specialist.'

Michael sat on the top step and listened. He knew everyone of his dad's stories off by heart. He'd heard them often enough over the Christmas turkey. His dad had just finished talking about those bloody Steel Drops. God knows why he's laughing, he thought. It was the use of those that had got him into trouble. If it hadn't been for using those, the BBBC wouldn't have been on his father's back all the time. First he'd had to drop out of the boxing game. Then he'd lost a well-paid job in football. It was probably that illegal substance that had put Danny McCoy into the position he was in today. Bankrupt!

The street door opened and Michael hurried down the stairs as quietly as possible.

'Well! Well! Well! Fancy seeing you here! Good God! You've grown up all right. You don't remember me, do you?'

'Hello! Who's there?' Danny was shouting down the stairs.

Putting a finger to his lips, Michael ducked round the banister.

Ashley Mitchell looked disconcerted but he didn't reply to Danny.

Danny didn't shout again.

Michael slipped outside and the ringmaster followed him. 'Now you're either Patrick or Michael. Never could tell you two apart.'

'As a matter of fact, I do recognise you, Mr Mitchell. And I'm Michael. It's a long time since we used to come and sit on those front seats.'

'Must be fifteen years at least. I was just popping in to see your dad. So what were you doing skulking around on the stairs?'

'It's a long story. I'll tell you over a coffee if you've got time but if you don't mind we'll go to that café in Church Street. I've just spent four hours in that one over there and if I go in again I think the owner will call the police.'

After Michael had talked to the ringmaster he went back to see Edward Briggs. He gave him a very large personal cheque. 'This should pull him back from the brink. But I don't want him to know anything about it. Anything needs paying in future just let me know. Give me that rates demand. I'll nip down to the Town Hall and pay it today. And don't look at me like that. Usually I've got no time for sentimentality in business but let's just say, these last few days have been a revelation as regards my father. I thought I had the opportunity to get him out of King Street and here I am paying the bills so he can stay there.'

'You're doing the right thing.'

'Well, let's hope I can persuade the family it's the right thing to do.'

'You won't have much trouble with your brother, Jack. He adores him.'

When Michael told his mother she looked a bit hurt. 'Do you think he just wants to be down there so he can stay out of my way?'

'Don't be daft, Mum. He's doing it because it's his life and he'd be lost if he couldn't talk about his days in sport to someone. Anyone! You knew when you married him: sport was his whole life. We were only ever second best. He can't help it. He eats and sleeps and breathes sport. I think it's even more important to him than wanting to live in Ireland. If we made him retire, I reckon he'd only last six months. And from what I've seen and heard, he'd be really missed. Half the population of Blackpool is popping in to see him: even those who are fit and healthy. You see, we always thought that using those Steel Drops ruined his life. We blamed them for everything that went wrong. But it wasn't so.'

'But he had to give up boxing because of that stuff.'

'No mum he didn't. He had to give up boxing because that bastard Abe Rosen shafted him. But I reckon Abe Rosen did everyone a favour. If he hadn't come to Blackpool, thousands of people would have been denied his expertise including footballers and show business folk not to mention Joe Public. And let's face it: Blackpool's been good to you, mum.'

Connie stared at her son in astonishment.

'Come on, mum. You know it's true and by the way, guess who paid for Billy Battle's funeral?'

'Not your father?'

'Yes. And not only his funeral. Dad also paid his nursing home fees and that wasn't any old nursing home he was in. That was a first rate one and it wasn't cheap. I know I've never really been close to Dad. It's taken a long time to see the real man behind all the schemes and scams. These last few days have opened my eyes and I'm finding I'm really proud to be his son. I just hope that after he's gone, everyone who's passed through his hands remembers him.'

EPILOGUE

Danny looked in his desk diary. Good! One last appointment for today and if the footsteps coming slowly up the stairs indicated, his next patient was already here. 'Take your time on those stairs.'

When she finally walked into the office she looked exhausted. 'Hello Danny. Thank God I've made it. I'm in such pain.'

'Now don't you worry. I'll soon have that back feeling better. Just go through. Get undressed and get on that couch. A nice bit of heat and ultrasound will soon get rid of all that tension. And while you're lying there I'll tell you what my boys did when they found out I was using that rubber suit.'

'How's that dancer you were treating last week?'

'She's just about ready to dance and she's already flown out to North Africa with her dancing troupe. She's not absolutely one hundred per cent but she'll be all the better for a little bit of sun on her back.'

'Honestly Danny. You do make me laugh. You sound just like you're talking about a racehorse."

Danny grinned. 'Well it's all much the same to me. Horses, greyhounds, showgirls. They all need the same sort of treatment. Bit of heat. Bit of ultrasound. Bit of a massage.'

Half an hour later, his patient was getting dressed. 'I feel heaps better Danny. I felt really depressed when I arrived but your tales have cheered me up no end. I've been thinking. Is it all right if I bring my tape recorder tomorrow? I'd like to record some of your stories.'

'Well, I wasn't expecting you as soon as tomorrow. You shouldn't have too much ultrasound all at once. I've put you down for next week. Same time, same day.'

'Well, if it's all right by you I might come tomorrow just to do some recording. I could sit in your office and we could talk. I can be resting at the same time. Is that ok?'

'Mmm! I don't mind if you do but why d'ya want to tape my stories?'

'Because if someone doesn't write them all down, it's like you would say; they'll be lost in the mists of time. So if I get them down on tape I can make it into a book. Of course I'll change all the names so no one who is still alive can sue us. Is that all right by you?'

'Course it is but you might be wasting your time. I don't reckon anyone'll want to read all about me and boxing and football and Ireland.'

'Well you might be surprised, Danny. So is it ok about tomorrow?'

'Aye but I might have to break off if there's any emergencies.'

He left her to get dressed and went back to his office. He slumped into his leather chair. His own back was killing him today. He'd had a fall when he was sixteen while training a horse for his uncle. His uncle had said at the time that one day that fall would come back to haunt him. Old injuries never go away.

323

Could do wi' a bit of physio mesel' he mused. The sun's rays cascaded through the window. The crystal pyramid on his desk splashed a rainbow onto the wall opposite. The little glass bauble was a favourite of his. He loved it. It reminded him of how the sun's rays had sparkled through that glass phial that he'd thrown to Billy Battle. 'Them bloody Steel Drops,' he muttered. 'They caused me no end of trouble and they changed the course of my life on two occasions.'

The woman was back with her coat on, ready to go. 'So what time tomorrow?'

Danny slid his diary across the desk, opened it at the following day and said 'How about four o'clock?'

'Perfect,' she replied and shuffled off down the stairs.

Danny stared into space for a moment and then he wrote…

Four o'clock. Jessica Porter